IN THE FAMILY

A gripping organized crime thriller

MARTYN TAYLOR

Published by The Book Folks

London, 2024

© Martyn Taylor

This book is a work of fiction. Names, characters, businesses, organizations, places and events are either the product of the author's imagination or are used fictitiously. Any resemblance to actual persons, living or dead, events or locales is entirely coincidental. The spelling is British English.

All rights reserved. No part of this publication may be reproduced, stored in retrieval system, copied in any form or by any means, electronic, mechanical, photocopying, recording or otherwise transmitted without written permission from the publisher.

The right of Martyn Taylor to be identified as the author of this work has been asserted in accordance with the Copyright, Designs and Patents Act, 1988.

ISBN 978-1-80462-202-5

www.thebookfolks.com

IN THE FAMILY is the first novel in a brand-new series of crime fiction titles by Martyn Taylor. Look out for the second book, MEN IN SUITS.

Further details about Martyn Taylor's books can be found at the back of this one.

Dedicated, as always, to M'beloved Cathie, without whom I would not be, and to the irrepressible Vic Watson-Logan, without whom this book would not be.

Chapter One

Barry Dance was a big man in every sense of the word, not just physically. He walked into a room, and everyone there suddenly felt smaller, their breathing restricted. Sixty years old, with cropped grey hair, he had a network of veins on his cheeks that spoke to an adulthood of living too well. He pressed the icon on the Range Rover fob and heard the locks click shut on the other side of the closed stable door. Then he slipped the padlock through the hasp, closed it and thumbed the numbered dials. That far out in the countryside some people didn't believe they needed to lock their doors, but the Dancer was a city boy, born and bred. He locked everything because there were people like him about.

He walked towards the farmhouse, his footsteps like gunshots, crunching the beige French gravel underfoot. The light above the front door did not come on as he approached, and he frowned, making a mental note to check the system. What was the point of having security precautions if they didn't work? He quickly opened the three locks, stepped inside and switched on the hall light so he could see to kill the alarm in the thirty seconds he had between opening the door and an automatic call being made to the security firm he owned in an anonymous industrial shed on Team Valley. He punched in the code and the red light turned green just in time.

Draping his leather coat over the newel post, he walked through into the lounge and poured himself a large Glenlivet, half filling a cut crystal tumbler with the whisky. He wasn't going to be driving again tonight so it didn't matter how much he drank. As the warmth hit his guts, he felt the stress and anger inside him just evaporate, leaving him clear-headed and relaxed. Why had he allowed himself to get so wound up because his children disagreed with him about the future of the family business? Kids, who needed them? Especially his. What had Garth yelled at him? 'I'll kill you!' They all knew so much better than he did because he'd been tipped out onto the streets at fourteen yet somehow made enough of himself to send them to the Royal Grammar School and university after that. Except for Barry Junior, of course. He'd made it on his own. Know better than him, did they? Yes, right, they didn't. He took another swig of whisky, savouring it and then letting it slide its fiery way down his throat.

Good Scotch, was there anything it could not dissolve or show in a better light? Another mouthful, which drained the glass, only reinforced the belief. The medicine worked, so he poured himself another dose.

Turning, he saw the man in the doorway which was such a surprise he almost dropped his glass. Ever since before he could remember, he had always known when anyone else was near, even in his sleep. It had been a survival trait when he was younger.

"Who the fuck are you?" he demanded, the words evaporating as he recognised his own shotgun in the man's hands, thousands of pounds of Purdey's very best over-and-under twenty-bore. It looked very much more at home in those hands than it did in his. He might not admit it, even to himself, but the Dancer was a lousy shot. He much preferred weapons that were extensions of his hands, weapons he could get up close and medieval with. "How did you get that?" The gun lived in a locked cabinet, the only key on his key ring.

His only answer was both barrels, fired in quick succession. The impact destroyed his face beyond all recognition and lifted him off his feet, the back of his ruined head slamming into the solid edge of the sideboard. Had he not already been dead, that blow would have killed him. Blood, torn-apart brain and pulverised skull fountained everywhere, creating a sticky red lake on the parquet floor beneath what was left of his head.

The killer waited until the Dancer's blood stopped pumping, then stepped forward and put the shotgun into the dead man's right hand. Standing back, he took out a mobile phone and photographed the body. Then, unhurriedly but without pausing, he left the house the same way he had entered it, through the front door having reset the alarm. He went around to the back of the farmhouse, over the three-bar fence, then set off through the trees and over the open moor to where his car was parked, hidden in a sparse copse of firs that were due to be cut down next week. Switching on the engine, he removed his gloves, dropped them into a Sainsbury's carrier bag and warmed his fingers before the air vents. He would dispose of the rest of his clothes when he got home. There was time enough for everything, if you were organised, and he was.

When he turned south onto the road and set off towards Newcastle, he switched on the car radio, and immediately began to sing along. "All right now…"

* * *

Sometime after the killer had left, a small dark-blue Citroën pulled up in the courtyard and a tall, slender young woman got out. She wore a clinging green dress, her dark hair piled on top of her head in a sophisticated version of the beehive currently fashionable with younger women. Quickly, she exchanged the flat shoes she used for driving for shoes that matched her dress, with six-inch heels. She strode to the door with a willowy, long-legged confidence few women managed however many aspired. Glancing at the gold watch on her left wrist, she knocked on the door and waited.

After a while she knocked again. When there was no answer she bent over so her face was level with the letter box, which she pushed open so she could call through it. "Mr Dance, Mr Dance, I'm Jessica. Mrs Bainbridge sent me."

No response came from inside the house, and no matter how she craned her head, she could not see inside.

Eventually she stood up and walked back to her car, shaking her head. She was sure she had come to the right place, but when she got her phone to check with Mrs Bainbridge, she discovered there was no reception that far out in the back of beyond. Shit. Deciding to give it one more try, Jessica went back and rattled the letter box. The noise was suddenly very loud in the silence. Surely, he would hear it even if he was in the bathroom. Nothing.

Jessica returned to her car cursing. She really, really needed that money. Then she laughed. Of course, she needed the money. Why else would she have come all the way out here to get fucked by a man she didn't know, except for the money? At least Mrs Bainbridge would give her a call-out fee and mileage. If she called in as soon as there was reception maybe there would be another client for her.

The Citroën spat gravel from beneath its wheels as she drove away as quickly as she could. Then only the silence remained.

Chapter Two

Katherine Dance – known to everyone as Kitty – yawned until her jaw cracked, rubbed her eyes with her knuckles and turned over to discover she was alone in bed. Barry hadn't come home last night. What a surprise. Well, fuck him. Not that Kitty had done that for a long, long time. Some things just got left by the side of the road during a marriage, and that was one of the items no longer required on their journey. It had been, once, and not just in a Saturday-night-with-the-lights-turned-off sort of way. Maybe if he'd been just a bit better at it – not even as good as he believed he was – she might not have had so many headaches, but the spilled milk had long since been wiped away. Kitty didn't care if he availed himself of younger, more athletic, more professional flesh, so long as he didn't use her money to pay for it. Whatever his faults, and God knew they were many, Dancer had never stinted her for cash.

She thought back to the time they had sat down with his lawyers and accountants to divide up his wealth in the most tax-efficient way and he had thrown up his hands, complaining, "Your attitude is that what is yours is yours and what is mine is yours, too!" She had looked at him. "It's called marriage, darling." And they had all laughed like she had cracked a joke. Kitty had never believed she knew the half of where his money was, but she had enough to keep her in the style to which he had allowed her to become accustomed, and he was always discreet. She could live with that. She did, comfortably heading towards luxuriously. At least he didn't pretend to play golf or indulge himself with some ridiculously noisy red Italian testosterone-mobile that couldn't drive over a speed bump, like some she knew.

In the bathroom, she conducted her daily inspection of herself for lumps, bumps and wrinkles. Her mother had died excruciatingly of breast cancer she had been too uneducated to detect early, like too many women of her class and generation, and Kitty was not going to allow that to happen to her. Nothing. Maybe there was the odd kilo or ten that hadn't been there when she was of the age to strut her funky stuff in a night club in search of Mr Right wearing little more than her underwear, but she could still wear a swimsuit and put Ekaterina to shame in that pool of hers, even if it did have a gymnasium attached. She'd never lifted weights or run on a treadmill in her life but she could still draw compliments from men worth being complimented by, which was a laugh, if she thought about it. The fact was, these days she liked her occasional bedmates the way Dancer liked his – young, anonymous and female. She was what she was, and didn't care for anyone else's opinion. Mrs Bainbridge was the soul of discretion.

Kitty had been people-watching for ten minutes in The Ajaccio when her daughter-in-law hurried over and sat down. Both women were tall and slender with blonde hair and fine cheekbones. They could have been mother and daughter rather than mother and daughter-in-law, although the many who thought they were sisters were doing Ekaterina an injustice. Underneath the dye, her luxuriant hair was so dark it was almost blue, and Kitty thought it was a shame she still had it bleached just because Barry Junior had had a very serious thing about blondes when he was alive. Not that Kitty Two – as the family called her behind both their backs – cared what anyone thought of her. She was her mother's child, and from what Kitty knew, Svetlana Ekaterina Rostropova was a formidable woman, even though they had never met. The Dancer had refused outright to attend his eldest son's wedding in Moscow, and because of that Svetlana Ekaterina had been conveniently indisposed at the time of Barry Junior's funeral.

"I'm not late, am I?" Ekaterina sat down, breathing ever so slightly more heavily than usual, the only indication she would ever give that she had hurried.

Kitty smiled. She was a lady of leisure, able to arrive early and make her daughter-in-law wonder whether she was late. Life was filled with little pleasures, if you knew where to look.

"I ordered you a mineral water and a Caesar salad," she said, taking a sip of her gin and tonic.

Ekaterina stared at her, wide-eyed. "Am I that predictable?"

Kitty smiled another of her smiles. "I am afraid you are, my dear."

Ekaterina reached for the menu, only to drop it back onto the table, unopened. "The Caesar salad here is tolerable, I suppose." She looked around as the waitress poured half a bottle of sparkling mineral water into a tumbler almost filled with ice and two wafer-thin slices of lime. She did not look at the waitress.

Kitty wondered whether Ekaterina knew that the Dance family owned twenty-five percent of the company whose name was on the label, and a similar proportion of the restaurant. Stupid question. Ekaterina, being Ekaterina, would know, even though she had nothing to do with that area of the family business. She might have married into the Dance clan but she was the only one of the children Kitty was confident could take care of Dancer's businesses as well as he could when the time came. All the boys were as ambitious as their father had been at their age but only Barry Junior had been as impulsive. Which was why he was dead. Ekaterina might play at being all fire and passion but inside she was as cold and calculating as any machine. Kitty was good at reading people and everything about her daughter-in-law was a pretence, an act, an illusion. Sometimes she wondered if Ekaterina knew where the imaginary creature ended and the real woman began. Kitty had never really liked her, but Barry Junior had very obviously loved her to distraction, and that was good enough for his mother.

They both took a drink.

"Have you seen the Dancer today?" Ekaterina said.

Nobody else would dare to use Barry's nickname to Kitty, but Kitty had long since ceased caring about that. She remembered the raised voices that had escaped the lounge yesterday and the door slammed heavily enough to make her wonder whether Barry had taken it off its hinges.

"Should I have done?" she mused, smiling.

Ekaterina shook her head. "I have had that oaf Cruddas on the telephone to me every thirty minutes, asking where he is. They had an important meeting this morning."

Kitty smiled in a way she hoped was enigmatic. She had never involved herself in Dancer's business dealings or wanted anything to do with his associates. Phil Cruddas had been 'an associate' before Barry gave up ducking and diving and being one step either side of the law in the scrap-metal business, and transformed himself into a legitimate businessman. If she never saw Cruddas ever again, it would be much too soon. A backstreet thug in an expensive suit with a silk tie was still a backstreet thug, and Cruddas was worse. He had started out as a copper, a bent one at that. Where Kitty came from, there was only one form of life lower than a copper, and that was a copper's nark.

"Sorry, can't help. I haven't heard from him since he stomped out of your little get-together yesterday. He's a big boy now, he doesn't have to phone home."

They exchanged pleasantries as Kitty attacked her carpaccio and her daughter-in-law made inroads into her salad. Then Ekaterina's phone buzzed. She glanced at Kitty, who nodded her permission to answer its summons.

"How many times do I have to tell you, Mr Cruddas? I have no idea where my father-in-law is."

That she used his title and surname made Kitty wince. When her daughter-in-law got all formal with you the best idea was to find shelter because the storm was about to break.

"If you do not believe me, ask Katherine."

She held the phone across the table. For a moment, Kitty looked at it as though it was a cobra about to strike, then she reached out and took the phone.

"Phil, how are you? Good to hear you after so long. How is that darling wife of yours?" She was aware the Cruddases were in the throes of a bitter divorce because he'd raised his fist to Jenny once too often. She also knew he had no idea that the ladies of the wider Dance clan, including Jenny, got together every fortnight for afternoon tea and the dipping in acid of the reputation of every man known to them. "Oh, oh dear, I did not know that. I'm most frightfully sorry to hear…" She knew he was not hearing her lies and it did not matter one little bit. Squirm, you bugger, squirm, she thought. Eventually, though, her patience exhausted itself.

"Sorry, Phil, but my carpaccio's getting cold. If you can't reach Barry, he's probably at his grandparents' old place. It's in Linden Square, out past Longhorsley. There's no reception out there and if he has unplugged the landline … No, Phil, I do not know the exact address but I'm sure you will be able to find it on a map." She trailed her finger across the red 'off' icon and handed the phone back to her daughter-in-law. "What were we talking about, Ekaterina?"

Ekaterina looked at her over the top of the dark glasses she had not needed since having laser eye surgery last year. Then she shook her head and laughed. "There are times, Mother dear, when I am grateful not to have any idea what goes on inside your head."

Kitty smiled and put a forkful of raw meat into her mouth. That makes two of us, she thought.

Chapter Three

The Dancer's murderer slept late and woke with the cotton-wool mouth and thumping head of a man who had drunk too much the night before and not hydrated himself properly after putting away the booze. He leaned forward with his forehead on the damp tiled wall as he pissed himself empty, and wondered why he hadn't learned his lesson yet. Anyone would have thought he would, a man of his age and experience, but what did they know about him? He'd got himself rat-arsed because he was alive and could do it while someone else never would again because of him.

Putting on a pair of shorts and a grey T-shirt that suggested he had been a member of the US Marine Corps even though he had never served in that military organisation, he put himself through a punishing regime of calisthenics that would have had a marine crying for mercy. His experience was that Americans talked the talk but when it came to yomping the miles carrying an eighty-kilo pack and a large-calibre machine gun they preferred to ride. Yanks, he shat them. When he was done, he stripped off his T-shirt and wrung it out in the sink. He took a bottle of water from the fridge, and drank it down carefully, not wanting any pain in his guts from being careless. Then he took a shower, shaved and looked in the bathroom mirror, feeling very much better about the man who looked back at him.

He might be a nasty piece of work, an ugly son of a bitch whom not even his mother loved anymore, not since he decked the bastard who claimed he was his new father, breaking the cunt's jaw and giving himself no option but to join up that afternoon. Nevertheless, his eyes were clear, his skin was toned and he didn't use any drugs other than alcohol. He dressed in dark-blue chinos, a pale-blue polo shirt, faded and frayed denim jacket and slightly scuffed, white trainers. Topped off with an NYC baseball cap and plain spectacles, anyone who looked at him would forget him before they looked away. The only way he could have been more anonymous in town was by being a barcode and wearing a Newcastle replica shirt. Just the way he liked it.

He breakfasted on cornflakes, and another litre of cold water taken from the fridge while he checked his social networks. Mork and Ali wanted to go to Doncaster for the races. He took a rain check on that. Tom reminded him that Thursday night was poker night in Gateshead. As if he could forget that. Apart from that, the world was quiet. He'd have to make his own entertainment.

Before that, however, he had yesterday's business to complete.

Taking a pair of purple surgical gloves from a box on the kitchen work surface, he snapped them onto his hands and went into the spare bedroom, in which was a single bed with the mattress still covered in the polythene the delivery guys hadn't taken with them, a folded wooden chair and an empty wardrobe. There was a plastic draw sheet on top of the covered mattress. On the bed were the overalls and trainers he had worn to do the job, plus a variety of odd clothes he had bought from several charity shops around Tyneside, strictly for cash. Tearing three heavy-duty black plastic sacks off a roll, he stuffed some of the clothes into each sack, then the overalls into one, boots into another, and the carrier bag with the gloves into a third. He bulked out each sack with more clothes and tied them closed with a double knot. Satisfied, he carried them outside the flat, locked the door and then walked down the four flights of stairs to the basement garage. He was the only resident who always took the stairs, which was one of the reasons why he did, not wanting to be seen.

The other reason was that he enjoyed the exercise. He was an exercise junkie, and took his fix wherever he found it.

Putting the bags into the boot of his gunmetal Ford Focus, he drove out of the car park and went on a long tour of recycling sites, dropping one bag into each of the 'Not for Recycling' skips at Dinnington, Morpeth and Ashington. Nobody looked at him twice. They could even look at the CCTV records and nobody would see him.

From Ashington he drove to Newbiggin and walked out past St Bartholomew's Church to where the low cliffs were rapidly eroding towards the caravan park that wasn't going to be safe in five years' time, less if there was another big storm. He took out the phone and punched in a number he had memorised for just this eventuality, attached the photos of the corpse to the empty message, and pressed 'send'. When he was sure the message had been delivered, he dismantled the phone, took out the battery and sim card, then dropped the phone onto a stone and ground it beneath his heel. He felt the plastic crack and shatter. Satisfied, he picked up the phone and tossed all the pieces – battery, sim card and all – into the waves beating on the rocks below. Taking a deep breath of sea air, he felt good and walked back to his car with a smile on his lips and a song in his head. 'All right now…'

Chapter Four

Phil Cruddas was lost out in the Northumbrian wilds, on roads that had no names, numbers or signposts, searching for an address he didn't know. He could have driven past it already, more than once. Had he taken a wrong turn somewhere? That was the story of his life. Then there was the fact his Audi mid-life-crisis-mobile was built for the autobahn, not these winding country roads with overgrown hedges on either side that left him driving down what felt like a tunnel. He'd lost count of the times he had held his breath, fearful this would be the pothole to rip out his suspension or his exhaust. Eventually, he came to the junction with the A697 and paused. Should he turn north or south? He turned south.

Moments later, he caught sight of a sign almost hidden by the hedges and undergrowth bearing the name 'Linden Lane'. He managed to turn right into the lane, drawing a blast of protest from the lorry going north. The lane down which the sign pointed was narrow – with scarcely room between the overhanging trash pines and other conifers for a car to drive down – but still better maintained than some he'd negotiated getting there. What was the boss doing coming out of this godforsaken place? Driving as cautiously as he could, he eventually came to a farmhouse and outbuildings surrounding a gravel yard at the end of the lane. The buildings were painted a blinding white, the woodwork a blue somewhere between royal and RAF, all of it glossy. Just about every other building he had seen out there had been dilapidated going on tumbledown. This was estate-agent ready, perfect, just like everything else about the boss.

Cruddas parked the car and got out. Other than the low rumble of the Audi's idling engine, everything was silent. Silence made Cruddas uneasy. Looking around, he saw no sign of the boss's car. If the boss was here, then so must it be. The Dancer wasn't big on walking. Cruddas walked over to the double-doored outhouse with a padlock on it, spun the dials to the boss's birthday and was surprised when it opened as he tugged on the steel loop. Opening the door just enough to see inside, he saw the big black Range Rover parked there, number plate BDD001, the boss's car. Cruddas's heart began to beat a lot faster when he saw it.

Turning away, he hurried to the front door of the house, hammering on it with the heel of his right hand and calling, "Boss, Boss!" until he noticed the black door knocker and used it instead.

No response came from within. His heart now beat fast enough to cause him a headache, breathing became an effort. Moving away from the door, he went to the nearest window and peered inside.

What he saw was an ankle exposed beneath a rucked-up trouser leg with a polished black shoe on the foot. The rest of the body was hidden behind a dark-brown sofa that looked as though it might be leather.

Cruddas ran over to the shed and looked on the perfectly ordered board of tools beside the car, finding a quarter hammer that would be perfect for the job. That it had only been used for driving in tent stakes these last few years did not mean it would not do the job. Taking a cold chisel, he went back to the front door and placed the blade on the centre of the lock, drew back the hammer and swung it onto the head of the chisel as hard as he could. If he misjudged the blow he would crush the fingers. He struck true and the lock vanished through the suddenly revealed hole in the door, rattling on the floor inside. The door still did not open, so he attacked it with the hammer, smashing out the bolts at the top and bottom. Only then was he able to push open the door and step inside.

The Dancer's body lay there, face gone and most of his head, too, in a pool of black congealed blood, a shotgun by his right hand. Cruddas had seen corpses before, murder victims, too, but never someone who had been a friend. Maybe not exactly a friend – the Dancer didn't have friends – but still someone close, someone he had spoken with about anything other than how bad the Toon had been on Saturday. He staggered outside and got to the courtyard fence before he doubled over and vomited up his guts. Not wanting to go back inside the cottage, he rinsed out his mouth with water from the yard tap and went to sit in his car to wait for the police, who were bound to be on their way after the security company responded to the alarm triggered by his breaking down the door.

The longer he sat, the more he regretted giving up smoking, not just for the nicotine hit but also for having something to do with his hands. Folding and refolding the foil packaging of the stick of chewing gum just didn't soothe any of the aches in his head. When a police patrol car approached cautiously down the lane, he almost jumped out of his car and ran towards them. As it was, he stood up, put his hands flat down on the roof of the Audi and waited.

The patrol car stopped at the entrance to the courtyard and the two officers got out and made their way towards Cruddas. Both wore flak jackets, had their thumbs hooked into their equipment belts and regarded at him with extreme suspicion.

"Mind telling us why you're here, sir?" said the taller of the two.

"My name is Phil Cruddas and I work for Mr Dance. This is his place. He hadn't been in touch all day and Mrs Dance said I might find him here."

The other policeman walked past and looked hard at the front door. "I take it your key didn't work," he said.

"I looked through the window and…" Suddenly, Cruddas couldn't speak anymore as the magnitude of what he had witnessed flooded through him.

"And what, sir?" asked the first policeman.

"Fucking well go in and look for yourselves!" Cruddas suddenly shouted, smacking the roof of his car so hard the sound made them all jump. "Look for yourselves," he whispered.

So they did, and while they were doing that, he got back into the driver's seat and fought not to shed the tears that were suddenly welling up in his eyes. The Dancer. The Dancer was dead.

Chapter Five

The case review that Detective Superintendent Joe Milburn had every Monday was running late in the afternoon, for all sorts of annoying reasons – most political rather than operational – so he made his opinion very clear when he sat down. "I do not intend to be late home today, so make it quick." He was a solid man, his huge fists planted on the table. Those in Forth Banks – and beyond – who did not respect him feared him, with good reason.

Detective Inspectors Penelope Darling and Colin Mountjoy nodded. They didn't want to stay any longer than they had to, either, although both would be surprised if they got home for eight.

Milburn pointed at Mountjoy. "You first, Eddie."

Mountjoy's first name was Colin but Milburn had called him 'Eddie' since the day they first met, and he had never worked up the curiosity to ask why. Mountjoy had just begun to run through the list of active investigations he was running when there was a knock on the door and Sergeant Peter Morton poked his head into the room.

"Excuse me, boss, but you need to hear this."

Milburn glared at Morton over the top of the spectacles he had taken to wearing since being promoted to the superintendent's job, which was essentially a desk job. Nevertheless, he tried to maintain the fearsome demeanour he had adopted as a street copper. "This had better be good, Sergeant."

The words, like the expression, were more for show than anything else. Morton was an old-school policeman, like Milburn. He would not have interrupted the super without a very compelling reason.

"It's Barry Dance, sir."

"The footballer? He's dead."

"No, sir. His father."

Milburn frowned. "The Dancer? Why should I want to hear about him?"

Darling and Mountjoy glanced at each other. They both knew Dance was at the top of the boss's bucket list of wrong 'uns he'd never collared and dreamed of putting away before he was retired.

"He's committed suicide. Just had the report in."

Milburn removed his spectacles and examined them closely. As he had already polished them on the back of his silk tie they were perfectly clear. "Committed suicide, you say. How?"

"Blew his head off with a shotgun according to the report, sir."

Milburn waved him away and waited until the door was firmly closed before looking to his inspectors. "Can't say I'm disappointed to hear that. What about you, Eddie?"

Mountjoy shrugged. "One less wrong 'un. Put out more flags."

"What about you, Pen?"

Penelope Darling was called 'Pen' because everyone on the job had a nickname and she'd decked the first trainee who had called her 'Bad Penny'. She'd been Milburn's right hand while he was an inspector, making sure all the i's were dotted and all the reports submitted to the right people in good time. She was a tall, strongly built woman with a hatchet for a nose and bright blue eyes, emphasized by her practice of wearing her hair pulled back so tightly most of the men thought it had to hurt. In Milburn's opinion, she was the best copper he had ever worked with. Not that he would ever tell her that.

"I can see the Dancer killing someone else…"

"He did, as a young man, probably more than one; we just never caught the bastard." Milburn shook his head.

"...but killing himself?" Darling looked at Milburn then shook her own head. "I don't buy that. He wasn't the type."

"In that case, Detective Inspector, you had better get out there and see what you can find, hadn't you?"

Mountjoy opened his mouth to say it was his turn to get the next big case, but he closed it as information about Barry Dance flooded into his mind. This was probably a case to steer well clear of and be grateful the boss had a better idea of his little pet's ability than everyone else in Forth Banks.

* * *

"Where are we going? The Dancer lives in Darras Hall," Darling asked as Morton dropped the Mondeo onto the Central Motorway and headed north-west, towards the A1.

"He had more than one place to go. This one's out in the wilds, past Linden Hall."

Darling frowned. What was a city boy like Dance doing out there?

"Seems like he has a cottage out there. He didn't turn up to the office today, so someone panicked, got the address from Dance's wife and went looking for him. He saw the body, tried to break in. The security company sent a patrol car out when the alarm went off."

The story seemed reasonable to Darling, up to that point. From what she knew about the Dancer, he kept business strictly within the family and a very few trusted bad lads, who had hitched their fortunes to his star a long, long time ago and had been with him ever since. She said nothing as they went north and then west at the Morpeth turning, towards Longhorsley and then on past Linden Hall towards Scotland. Darling liked the countryside, enjoyed it, went running or walking most chances she got when the weather was not foul, but rural Northumberland, midway between there and nowhere, was not a place she knew well, having had little cause to go there on business and none to visit it for pleasure. The communities were widely separated and yet closed – to outsiders, at least. There were secrets behind every door out there, every tree, secrets the locals wanted kept; secrets that sparked her innate suspicion, the nagging, insistent need to know what was going on that made her a copper.

Following the satnav, they found the farmhouse with no difficulty. There were a couple of patrol cars outside the gate with another car, a red Audi saloon looking very out of place, and an ambulance on the gravel. A fearsome-looking constable stood by the gate, thumbs hooked under the oxters of his body armour and his face bearing a discouraging frown that turned into a grin of recognition when he saw Darling.

"Didn't expect to see you here, Inspector, not for a suicide."

"There may be more to this than meets the eye, Stan."

The constable frowned, briefly, then grinned again and nodded, lifting the blue-and-white tape for Darling and Morton to enter. Stan Townsend and Pen Darling had joined the force in the same intake. That he remained a uniformed constable while she was a detective inspector did not make her respect him the less. Stan Townsend was a bloody good copper. It was in his blood. His father and grandfather had walked a beat when putting on the uniform was guaranteed to lose a man every friend he'd grown up with. Without Townsend and all the other uniforms, Darling's job would be a lot more difficult.

The body still lay where it had been found, although now it was covered by a blue plastic sheet against which the blood on the floor appeared dull brown. Darling stopped in the doorway, not wanting to contaminate the crime scene. Morton grunted as he bumped into her. At the sound, the paramedics turned towards them.

"You can't come in here," said the woman, stocky and competent-looking in her maroon overalls. "We're just about to clear him into the ambulance."

"I won't keep you," Darling said, taking her ID out of her pocket. "I'm DI Darling, by the way."

"I know who you are." The paramedic nodded. "I wouldn't have thought a suicide merited a visit from a DI."

"We're not sure it's suicide."

The paramedics glanced at each other and shrugged. If it was a murder, they weren't going to be taking anyone anywhere, and the chances were they themselves wouldn't be going anywhere for quite some time either.

"Would you move the sheet so I can have a look at the body, please?"

The male paramedic leaned over and pulled away the sheet.

Darling felt as though she had been punched in the stomach. Dead bodies were nothing new to her. Her first proper day on the job had involved helping to fish a twelve-year-old girl out of the Tyne. She still saw pale blonde hair plastered across a ghastly white face when she didn't need to. She was accustomed to the aftermath of violent death, but the first sight of a corpse never got any easier. Dance lay there, spread-eagled, the best part of his head blown away, blood, brain and pulverised bone everywhere. A double-barrelled over-and-under shotgun lay across his right hand, angled away from what remained of the head, thrown aside by the reaction to the blast.

She turned to Morton. "Sergeant, tell me why that is a murder victim."

Morton leaned past her, peering at the corpse for quite some time. Eventually, he said, "Looks like it could be a suicide to me."

Darling shook her head, disappointed he could not see what she did.

"Barry Dance was left-handed. The gun is by his right hand. Why would he use his right hand to pull the trigger?

How would he be able to pull the other trigger when he's already blown his head off with the first barrel? If he had put the barrels into his mouth or under his chin, the way most people do when they use a shotgun, why is there no damage to the lower area of his face? No, he was shot by someone else who wants us to believe he killed himself…" She nodded towards the shotgun in the wrong hand. "Someone who isn't quite as clever as they think they are."

"I'll get the SOCO team here," Morton mumbled.

"You do that. You can call the ME as well. He'll need to take a look."

The paramedics shook their heads. "Not much point in our hanging around."

"I don't think there is much you can do for Mr Dance, do you?"

Darling turned back to Morton. "Once you've contacted the relevant people, you can take as good a look around the house as you can without trampling on any evidence. In the meantime, I shall go and have a chat with Mr Cruddas."

She left the room without waiting for a response from anyone there. She was angry. All premature death saddened her, the waste of human potential. When someone had deliberately chosen to cause that death, her sadness went beyond that, to personal offence. Killing people wasn't just against the law, it was wrong – undermining the foundations of the society in which everyone lived believing they could expect not to be murdered. Darling couldn't claim that catching killers had been one of her prime motivations in becoming a police officer, but when she became a detective and got more involved with apprehending killers, it had moved up to being close to the top of the list of reasons she remained a copper, despite the endlessly increasing distractions from doing the job of catching the bad guys. Barry Dance might not be a great loss to society beyond his immediate family but that did not mean she lacked a personal, visceral need to find his killer.

Chapter Six

Phil Cruddas did not look at all happy when he saw Darling approaching. His expression did not lighten when she smiled at him and introduced herself. Time was, Cruddas would have known every detective on Tyneside by sight if not because they had spent far more time than he liked talking to him. Meeting a detective inspector he did not know, especially a woman who looked as though she might be half his age, made him feel distinctly old and out of the game. Which was probably just as well.

"You discovered the body, I understand."

Cruddas nodded. He'd speak when he had no alternative. 'Volunteer nothing to a copper' had been a motto all his adult life since he stopped being one himself, left the job and went over to the dark side – as Jenny had put it, laughing. Jenny was something else he would rather not think about just now.

"Exactly what relationship did you have with the da– Mr Dance?"

He paused for a moment. It was an article of his faith that no policeman ever asked a question they didn't already know the answer to. "I'm a business associate. The Dancer... Mr Dance and I were supposed to have a meeting this morning with some possible investors..."

Darling made no reply, waiting for Cruddas to fill the silence with something he didn't want to say. It was an article of her faith, as preached by Joe Milburn, that there was only one thing a guilty conscience could not tolerate, and that was silence. Give someone you were questioning silence and they would say something that would be useful just to fill it. Evidently Cruddas knew that, too, and continued to say nothing. Oh well, she thought, there is more than one way to skin a cat.

"You worked for him."

Darling nodded, and seeing his eyes open a little wider confirmed the men's relationship to her without him saying anything.

"Did he have any enemies?" she asked.

In the hesitation that followed, she could almost hear him weighing up the merits of telling the truth, the truth she knew anyway – that when he was starting out, the Dancer had made more than a few enemies, violent men in violent times, even if that was a long, long time ago – or the fiction that he was a successful businessman with fingers in a lot of pies, who was semi-retired now.

He nodded. "Of course, Mr Dance had enemies. Business is eat or be eaten. Some of his competitors didn't take kindly to losing out. Some may have made threats…"

Darling's notebook flipped open almost of its own accord. "Names? Places? Dates?" She clicked the cap of her pen and poised the exposed nib over the paper.

Cruddas shook his head. "I can't remember," he lied. "It was just talk." One of the functions he had executed for his boss over the years had been keeping records of everyone who might be considered any sort of a threat to him, his family, his associates, his businesses. He kept the file at the back of his shed, where he pursued his hobby of battlefield reconstruction; there, nobody would see it among the paints and the tools, the balsa wood and ply, the plastic sheeting and the ready-made trees. It was a long time since he had noted down anyone he considered a real threat. Most of them were just hotheads, all mouth and trousers, who made threats but would shit themselves if he produced the cosh and knuckleduster that always weighed down his jacket pockets, or the Glock 17 he also kept in a biscuit tin at the back of the shed. The Dancer had gone about his business as though he had nothing to fear from anyone or anything, and Cruddas thought he was just there to dot the i's and cross the t's by way of insurance.

Yet the Dancer was lying on the floor of the farmhouse with most of his head blown off and Cruddas could not escape the very uncomfortable feeling that he might be next.

"So, you can't give me a name?"

Darling's disbelief was clear from her tone and the frown on her face. He knew instantly that disappointing this copper was not a good idea. She might be a woman and a decent-looking one, too, but she was still a copper and Joe Milburn had sent her out to resolve this problem. If that bastard trusted her, it was good enough reason for Phil Cruddas not to. He ransacked his memory for a name he could give her to get her off his back, but came up empty, shrugging, showing her his empty palms.

"Do you think Mr Dance might have killed himself?"

Cruddas snorted so hard that snot flew out of his nose and phlegm out of his mouth to fall on the gravel between her feet.

"Kill himself? Mr Dance? Not on your life."

The ensuing silence drew on, with Darling clearly willing him to continue and Cruddas wondering what the hell he could say that wasn't going to land him in the shit.

"What makes you say that?"

"For a start, he was the Dancer. He wasn't frightened of anything or anyone." Cruddas hesitated.

When he remained silent, Darling prompted him again. "He might have had some terminal illness, cancer…?"

Cruddas shook his head. "Fit as a fiddle, was Mr Dance. Went to the gym three times a week. Dragged me with him sometimes, more often after Barry Junior died. He hadn't been to the doctor for as long as I had known him."

Darling scribbled down a note to check with Dance's family GP.

"No," Cruddas continued, "he used to say that when his time came they'd take him out kicking and screaming, and saying they'd made a mistake with the paperwork." He laughed. "He was a Catholic, you know?" he added.

"Catholic?"

"Yeah, RC, left-footer. Went to church every Sunday, along with Mrs Dance. He told me suicide is a mortal sin, whatever that is."

Another note went into Darling's book.

"Anyway, even if he did want to kill himself, I doubt he'd use a gun – not that one, anyway. And he wouldn't have done it out here, where nobody could see him. He was a bit of a performer, was Mr Dance."

"My sergeant will take a statement from you," said Darling. "You haven't spoken to anyone else about this, have you?"

Cruddas snorted again, produced a mobile phone from his inside jacket pocket and stared at it. "Not much chance, have I? There's no reception out here."

Darling walked back to the house. Cruddas hadn't said very much but he'd told her a lot.

Chapter Seven

The Dance residence wasn't the biggest mansion in Darras Hall, or the most ostentatious, but it was still behind an eight-foot wall with intercom-controlled wrought-iron gates and a decent-sized deciduous plantation on the other side of the wall.

"I am Inspector Darling of the Northumbria Police," Darling began. She had rehearsed her speech all the way back from the forest and was surprised when the gate swung open immediately. She drove around the curved driveway surrounding a lawn big enough for a cricket pitch and just as primped as the county ground at Chester-le-Street. It might not be quite as in-your-face as some she had seen in London but it trumpeted the large quantities of cash. Darling automatically suspected anyone in possession of money in large amounts.

She approached the big double doors and was about to tug the bell pull when the door opened and a woman appeared. She was Mrs Average wearing a pink floral-patterned pinafore with sensible short mid-brown hair and the hippy, stocky build of a woman who cleaned for the rich folks because she had several children of her own to raise rather than some perverse passion for polish and detergents.

"Yes?"

"Mrs Dance?"

The woman looked Darling up and down with a curl of disgust on her lip. "Do I look like the sort of woman Mr Dance would marry?" With the question went another, unspoken one. 'Do I look like the sort of woman who would marry Mr Dance?'

"I need to speak to her."

The woman stood out of the way. "She's in the garden room, straight through the dining room."

The inside of the house screamed 'money' as loudly as the outside. Money might not buy good taste, but what it could buy was space. Darling thought she had been in airport departure lounges that were smaller, although – at least – there was no pink marble and gilt decoration to be seen; just solid wooden furniture that went with the polished wood floors. There were no hunting prints on the wood-panelled walls of the dining room Darling walked through, just family portraits that looked as though they might flatter the sitter but not insultingly so. She stepped through the opened French windows and into a conservatory that was big enough to relocate to Kew. Small wonder Mrs Mopp had called it 'the garden room'. It was bigger than Darling's garden, and had far more plants, most of them succulents as far as her unpractised eye could see.

A woman sitting on a lounger turned towards Darling, her dark glasses tipped down onto the bottom of her nose. She wore a white sleeveless dress that looked so effortless it had to have cost a fortune. There was a hard-backed Val McDermid novel in her hands.

"Mrs Dance, I am Detective Inspector Darling."

"Pleased to meet you, I'm sure. Take a seat."

She nodded towards the lounger next to hers, which was between the two of them. Darling did not want to sit down. What she had to say would be best said with as much formality as possible. She sat down anyway, although she kept her feet planted firmly on the floor, and her knees pressed together as tightly as she could manage.

"Mrs Dance, I'm afraid I have some bad news for you."

Kitty shut her eyes for a long, long moment, then closed her book with the cover tucked in between the pages to mark her place and put it down by her side. "It's Barry, isn't it?"

Darling nodded. "I'm afraid so."

"Had an accident, has he?"

"Not an accident, I'm afraid."

"Murdered?" The colour went out of Kitty's face and Darling saw her squeeze her hands together so tightly that her knuckles were white.

"We believe he was murdered, yes."

Darling had brought bad news to many families and had seen it met in what she believed was every possible way from a 'shit happens' shrug of the shoulders to full-on hysterical sobbing that required medication. Kitty Dance's plain "Murdered, you say. Any idea who?" was one to be added to the list, close to the top.

"I suppose you want me to identify the body," she added.

Her composure did not shock Darling, or even surprise her, but it did tell her that Kitty's marriage might not have sustained the passion of its first days, possibly so much so that the first name on the list of suspects was Kitty Dance.

"That will not be necessary. Phil Cruddas discovered the... scene, and he has already made an identification. I believe he is... was a business associate of your husband."

"Business associate. That is one way of putting it" – Kitty laughed – "although I'd have thought you lot would think of him as a partner in crime."

Darling took in a deep breath. "Mrs Dance, whatever your husband may or may not have done, he has been the victim of a violent crime. Our interest is in finding who did it. Nothing else."

Kitty stared at her, then shrugged. "If you say so."

"Did your husband have any enemies?"

"Apart from every copper ever born? I wouldn't know. I never had anything to do with his business, and precious little to do with his personal life. We haven't been what you might call 'close' for a long time. We shared this house and our children; we attended the occasional public function together but not much else."

"I have been informed that you attended church together every Sunday."

Kitty shrugged. "So?"

Darling paused for a moment. "Your husband was found at a farmhouse near Longframlington. Did he spend much time there?"

"You're asking the wrong woman, Inspector." Kitty laughed. "As far as I know, it is a house his grandparents left him. I've never been there. I've never had the slightest desire to go there. To the best of my knowledge, it was somewhere he went when he wanted to be alone, or wanted one of his young ladies to entertain him so the noise wouldn't disturb the neighbours."

For a moment, Darling's forehead furrowed as she tried to understand what that remark meant until realisation struck. What was it with dirty old men hurting women?

"When did you last see him?"

"Yesterday afternoon, after he stormed out of a business meeting with our children."

Darling made an actual note of this. "Did he say anything when he left?"

Kitty laughed. "The last thing I heard him say was, 'Fuck the fucking lot of you!'. I knew him well enough to keep my head down when he lost his temper like that. He had a habit of breaking things when he lost it. Or people."

Darling surmised that Mrs Dance had the scars to prove it. Dance's reputation for breaking things and people when in anger was well known to her. It was one of Milburn's main reasons for wanting him inside. Crime was one thing to Joe Milburn, stealing things or embezzling things or even breaking things. But breaking people was something he could not stomach at any price, and he'd imprinted that conviction on Darling.

"Did you hear any of your children say anything that might have disturbed him?"

Kitty shrugged. "No more than usual." Then she appeared to remember something. "I think I heard Garth say something about killing him, but he couldn't have meant it. Just words. Like father like son when they lose their tempers."

Darling glanced at Kitty and saw a brittleness in her expression she had not noticed before. Instinct told her she would not get anything useful from her. It was time to move on.

"Are any of your children here now?"

"They have their own lives to live, their own houses." Something about her tone told Darling that Kitty had been bothered about this once upon a time, but no longer was.

"Could you give me their addresses and numbers?"

"You mean you don't have them on speed dial?" Kitty snorted.

Darling was about to tell her that her paranoia was entirely unjustified. Instead, she handed her notebook to Kitty and waited as she wrote down three names and addresses, Garth, Andrew and Ekaterina. She was about to say she thought they had three boys, only to remember that the eldest boy – Barry, like his father – had been a professional footballer who ended his career playing in Moscow and, when someone's boot blew out his knee, returned to Tyneside with a Russian bride, a bride he made into a widow within the year when he wrapped his Baby Bentley around a lamp post on the Coast Road. "Thank you, and thank you for your time. I'm sorry to be the bearer of bad tidings."

"Somebody had to be." Kitty smiled at her with an expression that could have passed for sincere. "I can't say it was exactly a surprise."

Something about that expression made Darling's 'copper's nose' kick in hard. The woman was lying to her – which was hardly unexpected, what with her being the wife of a man with a very shady history. Darling also knew that if she pursued those lies in the state she was in now, which was physically tired and emotionally drained – she might not show it, but seeing a dead body, any dead body, hit her hard, especially when the adrenalin wore off – she would probably not get anywhere and might well complicate things for the future. She didn't have to like Kitty Dance, but she had to keep her on their side.

"I'll almost certainly need to talk to you again."

"I'm not going anywhere."

With that, Kitty picked up her book and opened it again, dismissing her visitor. Darling nodded, got to her feet and walked out without another word.

* * *

When she heard the front door close, Kitty put down her book and stared out into the garden, not focused on anything specific. Eventually tears gathered in her eyes and began to roll down her cheeks, carving tracks through her make-up. She did nothing to staunch them. That the news was not exactly news did not mean the clenched fist twisting her guts was any less cruel. Dancer might have become a stranger to her over the years, but she had loved him once, spent most of her life with him, borne his children. A few tears were the least she owed the bastard.

Chapter Eight

The conference room in Forth Banks nick wasn't quite as full as the one at St James's when a new manager was introduced, but most of the seats were already filled with journalists, some of whom had notepads at the ready, others hand-held recorders, while one or two simply had their tablets in their hands. At the front of the room were four camera outfits, one each for the local BBC and ITV news operations, the others freelancers for anyone who would pay for the footage. Everyone there knew everyone else and they were dividing their time between gossiping and watching the door for whoever was going to sit behind the table with its white tablecloth and clutch of microphones. Silence fell as Milburn entered, followed by Darling and Jon Statham, the force's Press Relations officer. They sat down with Milburn taking the centre seat, the others flanking him.

"For those of you who don't know who I am," Milburn began, "I am Detective Superintendent Milburn." He nodded towards Darling. "This is Detective Inspector Darling. She will have day-to-day control over the investigation. Inspector."

Darling had been involved in press conferences before, but this was the first time it had been as the lead officer in a case as high profile as this. Swallowing, she leaned forward to speak, caught sight out of the corner of her eye of Milburn leaning back, and so leaned back herself. "Sometime after 19.30 on Sunday evening, a prominent local businessman, Mr Barry Dance, died at a family property at Linton View in Northumberland. At this time, our thoughts are very much with the Dance family." She paused for a moment as though she was thinking of the family and their loss. "There is still doubt whether Mr Dance was responsible for his own death, but at the moment we are working on the belief that he was, in fact, murdered."

There was a stir amongst the journalists as she used the word 'murdered'. Some of them called out questions, but Milburn put out his hand to prevent her answering them.

"All in good time, please. You know what the procedure is. Let the inspector finish her statement then make believe you're in school and put your hand up if you have anything to ask."

Milburn appeared aware that he was patronising them, and that they did not like it. They seemed equally aware that he didn't really care what they thought of him if they helped him get his job done.

Darling coughed into her hand and began to speak again. "As I say, we are treating this as a murder case, and we are pursuing several lines of inquiry."

"And you expect an arrest within the next couple of days," muttered one journalist in the front row to his neighbour.

"What was that?" Darling asked.

"Nothing," he said, shaking his head. "Nothing at all."

A middle-aged woman in the second row raised her hand. She had been a regular at police press conferences for more than twenty years and nowadays was a stringer for a major news agency.

"Yes, Margaret," Darling nodded.

The woman got to her feet. "Barry Dance had something of a reputation when he was younger. Do you think that might have had something to do with this?" She sat down again, wearily and warily.

"I know dancing is very competitive these days," Darling began. Her reply was drowned out by the laughter in the room. "Yes, I know that isn't what you meant. I should say that, at this time, Mr Dance's early history does not appear to be majorly important in this. It is, of course, only early days, and we will not leave any stone unturned in our investigation, even if it involves going over very old ground before he became a bone fide businessman."

The mutterer raised his hand. Jimmy Carlisle had been calling himself a 'crime reporter' longer than Darling had been alive, working for *The Journal* and *The Chronicle*. He was everyone's caricature image of a crime reporter, getting on in years, his face – especially his bulbous nose – bearing a red-veined testimony to the lifelong love affair with the bottle that would kill him, probably sooner rather than later. He even wore a grubby Columbo-style gabardine mac all year round. Despite his love of booze, he had an encyclopaedic knowledge of Tyneside crime and criminals that quite possibly surpassed even Joe Milburn's. There had hardly been a major trial in the last forty-odd years that had not seen Jimmy Carlisle on the press benches, scribbling furiously in his notebook. He proudly refused to rely on anything that might break down or have the battery expire.

"Jimmy… Mr Carlisle," Darling said.

He didn't bother to get up, although the faintest ghost of a smile flashed across his face when she called him 'Mr Carlisle'. "There are whispers about this being a professional killing, a hit if you like."

Milburn raised his hand to prevent her answering.

"Jimmy, we know each other fairly well, don't we?"

Carlisle nodded, warily. "If you say so, Chief Inspector… sorry, Superintendent."

"How long have I been investigating murders in Newcastle? You needn't answer that. Almost as long as you've been reporting them. Do you know how many murders I've investigated?"

Carlisle shook his head. "Not offhand. I could go and look it up somewhere."

Milburn laughed. "I'm sure you could, Jimmy, I'm sure you could. You know how to find out facts like that. It's one of the reasons you're good at your job."

Carlisle looked at his scuffed and worn desert boots. He didn't look as though he was buying Milburn's flattery.

"Now I don't know how many murders I've investigated and I don't want to know. I've investigated every kind of murder there is – men, women, kids; drunks killed in a closing-time fight; prostitutes killed because their customer didn't fancy paying for what he'd had; prostitutes killed because some weak-minded bloke had a down on women; women who weren't prostitutes killed because some weak-minded bloke had a down on women; gang members killed because they happened to be in the wrong place at the wrong time; druggies who couldn't pay for their fix; wives whose husbands thought they were playing away; husbands whose wives knew they were playing away. Et cetera, et cetera, et cetera. In all that time, I have only come across one murderer who killed because someone paid him to do it, and I picked him up in a pub in Birtley where he was pissed as a fart and boasting about it. I wouldn't call that a 'professional killing' or a hit, more amateur hour. This isn't America, Jimmy. This isn't a TV show. This is Newcastle. This is real life. This is real death. I don't believe in professional murderers and I don't believe this was a hit." He stared at Carlisle so intently that the journalist seemed to shrink in his chair. "Does that answer your question, Jimmy?"

Carlisle nodded.

"I'd be obliged if you'd tell me who was doing the whispering you heard," he added.

The journalist laughed. "I couldn't possibly reveal my sources, Mr Milburn."

Everyone laughed at that, even Milburn, who was still laughing when he bent over and spoke in Darling's ear. "I want to know who's been gossiping, Pen."

She wanted to know the same thing. This was not only a major inquiry – all murders were major inquiries – but Dance's connections made it very likely to be a sensitive one, too. She wouldn't be surprised if the Dancer's kids had the chief constable's home number.

When the laughter faded, she asked whether there were any more questions. There were, but none she could not handle. Eventually, the journalists' inquisitiveness was exhausted. There were, after all, only so many ways of asking questions to which everyone knew the answer was, 'There is nothing I can say about that'. Milburn got to his feet first and walked towards the door. Darling thanked them all for coming and reminded them that the police needed to know about any information that might come their way. Professional or not, this murderer was a dangerous… She almost said 'dangerous man' but caught herself and said 'dangerous person' instead.

On the other side of the door, she found Milburn waiting. "I heard that 'dangerous person'. Anything make you think our killer might be a woman?"

She hesitated. There was nothing yet to suggest the killer was a woman. Women did not tend to use guns to commit murder; poison and knives, yes, but not guns. From what she had seen of the murder weapon it was of a size and power to be more than most women could handle, unless they were experienced in using shotguns. That thought made her make a mental note to find out if any of the women in the Dance clan were shooters. She shook her head.

"But there's this scratching at the back of your mind that makes you wonder," he said.

Her jaw dropped open in amazement, only for her to close it again immediately. That was exactly how she felt, a scratching at the back of her mind, where her thoughts were that had not yet fully formed.

He grinned. "Good work, Inspector. Keep an open mind. It's far too early to rule anything in or out." With that, he turned and walked away briskly, leaving her to wonder whether she had just been chastised or complimented.

Chapter Nine

Darling stepped inside her darkened house, and dropped her bags on the hallway floor where they made a heavy thud. She closed her eyes, feeling the exhaustion flood through her now she could stop fighting it. This day hadn't been any more intense or demanding than most days. There hadn't been a breakthrough in the Dancer case, but she hadn't expected one. This phase of the investigation was gathering information. Some would be important. Some would be irrelevant. There was no way of telling which was which at the moment. As with any investigation, there were times she felt everything was out of control, that she was being submerged under the information coming in and would never rise to the surface again. Such moments came without warning and passed just as quickly.

She had experienced such a sensation in the early evening, sitting at her desk, reading through the daily reports she insisted on receiving from Morton and the other officers on the case. It was one of her strictest rules, that she would read whatever reports anyone put on her desk while that part of the investigation was fresh in their mind, in case there was anything she needed clarifying, or that suggested another line of investigation. She owed it to them.

However, it was difficult to stay at her desk and go on reading when there were flashes in front of her eyes and the world felt as though it had started rotating in the opposite direction. Stay she did, though, until every email was read. When she got up from her desk there was a pulsing ache where her spine joined her skull, and her vision was slightly blurred. It still was when she went outside into the station car park, the damp evening air doing nothing to relieve the feeling. Her car was parked there, but she ignored it. She was not fit to drive. Instead, she walked up to Grey Street and stood at the bus stop. She stood there long enough to be annoyed, when the bus eventually arrived and she was almost clear-headed enough to let it go past and go back to her car, but she didn't and when she got home she felt almost like a normal person, someone who had got the bus home from work.

There had been times when Darling would have gone through into the kitchen and cooked a dinner of a gin and tonic. One of the bargains she had made with herself after the police doctor gave her a right talking-to following her last annual physical check was that she would not drink during the working week, no matter what the excuse, what the temptation. Booze was an occupational hazard for coppers, and it also ran in her family. She was not going to go down that path. Caffeine would just keep her awake, so she made a pot of green tea and took it – together with a plate of cheese and crackers, and a very large orange – into the lounge. Then, she made herself comfortable on the leather recliner – her one concession to luxury – and turned on some piano music that was as good as ambient without being quite as vacuous, and relaxed.

Darling was just drifting off to sleep when the doorbell sounded, and again a short time later as she was getting to her feet. "Be patient," she called, only loud enough for her to hear. "I'm coming," she said, a little louder. The bell sounded again just as she was reaching for the doorknob. If this was someone trying to sell something…

Darling opened the door to find a painfully thin woman standing there – about her age, she guessed, dressed in a ragged denim bomber jacket and jeans, scuffed, half-laced Doc Martens on her feet, spiky blue hair everywhere, a dull sheen of drug dependency on her face, and bright hazel eyes staring up at her expecting recognition.

"Do I know you?" Darling asked.

The smile disappeared. "You did," she snarled. "In every way, particularly biblically."

Recognition dawned behind Darling's eyes and a chasm opened her stomach, making her feel as though she wanted to fall into it and disappear.

"Lizzie?"

The woman laughed, exposing worn and discoloured teeth. "Lizzie, that's right, Lizzie the Lezzie." Her voice was loud enough for the neighbours to hear, making Darling grab her arm and drag her inside, slamming the door shut.

"Doing well for yourself," Lizzie said, looking around at the prints Darling had on the walls. "No Mr Darling, I suppose."

Darling bit her tongue and clenched her fists. Robert was long gone and she didn't miss him one bit, but that didn't mean anyone else could mention him, and definitely not Lizzie Benton. Darling shoved her former lover into the sitting room, closed the door behind her and stood there staring at the woman, wearing her best 'mess with me at your peril' frown. "What do you want?"

"I just wanted to say hello to the only famous person I know."

Darling snorted. "A: I'm not famous, and B: you don't know me now, if you ever did."

"You were on the television, and that makes you famous."

"I haven't got time for this. I've had a long day, I'm dog-tired. So, say whatever you've got to say and get on your way."

"Oh, that is so disappointing. Still, if you don't want to talk to me I'm sure your boss will be interested in knowing your sexual proclivities."

Darling stepped towards her, right fist clenching, scalding anger flowing over the barriers of her self-control, almost convincing her she was going to beat the shit out of

Lizzie. Before that happened, however, Darling managed to calm herself.

"For your information, my 'sexual proclivities' are nobody's business but mine. Yes, I had a little fling with you…"

"Little fling! I was in love with you."

Darling snorted. "Be honest with yourself for once in your life, the only thing you have ever loved is what you see in a mirror."

"That's not what I'll tell your boss!"

"You don't know Joe Milburn. Unless I was breaking the law or threatening to scare the horses in the street, he wouldn't give a monkey's."

Lizzie laughed. "I wouldn't be so sure. Not once I've spoken to that ghastly old crime reporter on *The Journal*."

Light dawned on Darling. "You want some money!"

Lizzie clapped her hands, bouncing up and down. "See, you haven't lost it after all. I knew you hadn't."

"You've got a nerve, coming into my house and making threats."

Lizzie opened her mouth to protest, but saw Darling's expression and closed it sharply.

"What we did was have cheap, meaningless sex a long, long time ago," said Darling. "For me it was an experiment, one I haven't repeated since. I'd forgotten about it until five minutes ago. If you think you can con any money out of me, you've got another think coming."

The woman changed shape in front of her, shrinking, becoming even smaller than she was, twisting herself, winding her hands around each other, staring up at Darling like some cute puppy begging for treats.

"Oh, for fuck's sake, just get on with it," Darling said. "You disgust me."

It was clear to her that the woman only wanted money, and as she followed her slinking towards the front door she almost felt sorry for her, and was about to reach for her bag when she remembered what Lizzie would spend the money on. It wouldn't be a hot drink and hot food. If she was lucky, it would be on the booze that had brought them together so long ago and then just as quickly torn them apart. If she was unlucky it would be on something she boiled up in a spoon and then injected into her arm. Darling didn't make moral judgements about drugs. There but for the grace of God, and what really was the difference between the acceptable drugs and the illegal ones? They all ruined lives. While she did not judge, neither was she prepared to enable. Lizzie would have to do without whatever money she had thought she might get from her former flame.

On the step, Lizzie turned around for one more try. "I really did love you, you know."

The only way she could have made herself any more pathetic would have been to lean on a Tiny Tim crutch and tuck one leg out of sight.

Darling sighed and shook her head. "No, you didn't, Elizabeth. I'm sorry things don't seem to have worked out for you but none of that is my responsibility. Now, if you don't mind, I need to get some sleep. I've got a murderer to catch."

She closed the door on Lizzie's shouted response that accused her of being an uncaring bitch. There was also something about working girls that she didn't entirely catch. Darling walked through into her bedroom and fell on the bed, fully clothed. There were many things of which she was in need. Being reminded of when she was young and innocent and stupid was not one of them.

Chapter Ten

Darling had been at her desk less than an hour when she got a telephone call from Jimmy Carlisle. She closed her eyes and sighed before accepting the call.

"Mr Carlisle, what can I do for you this bright and sunny morning?"

The rain was lashing down outside. If her blinds hadn't been down, she would scarcely have been able to see the other side of Forth Banks. The *Journal* building, where Carlisle was probably calling from, was just a short walk away. He laughed, a short, gruff noise – the sort she imagined pigs made.

"I was wondering whether you would care to comment on a conversation I've just had with an old friend of yours."

She counted to ten before she replied. "I presume you've been speaking to Lizzie Benton."

He didn't respond but she still heard him nod.

"Well, I wouldn't describe her as a 'friend'. She is someone I knew in college more than fifteen years ago. I was much younger than I am now, and she was much more glamorous."

He huffed again. "Glamorous. That's not a word I'd use to describe her now."

"To cut a short story even shorter, she made a play for me and I fell for her very hard. It must have lasted, oh, a good week before I found her with someone else. That was the total and full extent of my lesbian love life. I've never made a thing about it, but neither have I ever concealed it. From what I saw, I wasn't very unusual. As you probably also know, I was married once, and I'm now divorced. I've never made a thing about that either. I don't believe either features of my life have any impact or influence upon my capability as a police officer. Neither do my superiors, I believe."

Her superior officers might be ageing, old-fashioned northern men who still harboured doubts about women who did anything but stand in the kitchen with an infant on one hip while stirring a stew on the stove with their free hand, but if they were she had never seen it. They had never required anything from her but competence and professionalism or had ever treated her any less than professionally.

"Aye, Inspector, I dare say you're right. I just thought I'd have a word to the wise about the woman. She struck me as being a very loose cannon, if you see what I mean."

It was Darling's turn to laugh briefly. "Am I to expect something to appear in *The Chronicle* about your conversation?"

"Only if it is a very, very slow news day. Any progress to report?"

"You'll be the first to know when there is, Jimmy."

He snorted with laughter. "I very much doubt that, Inspector. Joe Milburn would want to know the reason why, and I, for one, would not want to be the one to tell him."

They both laughed at this, but before she was finished the connection was cut and she found herself looking at the handset. Was her laughter that off-putting? Chuckling, she returned to rereading the pile of reports on her desk, hoping she could find something there that would open up the Dance case, something she had not discovered on first reading. The magic forty-eight-hour line had been crossed and, if she was brutally honest with herself, they were no closer to finding the murderer than they were when Dance's body was found. She would be damned if she would allow this to distract or discourage her. Police work – all investigation – was about dealing with the reality at hand rather than chasing after wishes. Statistics were sometimes useful in giving a direction to explore but she disregarded the passage of time. She would leave superstition – however scientifically based – to her junior officers on the investigation, and never give them the slightest hint she might share their beliefs.

Chapter Eleven

Darling had never liked Wolstenholme, the medical examiner who was older than Methuselah, twice as pernickety and made no secret of his conviction that, wherever a woman's place was in the world, it was not in policing. Her way of tolerating his antediluvianism was to call him 'Neanderthal' behind his back and remind herself all that mattered was that he did his job. She had never heard any misgivings about his professional competence. That he wore gold cufflinks shaped like horses' heads and had a dividers-and-set-square gold charm hanging from the watch chain that crossed his huge belly was immaterial. He took a sheet of paper from his pocket and unfolded it onto her desk, smoothing it in that deliberate, irritating way he did everything.

"This is a synopsis of my post-mortem examination report. Mr Dance died because of catastrophic blood and tissue loss due to the impact of two shotgun shells discharged at close range. I found no evidence of gunshot residue on either hand. Make what you will of that. Neither did I find any sign of powder burns on what was left of his face, which I should expect to find in the case of a self-inflicted wound."

Darling made no mention that he was confirming what she had noted during her very brief and distant inspection of the corpse at the cottage.

"From my examination of the body, and the extent of the damage caused to a relatively restricted area of the skull, I estimate Mr Dance was standing between six and eight feet from the barrels of the shotgun when they were fired. Twenty-bore pellets do not spread very much over that sort of distance."

Darling thought back to the sitting room in the farmhouse, looking at the Dancer's corpse lying there. Six to eight feet would be the distance between the killer standing in the doorway and Dance standing in front of the dresser that occupied most of the space between the windows on the wall opposite the door, with a two-seater leather settee between it and the door. She took a deep breath.

"I take it you would not support the initial theory that Mr Dance committed suicide?" she asked.

Wolstenholme's lip curled downwards as he laughed derisively. "The deceased would have needed twelve-foot-long arms to pull the triggers on that shotgun from the necessary distance. He would also have needed to shrink them back to normal size in the millisecond between the gun first being fired and him dying. Then there is the fact that one shell would have killed him before he had the time to pull the second trigger. My professional opinion is that Mr Dance was killed by someone other than himself."

She smiled and inserted the paper into the folder she was carrying. "Thank you, Mr Wolstenholme. You have been a great help to me, as always. I never really bought the suicide theory."

The pathologist shook his head. "Which isn't to say he wasn't doing his best to kill himself in all those ways of excess to which a wealthy man is prey. The fingers of his left hand were heavily discoloured by tobacco, although I confess I found no evidence of lung cancer. His liver, however, was twice the size of a healthy man of his age, and I have no doubt that my surgical colleagues would have taken one look at his arteries and rushed him into the Royal Victoria for a heart bypass operation. One look at the veins on his cheek and nose would have told anyone Mr Dance was too good a friend of the grape and the grain for his continued health."

Darling wondered how Wolstenholme could call the pot 'black' with such a straight face. His predilection for alcohol in all its disguises was clearly written in the tracery of red across his own face, but she told herself sternly that it did not matter. That he was an obnoxious, judgemental old man did not matter, either. All that mattered was the quality of his work. "Thank you."

Chapter Twelve

"Nothing?"

Sergeant Rose McCreavie, the head of the SOCO team, shook her head. "We found just one footprint that could not be accounted for by either Dance or Cruddas." She removed a photograph from her file, showing the imprint of a right foot half on the gravel that surrounded the cottage, half on the earth between the gravel and the three-bar fence that ran around the sides and back of the farmhouse. "It is a size thirteen."

McCreavie was a thickset, fair-haired woman who resembled many people's idea of the way Mrs Claus would look: rosy-cheeked and always smiling. She had seen and analysed more of the bloody remains of what men and women did to each other to wipe the smile off most people's faces on a permanent basis, but seemed to have a way of not letting it show.

Darling admired her immensely, not just for her relentless professionalism. She had somehow remained married to the same man and they had raised three well-adjusted teenagers who did not do class-A drugs, mug old ladies or worship whoever had won the latest television talent show. Darling could never tell McCreavie that.

Darling leaned forward, peering. "There doesn't look to be much wear on it."

McCreavie nodded. "No wear at all." She sat back, puffed out her cheeks and shook her head. "It is a brand-new shoe, but that pattern on the sole is one Adidas haven't used in five years."

"A new shoe that's five years old?" Darling shook her head, hoping to dislodge the very unwelcome suspicion creeping up on her. "I'm investigating a murder where the killer appears to have got into a locked and alarmed house belonging to a man who was known to be extremely cautious; they killed the man with their own shotgun and then got away leaving not a shred of evidence, except an improbable shoe print. It appears to be a very carefully planned and executed crime. If this was a television show, somebody would say, 'Looks like we're dealing with a professional here,' and they'd go and look at various databases to find the best match before picking them up and interrogating them so cleverly they broke down and confessed in good time for the closing credits and the advertising that paid for the sets, the talent, and the producer's cocaine."

McCreavie laughed. "Only this is real life in Milburnland and there's no 'professional' killers sitting around waiting for contracts to get rid of business competitors or errant lovers."

Darling nodded, glumly. "There's some killers cunning enough to evade us for a long, long time, maybe even for ever. We're only human. There's also a few thugs who have conned those with more money than sense and a desperate estimation of their own entitlement into believing they really were professional hitmen. They might even be able to kill someone, but keeping their mouths shut in the pub afterwards is beyond their capabilities."

"Yet it appears you're confronted with exactly that creature of fiction."

"No fingerprints in the house or on the gun?"

McCreavie opened her file again and took out a couple of sheets of paper. "There are no fingerprints on the gun, anywhere, not even the deceased's."

Darling frowned. That was odd. She would have expected anyone who possessed such an expensive shotgun to be a keen user. She made a note to ask the family about that.

"Most of the prints in the house are Dance's. There are a few that belong to Mr Cruddas and a few we haven't identified yet."

Darling nodded. "Anything else of interest so far?"

McCreavie sucked on her bottom lip for a moment then decided it was time to speak up. "I can't be positive yet, and Cruddas did some serious damage to the lock when he smashed it out of the door, but I found no evidence on the barrel and tumblers that suggest it had been picked."

Darling nodded. The killer had to have got into the house somehow and if they hadn't broken in or picked the lock, that left just their having a key. The Dancer didn't seem to her to have been the sort of man who would hand over the key to his love nest to anyone, let alone anyone who might want to kill him.

McCreavie went on. "The gun cabinet, though, that was definitely picked. Not that you'd need much skill to pick that lock, just a bent paper clip and a bit of patience."

Something else Darling shared with Superintendent Milburn was a hatred for guns that bordered on religious passion. As far as she was concerned there was no need for anyone to have a firearm in their home, even if they did keep it in the required locked, fireproof cabinet. Sometimes she thought she might make an exception for farmers, only she had been involved in enough cases where a stressed-out farmer had gone berserk on his family and friends with a shotgun, or just put it under his own chin, to question even this justification.

"Then there was the alarm. According to the internal record, it was activated twice on Sunday and once on Monday. Both times on Sunday it was turned off with the key code before it would sound at the security company.

On Monday, Cruddas knocked the door in and the company alerted a patrol car, which attended the scene," McCreavie added.

It was Darling's turn to suck her bottom lip. "So, it appears that whoever opened the door also knew the code for the alarm. Who else, apart from Dance, knew the code?"

McCreavie grinned. "You're the detective, Inspector." Then she grinned a little more widely and began to sing, "I'm just looking for clues at the scene of the crime." Looking away from Darling's blank expression while chuckling at her own wit, McCreavie delved into her file again. "If I were you, I'd ask them." She pushed an evidence bag containing a business card across the desk. "This was in the alarm." The card was that of Wayfarer Security, and the address was on Western Avenue in Team Valley.

Darling nodded. "Looks like someone will be paying them a visit." She made a note of the address and telephone numbers in her notebook. "How long before you've processed the scene?"

McCreavie snorted. "How long is a piece of string? It'll be done when it's done. I haven't exactly got a CSI budget, you know."

Darling grunted. Budget cuts were the bane of everybody's life. As far as she was concerned they were long past the point of trimming away the useless fat. They were well into slicing bone and muscle now. "Thanks. Keep me posted."

Taking that as her cue to leave, McCreavie gathered up her file and closed the door quietly behind her, leaving Darling to stare into the distance.

Darling tapped her teeth with a pen, planning her next move, which would be to talk with Dance's boys, singly rather than together. And then there was the daughter-in-law. She had no doubt they would already have rehearsed their story of the meeting with their father. There was nothing she could do about that. She would just have to be cleverer than them.

Chapter Thirteen

Kitty prowled the lounge as she waited for her sons, wearing a figure of eight in the carpet as she went around the four-seater sofa – on which she never sat because getting out of it entailed making an undignified spectacle of herself – to the window that looked out onto the drive, where she paused and took a sip from the vodka in her glass before starting another circuit of the room. It was only when she raised the glass to her mouth and discovered it was empty that she realised what she was doing, cursed, went back to the kitchen and filled the glass with tonic water – just tonic water. Let them think Mumsie was hitting the booze if they liked. Nobody could blame her.

Turning away from the window, she walked to the wall of framed photographs on the other side of the room, photographs that detailed years of family life. The first photos, in the top row at the left-hand end, were the ones of Barry and herself in the formal, slightly absurd dress they had worn to compete in ballroom dancing competitions at the Mecca and other halls. Compared with the strategically placed wisps of netting and sequins the female dancers wore on *Strictly*, Kitty looked almost Victorian with her half-dozen underskirts and a blonde beehive hairdo that hurt your fingers if you tapped it. God, she had been so young, and a real looker. Yes, she had been a looker, and so was Barry – tall and dark and handsome, with those evil eyes of his sparkling as bright as any of the lights. He was a better dancer than her, which was why he was known as the Dancer wherever he went, and he'd worked her hard to get to the standard they needed to achieve to win the contests and take home the prize money, which he liked as much as he disliked getting beaten.

What else she remembered of those days was how hard he worked at making her look good, even if it was at his expense. "They come to see you, Kitty, you not me," was what he told her. "I'm just the gorilla on your arm." Which she had assured him was not true and which she didn't think he believed anyway. Whatever, it had worked, until the day she told him he was going to be a father. They only ever danced together after that at birthday parties and weddings. Sometimes she had missed the thrill of the competition, the bright lights and the applause, but she had no more spoken of it than he had. Which was not at all.

She was surprised when Garth and Andrew arrived together in Garth's car. Andrew did not enjoy the way his elder brother drove, which tended to be the way his father drove when he was that age, as though today might be his last day alive and he was intent on squeezing every drop of enjoyment from it. But she knew that Garth didn't care what Andrew thought, something else he shared with his father.

Kitty went to the door to embrace them. Garth wore jeans and a polo shirt that showed off his physique. That he smelled of shampoo and aftershave told her that he had not forgone his daily workout at Cooper's gym, even though his father was still in a refrigerated drawer in the RVI mortuary. While she'd never actually heard her son say his body was a temple, he did take fitness to an extreme. As a child, he had always tried to compete with Barry Junior, and when it became clear even to him he would never compete with his brother in terms of footballing skill, he had determined to make up for that with physique and fitness. Not that he had succeeded. Barry Junior had done it all so effortlessly, not caring how much of a clod he had made his brother look.

Kitty had at once enjoyed her eldest son's superiority and despaired at his total incomprehension of what this did to her middle son, who worshipped the ground Barry Junior floated over. That, though, was a long time ago.

Andrew's concession to physical fitness was to play golf, very badly, with his clients and the few friends he had. The Dancer had always scorned golf. The tie loosened at his neck was his only concession to the day that had passed. Andrew could make a high-class store mannequin wince with envy. His trouser creases could draw blood if you were not careful.

"If you want a drink you know where everything is. Help yourselves," she said.

They all sat in silence until Andrew shook his head.

"This is ridiculous. Why are we here? I have things to do…"

His voice petered out as Kitty put her glass onto the table by her chair and leaned forward, her serious expression one that both her sons recognised and wished they weren't seeing now. She might never have scared them the way Dancer could when he was so minded, but they could recognise the time when taking liberties was not a good idea.

"Yes, we all have things to do," she said in a low tone they could only just hear. "What I want to know is what you are doing about it."

"About what?" Garth looked at her, blank-faced, then seemed to realise what she meant. "Oh, the murder, you mean. We're leaving that to the police. They're the professionals."

Andrew caught sight of the thunderclouds that boiled in his mother's eyes and looked away, as though he could hear her counting to ten before she bit off her elder son's head.

Garth looked from her to him and back again, his eyes opened wide, as if asking, 'What did I say?'

"Leave it to the police," Kitty eventually whispered. "Leave it to the fucking police." She looked up, craning to hear something, seeing just their shocked surprise at her use of an obscenity. "That sound, can you hear it?" She glared at Garth. "That's the sound of your father turning in the grave you haven't even put him in yet. Turning in his grave that his sons should want to leave anything to the plods, let alone his murder. Shall I tell you what he would be doing if it was one of you lying in the morgue? Shall I?"

Garth stirred in his seat, making the ice in his glass rattle.

"He'd be out there kicking doors down, shaking trees, asking nasty questions of anyone who got in his way until he found out who did it. Then he'd tear them to pieces with his bare hands. That's what he'd be doing. That's what he'd be doing for you!"

She sat back, glaring at them, before taking a mouthful of her drink and savouring it as though it really was vodka and tonic.

"Mum, we're not like Dad," whined Andrew.

His tone snapped the last of her self-control.

"Damn fucking right you're not!" she screamed, and flung her empty glass at Andrew's head.

He was so shocked he did not move. Had he flinched to his left, the glass would have struck him smack on the forehead, right between the eyes. As it was, it hit his shoulder and rebounded up into the air before falling onto the thick carpet, where it rolled around until it stopped, dribbling out a trail of tonic drops. Had it not hit him it would have hit the picture window behind him. Andrew stared at her, seemingly unable to comprehend what had just happened.

"The world's changed, Mam," said Garth. "Nobody's like that anymore. Even Dad hadn't been like that for donkey's years. He was a businessman, not a gangster. He didn't have enemies, not like in the old days."

Kitty almost said that was because Dancer had buried them all, but found she couldn't say anything. The rage had left her, just like that. There was nothing left to say to her sons. That they were right only made it harder to bear.

She got to her feet and walked towards the hall. "I'm going to bed. Let yourselves out."

She didn't wait to for their replies, or give them her customary goodbye of a peck on both cheeks. Let them make no mistake. She was angry with them. She was angry with the whole world. Kitty wasn't going to let them see her shed tears, which did not come until she closed the bedroom door and lay down on the bed. After a while, Kitty wondered why she had not invited Ekaterina to their little soirée and realised she did not have an answer to that question, other than that her daughter-in-law frightened her in ways her sons never could.

Chapter Fourteen

Darling's shoulders ached as she glided the last metre into the wall and allowed her feet to touch the pool floor. Twenty lengths was hardly the workout of an Olympian, but it was more than she'd managed in three weeks, and she'd had to cancel a meeting to steal even this much time from her increasingly crowded schedule. It was six months since Dr Parasararthary had read her the Riot Act following her annual physical.

"Keep eating the processed, salt-laden, high-sugar rubbish you push down your neck, keep drinking the alcohol…"

Darling had tried to protest, saying that by coppers' standards she was virtually teetotal, but on opening her mouth she discovered she hadn't the brass neck to say anything.

"…you keep not exercising and I guarantee you will not live to collect your pension. You are a good fifteen kilos overweight and your blood pressure makes me surprised you haven't got steam coming out of your ears."

"But—" she had begun, knowing there wouldn't be any buts, and there weren't.

"Detective Inspector Darling, just you hear me out. You have a demanding job that I wouldn't have for all the tea in wherever it is they grow it these days. You are subject to pressures that most of us do not even know exist. I am told you are good at that job. I know it is an important job. If you are to thrive and do that job as well as you can, you have to get yourself fit. It is possible. You should eat properly, not just a bacon sandwich snatched from the canteen and eaten on the run. It is possible. You need to lose weight. It is possible. If you want it. Your body and your mind are the tools you use to do your job, the job I believe you enjoy and I know fulfils you because you have told me so. Would you let the car you use to do your job get a flat tyre, or not get its ten-thousand-mile service? No, of course you wouldn't. Would you let the computers you use to do your job get a virus and go offline because you didn't take the time to activate the anti-virus software? No, of course you wouldn't."

She had bowed her head and raised her hands, acknowledging defeat. "I hear what you say, Doctor—"

"Do you?" he carried on. "Do you really? I mean, do you really hear me? Well, here's the deal I will make with you. Lose those fifteen kilos. Get regular exercise. Bring your blood pressure down. Do those simple things, and I will not pull you off active duty on health grounds."

"What?" Darling jumped to her feet. She would have loomed over Parasararthary, only the doctor jumped up as well, and he stood a clear head and shoulders taller than she did.

"I can do it. You know I can do it. And I will. I am not concerned how many thieves' collars you feel. I am concerned about you dropping down dead or, worse, having a stroke that disables you." He'd picked up the card-backed file and dropped it onto the desk. It made a startlingly loud noise. "I know your family history even if you appear to have forgotten."

There was nothing Darling could say to that. Heart disease ran in her family, and ran fast. Her father had died of a heart attack aged fifty-two. Her brother Steven hadn't even survived that long.

"Now, do I have to write it all out for you?"

He hadn't written it all out for her, and she had tried to eat better and exercise, even being surprised that she seemed to sleep better for reasons she did not understand. Then the sky had fallen in at work when Collister just walked out and Bullimore sent in a long-term sick note because of stress, and suddenly all her good intentions were left behind, all her good work undone.

It had taken a chance encounter with Dr Parasararthary in a corridor at the Crown Court – they were giving evidence in different cases – to get her back into the city centre swimming pool that she used. 'Feel the burn' was what the fitness freaks told her, and feel it she did, as she stood up with her back against the shallow end and rotated her shoulders to ease the pain.

Another swimmer came front-crawling towards her, knifing through the water, breathing to his right every other stroke, looking like a pro. He touched the wall with his left hand about a yard away from her before tumble-turning and setting off back up the pool, doing breaststroke this time. Something about him seemed familiar, although she could not think what it was until he came back alongside her, turned without pausing and butterflied his way away. Then she realised. There was a long, thin scar on his back that reached from his shoulder down and around his scapula. It was the relic of a fight on Byker Terrace at chucking-out time one Saturday night fifteen years ago. He was also missing two fingers on his left hand.

She and Paul Reid had been an item, briefly, several lifetimes ago. They had burned intensely for a few weeks after graduating from Police College, then she had introduced him to Marianne Marshall at a party; she might as well have ceased to exist for him right then and there, even though she was standing right beside him. They'd gone their own ways, taken the blows that life had swung at their heads, and while her love life hadn't been exactly roses, she hadn't taken the literal and metaphorical kicking Reid had from Marianne and her entire family.

He came to the wall doing backstroke, allowed himself to sink beneath the surface and then re-emerged, removing his goggles with one hand and raking his hair back with the other. His hair was still as thick and black as it had been when they'd been coppers together, a bit longer perhaps.

"Hi, Paul, long time no see," she said, trying to sound friendly.

He turned to look at her and the smile of recognition seemed genuine enough. "Pen! You're looking good." He reached out and embraced her, kissing the air beside both her cheeks.

She found this astonishing – the Paul Reid she had known would have laughed his socks off before doing anything like that.

He stood back and looked at her, appraisingly. "I hear congratulations are in order," he said. "Detective Inspector Darling. Well-earned and not before time."

She wasn't sure whether he was sincere or just playing a game, but she smiled and nodded her thanks. "You're looking fairly good yourself."

He glanced at himself. "Living the monastic life, swearing off the booze and exercising regularly will do that."

She laughed. "You're welcome to it. I like mine as it is."

"So do I," she thought she heard him whisper just about under his breath, but she decided to let it go. Life was complicated enough without ploughing up old ground.

"What are you doing these days?" she asked.

"Still in the private detective business, you know."

"Oh, yeah."

Darling couldn't remember exactly why Reid had left the force, yet even though she had spent a lot longer in Milburn's shadow than he had, she wasn't of the opinion that all private investigators were superannuated wazzocks playing at still being coppers and getting divorce material for greedy not-so-young-anymore wives, just most of them. Even so, they could be a source of information.

"I hear you've got the lead in the Dancer case," Reid said, grinning.

Darling shook her head. "I can't tell you anything about that, you know I can't."

"I'm not asking. I don't want to know."

They both knew that was a lie. Reid was a detective. He had curiosity running through his veins rather than blood. He wanted to know everything about everything.

"Have you heard anything?" she asked before she could stop herself.

He glanced at her, all sorts of questions roiling behind his eyes. "Like what?"

"Oh, nothing, anything. Just… just, well, you have your ear to the ground in places I don't go…"

He held up his outspread hands, pleading. "Pen, I'm legitimate these days. I don't walk on the wild side. I don't associate with criminals… well, not any more than I can manage."

"I shouldn't have asked. Forget I ever did." Pen felt her cheeks colouring and wanted to just dive in and swim to the other end of the pool, under water.

"No, that's okay. Murder is murder, even if the dead man was the Dancer. All I've heard is that whoever did it seems to have left no evidence."

"I wouldn't say 'no evidence'," Darling cooed, knowing this would sink a barb into Reid's curiosity. If she said there was evidence, he would want to know what it was – not that she was going to tell him. He would also want to find more evidence because he had always been too curious for his own good. Curiosity was what had cost him those two fingers. Once the infection was in your blood, you were never cured of it. There was also the possibility that, if he started whispers on the other side of the street, even if he did not come up with anything, something might be shaken loose. Darling knew she was using him, and didn't care. Until a couple of minutes ago, she had forgotten he existed but now he was an asset in her investigation, and if there was one lesson Joe Milburn had hammered into her – just as she was sure he had hammered into Reid – it was that you made use of any and every asset you had.

Reid looked at her for a long while without saying anything, then smiled, just a little, and nodded, just a little. "Once a copper, always a copper."

Then he pulled his goggles down over his eyes, dived forward and began a fast, splashy front crawl that sent water fountaining into her face, making her splutter and laugh, and then turn around to haul herself out of the pool. She had to go back to work, tomorrow morning at least. And when Reid went back to his work he would be working for her, whether he knew it or not.

Chapter Fifteen

Garth Dance was his father brought back to life, only taller, not yet so fleshy, with a smooth skin that screamed 'pampered by product', a haircut that cost more than Darling spent on cosmetics in a month, and no scars on his knuckles. Barry Dance had fought his way up from a backstreet scrap-metal yard – sometimes literally – to make sure his eldest son had to do none of that. There had been a time, when Garth was thirteen, that his father had been called to the Royal Grammar School to be told that his son was guilty of bullying a classmate for reasons nobody could quite articulate. Barry Dance had listened while

Garth's housemaster had explained that the school did not tolerate bullying under any circumstances and that Garth would have to serve four Saturday mornings in detention. He had nodded, said that it seemed fair enough but, if the teacher did not mind, he would give his son a lesson about bullying he would never forget.

They drove home to Gosforth in silence, and Barry sent his son straight up to his room – "no dinner for you, my lad, and I'll see you later" – before going into his study, pouring himself a first small Scotch and switching on the TV to watch the local news. Three hours later he went up to Garth's room and entered without bothering to knock. The boy was lying on his bed, reading *Julius Caesar* with a notebook and pen by his side.

"You're going to teach me a lesson about bullying I'll never forget, are you?" Garth said, putting aside his book and getting up off his bed, standing nearly tall enough to look his father in the eye, trying to affect a nonchalance he didn't really feel.

When he glanced down and saw the belt wound around his father's right fist with the buckle showing, that nonchalance escaped him with the sound of a long liquid fart. His father wrinkled his nose and shook his head.

"Think you know everything, don't you, son? Think your dad's still just the backstreet thug he was, don't you? Think I'm going to give you a beating because some know-nothing little ponce of a teacher says you're a bully, don't you?" He laughed, and unwound the belt. "If I was going to hit you, boy, it wouldn't be anywhere that anyone else might see the marks."

He pushed Garth in the chest so suddenly that the boy could not keep himself from sitting back down on his bed, looking up at his father with astonishment.

This was the first time in as long as Garth could remember that his father had spoken more than half a dozen consecutive words to him. He had the distinct impression that his father did not really know what to make of him.

"The lesson about bullying you will never forget is the same lesson you need to learn about anything else that the likes of your teachers turn their noses up at. Know what it is?"

Garth shook his head.

"Don't get fucking caught."

With that, he tapped his son lightly on the cheek, almost a gesture of affection, and left him.

Garth had never forgotten the lesson, although he considered himself far more subtle an operator than his father had ever been.

He watched as Darling and Morton took their seats on the other side of his desk before sitting down himself. His executive chair had been made to measure, and had been as stupidly expensive as it was exceedingly comfortable. It was on a three-inch plinth that ensured he would look down on anyone sitting on the other side of that expanse of deeply polished mahogany. Some might say it was an adolescent trick, but Garth liked it. He sat and waited for the inspector to break the silence, glancing from Darling to Morton and back again. This was his office. He was in control of everything in here, but a nagging suspicion grew in him that he was not in control of this encounter. He had just about exhausted his control when the inspector spoke.

"I am sorry to make your acquaintance under such inauspicious circumstances, Mr Dance," said Darling.

His father had been murdered. Circumstances didn't get any more inauspicious! Garth was just about to say something when she continued.

"Did your father have any enemies?"

"Enemies? My father was a businessman! He had competitors, not enemies."

Even as he spoke, Garth realised he had answered without thinking, forgetting another lesson his father had taught him, which was never trust a copper if they asked you a question. Coppers never asked innocent questions, not good coppers, which were the only ones he needed to concern himself with. All coppers had ulterior motives, an agenda that was based on the need to prove you guilty of something; anything.

You needed to think before you answered a copper's question, think quickly if you could, and the best answer was something as close to the truth as you could manage, close enough for you not to have to try and remember how you'd answered that question when they asked it again, slightly differently, looking for you to give them a gap in your defences through which they could slip a blade of logic and pry you apart. The question that was always on a copper's mind when they asked a question to anyone – even a smiling little old granny who wouldn't melt butter in her mouth – was 'Why is this lying bastard lying to me?' And they were good at discovering the answer to that.

'Never underestimate a copper' was another lesson Garth's father had tried to teach him, especially if Joe Milburn sent them, because they were liable to be as good at their job as he was, just as tenacious, just as sneaky.

Garth had forgotten that lesson as well. He swallowed hard, trying to keep himself from saying anything else.

"Of course, Mr Dance." Darling nodded. "He was a very successful businessman and you seem to be following in his footsteps."

Garth opened his mouth to ask why she said that as though it was an accusation rather than a compliment, but he managed to close his mouth before any words could escape. Think before you speak, bonehead! He snarled, silently to himself.

"Nevertheless, he was murdered in a way that suggests his murderer was highly skilled in the dark arts of homicide. Do you have any comment to make about that?"

Why the fuck are you asking me questions like that? Garth almost raged, but caught himself again. His reply was to shake his head, volunteering nothing.

"I understand there was a disagreement at the meeting your father attended on Sunday with you and your siblings, a disagreement that led to raised voices and his leaving the meeting in a state of anger."

"Who told you that?" He could not prevent those words being spoken, his voice half an octave higher and harsher than the deep brown manly tone he usually affected.

"Witnesses," Darling replied, so calmly it stripped another layer from his control.

"Who?" he demanded.

She shook her head, smiling. "Oh, I'm sure you don't expect me to divulge that to you, now do you?"

Short of his father speaking to her from the mortuary, the only witnesses to their father storming out of the room yelling, 'you are fucking mad, the whole fucking lot of you and I've had my bellyful of you! I wish you were all dead!' were himself, his brother Andrew, and Ekaterina – their sister-in-law. Had Darling spoken to them yet? He didn't know.

"We all have our opinions, Inspector, and none of us are shy in voicing them, even to our father. That's the way he raised us."

"I'm sure," Darling murmured in a soft voice, as inexpressive as that utterly neutral smile that was beginning to make Garth feel angry.

He would make her regret it if she forced him to lose his temper. Then he glanced at the other detective, sitting watching him with the same appraising look she wore, and he realised he wasn't capable of making her regret anything. She wasn't at all like the working girls he met around town. She wasn't like them at all. If he raised his hand to her the way he sometimes did to them, the chances were the sergeant would enjoy breaking his head.

"What were you discussing?"

"Business." It was the truth, if not the whole truth. Business had been all any of them ever talked about when they got together for a long time. They weren't so much a family as a corporation. "The future of the family businesses."

"Of course."

She wrote something in her notebook. It didn't look like words. Could it be shorthand? Garth wondered. Did they still teach police officers shorthand?

"Do you often have violent disagreements when you discuss business?"

Garth counted to five before answering. "We are all people of strong opinions, Inspector. Sometimes others disagree with those opinions, but we all respect our right to our opinions and to voice them aloud. The discussions can be passionate." How much more passionate could things get than a father wishing his children dead? "When tempers cool, we usually come to an amicable agreement."

"And did you? Come to an amicable agreement?" asked Darling.

"Did you kill him?" asked Morton, apropos of nothing at all.

"Did I what?" Garth demanded, levering himself halfway out of his chair before realising he had let the copper get to him, made him respond without thinking, and subsiding again. "What sort of fucking question is that?"

"One we have to ask," oozed Darling.

"One you have to answer," finished Morton, his face devoid of expression, his eyes boring into Garth.

"No, I did not murder my father," sneered Garth. "And I have no idea who did."

Darling nodded. "Of course you do, Mr Dance." She produced a card and held it out to him. "If you think of anything, I can be reached most of the time on one of these numbers," she said. She got up and went to the door, turning back just as Morton reached out to open it. "How is business, by the way?"

"Business is good, very good," Garth replied.

"Oh, just one more question. That is a very expensive shotgun your father owned–"

"Pair of shotguns. It is a pair of shotguns," Garth snarled. "You buy shotguns from Purdey in pairs."

Darling glanced briefly at Morton. "I did not know that."

"You learn something every day," Morton muttered.

Darling turned back to Garth. "How proficient was your father with his shotgun?"

He laughed. It was not an agreeable sound. "He couldn't hit a barn door from ten yards," he sneered. Shooting was one of the few activities at which his attainments exceeded those of his father, and that the Dancer didn't give a flying fuck about it only made his anger more piquant.

"One more thing, what did you do after this business meeting of yours broke up?"

Garth shrugged. "I went home."

"Straight home?"

"Why should I go anywhere else? I have a wife and a family. I like to spend time with them."

"Really?" Darling nodded, closed her notebook and put it back in her bag. "I'll be in touch," she said, walking out as Morton held the door.

* * *

Darling and Morton did not speak as they left the building and got into the car.

"What do you think, ma'am?" he asked, eventually.

"Stop the car, Sergeant."

Morton jerked his attention back to the car and swung towards the side of the road, braking so hard they were both hauled back by their seat belts. Fortunately for him, there were no other vehicles nearby in the left-hand lane and he came to a safe stop, half on and half off the pavement.

"What's up, ma'am?"

"For a start, Sergeant, you can stop calling me 'ma'am'. 'Ma'am' is Her Majesty, Mrs Windsor. You call me 'guv' or 'Inspector Darling' or – if there's something you really want – Pen. Understand?"

"Yes, ma– guvnor."

"What is up is that I have something to say to you and you are going to sit there while you read, learn and inwardly digest every word. Understand?"

Morton nodded, unable to speak for just about the first time in his life.

"Here is some news for you, Sergeant. I don't care what you think of me. I don't care what anyone in the canteen thinks about me. The people whose opinions I care about don't eat in the canteen anymore. Do I make myself clear?"

Morton nodded again.

"I can't hear you, Sergeant."

"Yes, guvnor."

"Good, now that we've got that out of the way, let me say that I don't care if you are an unreconstructed male chauvinist pig."

Morton's jaw fell open, although he closed it again quickly enough. Darling wondered whether he had ever heard the term before.

"The only thing I care about you, Sergeant, is that you go on being what you are."

He shuffled in his seat. "And what's that?"

"A bloody good street copper, Sergeant. That's what Mr Milburn tells me you are – that you know the patch, know people, know how to talk to them and get them to tell you what they don't want you to know. That's why I asked for you on my team. If you remain that, then we are not going to have any problems. To do our job we don't have to be friends, just professional."

Morton nodded.

"One more thing, if you think I'm wrong, you tell me. You don't go behind my back to Joe Milburn 'cos he won't listen, you don't flap your lips in the canteen. You bring it to me and I promise you, we'll have a serious talk about it after, where we'll both agree that I was right all along, as Brian Clough used to say about Martin O'Neill."

The empty expression in his eyes told her he did not get the joke, the joke she had so assiduously collected and kept for just this moment. Oh well, nothing ventured, nothing gained. Even on Tyneside, not everyone was a football fan.

"You do your job, Sergeant, and I'll even forgive you being a Mackem."

This seemed too much, even for him. "I'm not a Mackem," he said. "I am not a Mackem!"

"If you're not a Mackem, what are you?"

"Inspector Darling, I am a Sandancer!"

They stared at each other for a long while until they both began to laugh, laugh uncontrollably, until she took a tissue from her jacket pocket and dried her eyes.

"I think we had better get back to work, Sergeant, before anyone sees us and gets the wrong idea."

He said nothing in reply, which Darling decided was probably just as well.

"First thing you do when we get back is check Garth Dance did drive straight home and not by way of Linden Lane."

"You think he could have done it? Helluva thing, killing your own father."

"I don't know he didn't do it, so I'm going to keep an open mind and keep on looking for evidence, the old-fashioned-copper's way."

Chapter Sixteen

They were almost back to Forth Banks when a call from the office came for her to go to an address just off Chillingham Road, Newcastle's 'student quarter'.

"What's it about?" Darling snapped. It seemed like a reasonable question, and she frowned when she got the reply.

"Can't tell you anything, just Mr Milburn wants you there ASAP."

Shaking her head, Darling told Morton to stop. "I'll take this car, you go to the station, pick up another one and get yourself to Wayfarer Security. I want to know how our killer could get hold of Dance's security code. I don't get the impression he was the sort of man who would give something like that to anyone."

Morton said nothing, and did as he was told, and as Darling drove off towards the Central Motorway she had a clear sight of him in her rear-view mirror striding towards the station. She wondered whether he would slow down when she was out of sight, but before she could think of an answer, she was on the Central Motorway and had to give her full attention to the traffic, much of which seemed to have forgotten how and when to use indicators. Once again, she offered up a silent prayer and prepared for all the idiocy she would encounter.

Darling found two marked police cars parked outside a dingy house on Lesbury Road, an unkempt privet hedge spilling over the front wall – the paintwork faded in colour almost to grey – and curtains drawn at every window. There were a couple of unmarked cars nearby that were out of place there, too big, too new. She presumed one belonged to Milburn. Parking as near to the house as she could, Darling went to the gate and opened it. It squealed loud enough to wake the dead.

A uniformed constable whose name she could not remember glared at her for a moment, then essayed a salute, mumbling something that sounded like 'ma'am' to her. She decided against giving him the lecture she had just given Morton and brushed past him on her way into the house.

"Mr Milburn is upstairs," he called after her.

"Thanks," she said as she put her first foot onto the bare wooden stair and felt it give just a little beneath her.

The house smelled of damp and decay, unwashed people and inadequately washed clothes, spicy food, milk that had gone off, and every recreational narcotic known to man. For a moment, she wished she had one of those oranges studded with cloves Elizabethan ladies used hold beneath their noses, but the thought left her as quickly as it had come. She didn't have one so she would have to do without.

It was as she put her foot on the second riser and her hand towards the banister for support as it, too, sagged that she realised she had forgotten to wear plastic gloves, something that should have been an autonomic reflex on entering any potential crime scene. Had she touched anything with her hands? She wondered as she took a pair of purple gloves from her bag and snapped them onto her hands with practised facility. As she climbed the stairs, she decided she hadn't.

The first two doors on the landing were closed. The third, towards the back of the house, was open and another uniformed constable stood guard outside. As she approached, he cocked his head towards the open door. "He's in there."

She nodded her thanks and went inside.

The room was tiny, mostly occupied with a single bed that had bedclothes that were hanging off and onto the floor. Darling had lived in some pretty grotty places while she was at college but nothing quite so squalid as this. It was positively Dickensian. Milburn stood in front of the bed. Detective Constables Cope and Matthews were also in the room, trying not to get in the superintendent's eyeline. That wasn't easy. Darling could just see a painfully thin bare leg hanging down from the bed and onto the floor. It was filthy. Instinct told her whose room this had been, whose corpse was on the bed, but she said nothing, just walked up behind Milburn.

"You wanted to see me, sir." Her voice was completely neutral.

He turned towards her, then stood aside so she could see the corpse. Lizzie Benton lay sprawled on her back, wearing knickers and a sports bra that had both been white a long, long time ago. She stared at the ceiling and a syringe dangled from the crook of her left arm. There were needle marks all over her body.

"Do you know her?" Milburn asked.

"Her name is Elizabeth Benton. I knew her at college," Darling answered without hesitation.

"At college?"

Once again, she answered without hesitation. There was no point at all in trying to flannel Joe Milburn. He saw through well-rehearsed simulation, never mind something made up on the fly.

"I hadn't seen her since then until she turned up at my door the night before last, asking for money."

"A coincidence, don't you think?" Milburn did not believe in coincidence, just enemy action.

She laughed. "She'd seen the press conference on the evening news, thought she could blackmail some cash out of me."

Milburn frowned. "Blackmail?"

She could have asked to have the rest of the conversation somewhere confidential, somewhere Cope and Matthews and the uniform outside the door wouldn't hear everything she said, but she wanted her version to be the one that went around the canteen, not one that had evolved into 'send three and fourpence, we're going to a dance' through the multiple mouths of everyone in the station.

"She and I had a very brief fling, lasted a whole week. I was very young and impressionable back then. I hadn't thought about her from that day until I opened my front door on her."

All three men turned to stare at her, taken aback by her bluntness, which was one more strike for her, more evidence she really was as no-nonsense as she tried to appear.

"Did you give her any money?"

It was time for her eyes to widen a little. "Give her any money? Of course not. Why should I give her any money?"

"That would explain this, then." Milburn held out a clear evidence bag inside which was a torn scrap of paper.

'Penny Darling is to blame' was written there in a dull, reddish brown ink in Lizzie's spiderlike handwriting that Darling realised could well be dried blood, with a pain in her stomach that was like a punch. She didn't try to take the note, didn't say anything more about Lizzie's final attempt at revenge.

"She must have got some money from somewhere," he said, "to be able to afford her fix."

Cope intervened. "It looks like she got herself some of the really good stuff that's going around."

Darling suddenly recalled a briefing the previous week about a batch of uncommonly pure heroin that had hit the streets lately. Given that most of the junk that was peddled on Tyneside streets was so impure, so cut with talcum powder and God only knew what else, the new stuff was too much for long-term addicts like Lizzie. She was the fourth death Darling knew about, and she probably wouldn't be the last.

"Is there anything else you want me for, Superintendent?"

There was no reason for her to address him by his rank in a room where no civilians were present, except that it sent several coded messages back and forth between them. Yes, she understood why he had dragged her there when she would have nothing to do with whatever investigation there was, and she was grateful that the note hadn't been presented to her in an interview room with the tape recorders going. On the other hand, she was somewhat busy with a murder investigation and this exchange could even more easily have taken place over the telephone while she was busying herself with something of more immediate importance than a pathetic junkie whose sun had finally set.

Milburn gazed at her for a moment. Darling had no idea what was going on behind those eyes. "I'll want your report detailing your relationship with the deceased and your recent dealings with her on my desk by the time I get back to Forth Banks. Is that understood?"

"Yes, sir.

He nodded and turned back to the corpse.

Darling considered kicking him in his amply padded rear. Instead, she mumbled, "sir," and left as quickly as she could without actually running.

Chapter Seventeen

Wayfarer Security was a nondescript aluminium-sided light industrial shed with blinds at the windows.

There were two cars in the small car park, a pink Peugeot hot hatch and a dark Focus, so anonymous it was almost invisible where it stood with no other cars near it.

Morton opened the door and walked in. The woman behind the desk was a bottle-blonde in her late thirties wearing an almost-sheer white blouse that was two sizes too small and revealed very clearly the black Wonderbra she wore underneath it. There was so much gold about her person, the only appendage that didn't have at least one gold ring on it was her third finger, left hand.

She smiled at Morton, an expression that momentarily curled her lips but went nowhere near her eyes. "What do you want?" she asked, rather than the 'Can I help you?' a potential customer might have expected.

Morton's years of experience as a copper had taught him you could tell a lot about a person from the way they greeted him. This one might have an invisible sign above her head proclaiming 'Receptionist', but she wasn't accustomed to dealing with random members of the public, and didn't like it when she had to.

He took out his warrant card and showed it to her. "I'm Detective Sergeant Morton of the Northumbria Police. We are investigating the death of a Mr Barry Dance whom we believe to have been a customer of this company."

She shook her head. The smile had entirely disappeared. Morton raised his estimate of her age to early forties. "I can't discuss anything to do with customers with you."

It was Morton's turn to smile, and his expression was even frostier than hers. "That's good, because I don't want to discuss your confidential customer with you. I want to discuss your confidential customer with your boss, just to see if he has any information that will help us find Mr Dance's murderer."

"Murderer?" Her voice scarcely escaped her mouth, and Morton saw her fingers go white beneath all those rings. Had she been out of the country the last couple of days? Didn't she watch the local news?

Just then, the only other door in the reception area opened and a young man appeared. He wore a white shirt so dazzling Morton almost had to close his eyes, together with black dress trousers, highly polished shoes and an MCC egg and tomato striped tie clipped to his shirt with a gold cricket-bat pin.

"Sergeant, I'm David Tucker. Can I help you?"

"Are you the boss?"

He smiled, just a little wanly, and shook his head. "No, I'm afraid I'm not the boss. She is very rarely here."

Morton was about to reach into his jacket pocket for a card when Tucker continued.

"On the other hand, I can answer any questions you have about the late Mr Dance's accounts with Wayfarer. Come on through, Sergeant. I don't want to waste any of your valuable time."

There was something about his tone that put Morton on his guard. His ordinary assumption was that everyone lied to him. Mr Tucker wanted to waste his time. The question was why.

Morton had long since given up questioning his suspicious inclinations, his paranoia. They saved time and he was a busy man.

"Bring us some coffee, please, Jackie," Tucker said over his shoulder as he turned around. "The good stuff."

"Right away, David." The 'David' made the man wince, ever so slightly.

The office into which he followed Tucker was totally undistinguishable from dozens of other offices on the Teams and everywhere else in the country. There were four computer desks, although only one computer appeared to be switched on. The mesh-backed chairs came from the same supplier as the thousands of identical chairs he had seen on the Cobalt and Quorum call-centre farms. On the wall above was a big, flat-screen TV silently showing the BBC News channel. Along the rest of the wall were half a dozen fireproof filing cabinets, all identical café-au-lait-coloured with four drawers. They had the same ones in Forth Banks.

Tucker suddenly turned around. "How can I help you, Sergeant?"

"Wayfarer provide security facilities for Mr Dance's property at…" He reached for his notebook to remind himself of the address where the Dancer had been murdered.

"We provide security for all the Dance properties. It would be surprising if we didn't."

Morton ticked off another reason for him to dislike the man. He did not appreciate being interrupted while asking a question. "Oh, why is that?"

"Wayfarer is a Dance company."

"I see." Morton nodded and made a note in his book. "It appears as though the person responsible for Mr Dance's death opened the front door lock and reset the alarm system before the alarm was raised here. Can you suggest how that might have happened?"

"That's not possible."

"Oh?" Morton inclined an inquisitive head. "How so?"

"The Dance properties are equipped with Keytec 1020 alarm systems. Even though I say it myself, it is state of the art and I fitted it in the Linden Lane property three months ago. Resetting the system in the time following the door being opened for whatever reason and the alarm being triggered here requires the inputting of a six-digit code on the keypad in the property within thirty seconds. Whoever reset the alarm knew the code."

"How could they know the code?" Morton felt as though he was leading Tucker by the nose towards a trap he had no idea was in his path.

"Mr Dance would have had to tell him…" The man's voice petered out as he realised what he was saying.

Morton smiled. He hoped it was a wolfish kind of smile. "Let's assume Mr Dance did not tell the man who killed him the code. How else could he have got it?"

Tucker's brow furrowed as he thought for a while. Morton believed it was not something he did very often. Then he shook his head. "I don't know."

"Oh, surely you have copies of the codes here, in case Mr Dance ever forgot."

The man nodded. "Yes, yes, of course we do."

"Show them to me."

"I can't."

"Can't or won't?" Morton made no attempt to disguise the mistrust, the antagonism, the threat in his voice.

"I can't show them to you."

"Surely, it is just a question of calling up whatever file it is on that computer of yours?"

Tucker shook his head. "The numbers aren't on the computer. If they were on the computer, a hacker might be able to get in and find them."

The policeman snorted. "Surely a security company has systems that are invulnerable to hackers!"

Tucker shook his head again, sighing. He had been through this so many times. "There is no such thing as an online computer system that is impenetrable to hackers. It is common knowledge that hackers have got into the Pentagon systems, into GCHQ, into the Kremlin, and those are the ones anyone on the edge of the know knows about."

Morton stood for a while contemplating this information. "If they aren't on a computer, where are they?"

Tucker walked over to a desk that did not have a computer terminal on it and had a much more expensive chair than the others behind it. He knocked on the desktop. "They are in here, on a bunch of record cards wrapped up in elastic bands and put inside a locked drawer."

"Well open it, then."

"I can't."

Morton counted to ten. "Again, I ask you, can't or won't?"

Tucker chuckled. "This is the boss's desk. The boss is the only one who has a key."

"This is a murder investigation we are talking about."

This time Tucker laughed aloud. "Officer, I'm sure that in your world you are one scary fellow and you can intimidate just about anyone into doing or saying anything you please. Well, let me assure you that in my world you are nothing like as scary as my boss. Break into Mrs Dance's desk? You have to be joking."

"Kitty Dance?"

"Ekaterina Dance. Not that I'd call her that to her face. I wouldn't dare. To me she's 'boss'."

"So, the reset code for Mr Dance's house was known to himself and his daughter-in-law?"

"And anyone else he told it to."

Morton nodded, and scribbled in his notebook, a quick reminder to do some digging and find any dirt there was to be found on Mr David Tucker. "Thank you for your time, Mr Tucker. We may have some more questions for you."

Just as he reached for the door, it opened as Jackie used her commodious backside to push her way in, carrying a tray bearing coffee cups, a cafetière and a jug of milk. Morton pushed past her.

"Don't you want your coffee?" she wailed.

"Duty calls," he muttered, and left.

Chapter Eighteen

Andrew was not like his father or brother. He was a slim man with already-thinning blonde hair, and pale, watery blue eyes. As Darling introduced herself and shook his hand, she was almost afraid that she might crush his long, delicate fingers if she squeezed as hard as was her habit. In the police world, a woman learned very quickly that she had no option but to win the 'more macho than you' hand-shaking contests. Her immediate question was whether Andrew and Garth shared the same father, but she dismissed the thought for the time being. Whether the children were as related as their parents claimed would become germane to her investigation only when all the obvious avenues had been explored.

Darling glanced around his office, all wood panelling and discreet carpeting, bookcases filled with bound law reports and a few still in their monthly editions. She decided this was for show, to reassure clients that he kept abreast of the latest developments, something he could not do if he only downloaded from the *New Law Journal* website. Not that there was a computer on his desk, his sumptuously gleaming mahogany-topped desk, with its A1-sized leather-bound blotter with a matching pen-and-ink stand. It was even more ostentatious than the one in his brother's office. The shining silver letter opener lying across the trough in the stand looked as though it was sharp enough and pointed enough to do serious damage to something far more resistant than an innocent envelope. The whole effect was Dickensian. All that was required to complete the look was for Mr Dance to be wearing tight white riding breeches and a cutaway red coat, and sporting luxuriant whiskers. He was, of course, dressed in a three-piece business suit of anonymous charcoal grey that probably cost more than she spent on clothes in a year, and he was so closely shaved his cheeks and chin gleamed.

The entire effect of the office was an artful pretence, a sham. Which probably meant he was, too.

"I imagine you know why we want to see you." She kept her voice neutral and used the plural 'we' to tell him she was a detective with the weight and heft of the police force behind her, not just some woman barging in on him, in case he believed he could just dismiss her out of hand.

"Don't let any of the bastards believe you're 'just' a woman. You're a copper, first, last, always. If you don't forget that neither will they." This was a lesson Milburn had imparted when she first joined his team, one of the many lessons she had taken from him.

"There's nothing I can tell you," Andrew said, leaning back in his chair and crossing his right leg over his left.

"Allow me to be the judge of that," Darling said. "You cannot tell how significant even the tiniest detail may be at the end of the day, when we have the big picture. We understand there was a family meeting on Sunday afternoon that ended in some disagreement?"

Andrew snorted with laughter. "The old man lost his temper because he didn't get his way. As per usual. It didn't mean anything, just that he couldn't accept that the three of us have voices equal to his in the family businesses. He stormed off, swearing at us. We just got on with it."

"So, the three of you could make business decisions without your father?"

He blanched, as though she had just suggested that every *i* did not need to be dotted and every *t* crossed in a contract. "Good heavens, no. All decisions have… had to be unanimous." He paused for a moment, looking inward, thinking. Then he brightened. "Of course, the three of us can decide now." Even the darkest cloud had a silver lining.

"What did you expect would happen after your father 'stormed off, swearing at us'?" Her mimicry of his voice was sufficiently accurate to make him frown, as if wondering whether he was being mocked. "How would those important business decisions you had come together to consider get made?" said Darling.

Andrew shook his head, breathing heavily through his nose. That simple gesture told Darling that Mr Andrew Dance did not enjoy family gatherings, that he disliked at least some members of his family, although not necessarily the obvious choices.

"What we... what I expected to happen was that father, dear father, would go somewhere, drink himself to sleep and then call us all together – again – on Monday evening, and he would agree to everything he had called 'a betrayal of everything I hold sacred' on Sunday. Not that he held anything sacred that did not have the Queen's head printed on it."

Darling did not know whether his mimicry was as accurate as hers, but she didn't need to know that to understand Andrew Dance believed his father was a cantankerous old bastard who really should get out of the way and allow the younger generation to run the ship.

For a moment, she felt a pang of sympathy for the Dancer. She wondered whether he had known he was a dinosaur stumbling towards the tar pit of history rather than trumpeting his dominance over the forest of gigantic ferns. Then she wondered where she was getting these crazy thoughts.

"What did your father take such particular umbrage to?" Umbrage. Now there was a word she had not even known she knew but that seemed appropriate to this moment.

"It was nothing specific, just our general attitude towards the companies. Times are tough, as I am sure you are aware. Competition is fierce. Garth and Ekaterina were proposing that the family businesses should adopt a more aggressive stance towards our competitors, and our suppliers."

"And your father disagreed with this?"

Andrew nodded.

Darling wondered what sort of 'aggression' they could have proposed to get Barry Dance saying 'no'. In his youth, he had not been averse to breaking fingers, knees and heads in the name of profit. At least one of his competitors had ended up dead. Had they suggested bombing competitors' offices?

"What about you? What did you think?"

His hesitation, his glance at his perfectly manicured nails, that ever-so-slight downturn at the corners of his mouth were enough to tell Darling that Andrew Dance believed no one else in the family gave a toss what he thought.

"I agree with Garth and Ekaterina," he said. "The business environment is growing more competitive by the day. Only the strong are going to survive, and we Dances are born survivors."

He spoke with a confidence and resolution that still sounded as true as a cracked bell to Darling. She thought of suggesting that he tell that to his father, but didn't. She was not going to waste that line on someone who was a bit player in this drama, a walk-on spear carrier without a line, a redshirt, whatever high opinion he might have of himself. Whoever had killed the Dancer, Darling didn't think this limp-wristed little weasel had any responsibility for such a decisive act.

Darling continued asking seemingly serious questions and taking careful note of his answers, even asking follow-on questions as though in search of a full, coherent picture, a 'big picture' in which Andrew Dance was more than an irrelevant stick figure in the farthest corner from the blaze that was the murder of his father.

Eventually she took her leave, saying they would probably require a formal statement from him and would be in touch.

"Any time, of course." He smiled, exchanging business cards with her as though kissing the air beside either of her cheeks, an automatic, unthinking reflex. "Anything I can do to help. Anything."

What do you think? she asked herself, walking to the car. Straw, that's all he is. "Any way the wind blows." Her attempt at singing sounded nothing like Queen. It sounded nothing like singing. *He pretends he's important but deep down he knows he's not.*

Chapter Nineteen

Kitty looked around the dinner table. It was the first time she had ever sat at the head of the table with all her children seated there. Well, her two surviving sons and her daughter-in-law. The head had always been the Dancer's place, as the paterfamilias. For all his faults, he had always done his best to provide for his family. Their home, their food, their clothes, their lifestyles were testimony to that. While the children might have fled the nest and imagined they were making their own ways in life, the truth was they had all been in orbit around their father. Now he was gone, there was a distinct possibility they would all go spiralling off on their own. Kitty was not going to permit that. There were very few promises she had made to Barry that she had not broken – love, honour and obey had long since crumbled to dust – but keeping the family together was one she very much intended to honour.

Sitting there they were all looking to her.

"Okay, this meeting of the Dance family is called to order."

She laughed. They didn't. Well, fuck them for having their thumbs up their arses, she thought. She held up an A4 manila envelope. "This is your father's will." She nodded towards Ekaterina. "Your father-in-law's, just in case you were wondering." Her daughter-in-law's smile was as warm as the vapour boiling off a flask of liquid oxygen. "I think this is the time to read it."

If she hadn't had their attention before, she did now. Kitty opened the envelope with exaggerated slowness, as though she did not want to damage it beyond reuse.

Eventually, she removed the single page and began to read aloud.

> This is the last will and testament of William Barry Dance. Being of sound mind and body, I appoint Trevor Austin Sinclair of Bodiam and Mallet Solicitors, to be my executor, who shall be entitled to remuneration in accord with the scale of fees agreed by the Law Society at the time of my death…

"Get on with it, Mother," snarled Garth, his voice a dead weight of frustrated anticipation.

"If you insist." Kitty smiled. "If you want to be like that…" She pantomimed reading the next paragraph, tracing the words with her finger. Then she looked up and smiled. "All your father's worldly goods and possessions go to me."

If it was possible for the room to become any more silent than it already was, it did. The temperature felt as though it fell a good ten degrees.

"Is that all?" asked Garth, eventually.

Kitty nodded. "You'll just have to wait until I die and my will is read to see whether you get anything or I leave everything to the Newcastle Dog and Cat Shelter."

"Oh, don't look so angry," she told them. "You are all well off already because of your father and you have no reason at all to think I would leave you out of anything, no reason at all."

Garth and Andrew looked convinced, but Ekaterina's expression was utterly impassive.

"What's that written on the back of the will?" Garth said, pointing.

Kitty made a questioning face and then turned the sheet over. "It looks like something additional to the will."

"That's called a codicil," smarmed Andrew. Being a solicitor, of course he knew about things legal. "To be valid, it has to obey the same formalities as a proper will."

"What do you mean?" demanded Garth, who was growing more obviously uncomfortable with each second.

"It has to be dated, signed by Father and his signature witnessed by two independent witnesses who are not beneficiaries of the will."

Kitty pushed her reading glasses back down onto her nose and read what was there.

"That is definitely his signature, and the witnesses are Phil Cruddas and Trevor Sinclair, so it looks as though this is valid…"

"Get on with it!" the boys chorused.

"It says that all his executive powers in all Dance enterprises are to pass to Ekaterina, and not me."

"What?" All three spoke at the same time.

Kitty saw fury in Garth – the same fury she had sometimes seen in his father a long, long time ago – disbelief in Andrew and bewilderment in Ekaterina. There was no doubt in her they were all as surprised by this as she was.

Before anyone could prevent him, Andrew snatched the document from her hands while taking his reading glasses out of his pocket and putting them on his nose to study it with the close attention he gave to all legal documents. After a while, he threw the will onto the table and removed his spectacles.

"Looks kosher to me." He sighed, turning his attention towards Ekaterina, who was already under the full weight of Garth's scrutiny.

"Why didn't you tell us?" he asked.

"Tell you what?" Ekaterina replied. "This is the first I have heard of this."

Garth shook his head. "I don't believe you. Dad wouldn't do something like this off his own bat. His family business was for family only. He didn't think of you as family."

"That isn't true," Kitty intervened. "He was very fond of Ekaterina, very fond indeed."

"She must have put the idea in his head!" Garth protested.

Andrew nodded in agreement.

"We never talked about it," said Ekaterina, her voice low and even. "Never."

Intuition told Kitty she was telling the truth. While Ekaterina was very good at hiding things, Kitty believed her in this. The news had come as a shock to her no less than it had to both the boys. It frustrated their obvious ambitions – and why should they not have expected to take control of at least some of the family empire? They were as surprised and angry as she would have expected them to be. Ekaterina was as controlled as Kitty had ever seen her, and her first impression of her daughter-in-law had been that she was a calculating, controlling little madam who was not to be trusted, although her eldest son obviously worshipped the water she walked on and that had been reason enough for Kitty to hold her tongue. It still was.

"There is no point in getting into an argument over it," Kitty said.

Both her sons glared at her as though getting into a serious argument was the only thing to do.

"Your father never did anything without a reason…"

"I think we all know his reason for doing this," snarled Garth. "To fuck us over good and proper."

Kitty shrugged. That might be true. Certainly Dancer had grown less and less enamoured of his sons and their abilities as the years had passed, but he had never discussed this with her. "You cannot know that."

"Oh yes we can!" said Garth.

For a moment, Kitty saw her Barry in their eldest surviving son, and knew that if she let him totally lose his temper there would probably be consequences they would all regret. A chill went through her as she wondered whether she had actually heard Garth shouting that he would kill his father. "If I do not know why he did this then neither do you."

Garth's response to this was to glare at his mother in a way he never had before, making her wonder whether he knew how distant she and Dancer had become these last couple of years; whether he was prepared to risk everything by giving in to his temper. Only when he turned away and his shoulders became less rigid – a gesture that was his father through and through – did she realise she had won this skirmish, and that a skirmish was all it was. His father had never forgotten anything and had forgiven nothing. Neither would Garth.

"What we have to do is take this to Trevor Sinclair and see what he makes of it," Kitty said.

This time she thought it was Andrew who was going to object, his professional pride piqued by someone else being appointed executor. He relaxed after a moment's thought and nodded.

"If anyone can find a way around this, it is Trevor Sinclair," Andrew said, grudgingly.

Who says we want to find a way around it? Kitty thought, but did not say. She wasn't sure she did and she was damned certain Ekaterina did not. "That's decided, then," she said. "To Trevor it goes."

To say this met with her children's whole-hearted agreement would have been stretching things to breaking point, but nobody objected when she replaced the will in its envelope and pressed it down flat with several strokes of her hand. She had no idea why she made that gesture, only that it seemed appropriate, a line drawn under the problem. "Would anyone like some tea?"

Suddenly Garth turned towards Ekaterina. "You were fucking him, weren't you, you cunt."

In an instant, the temperature in the room matched that of a Northumberland moor on a cloudless night in February. Kitty saw her youngest son's jaw drop open and his eyes open wide. She could almost hear Ekaterina weighing up her responses behind her impassive eyes. Kitty felt a wrenching in her own stomach, a reaction to the stupidity of her son.

Ekaterina's right hand lashed out and smacked Garth across his cheek with a crack that filled the room. "Don't you dare insult me!"

Kitty watched Garth's fists clench, and hoped he wouldn't do anything even more stupid than he had already done. Ekaterina might be a head shorter than Garth and little more than half his weight, but Kitty believed she knew her daughter-in-law well enough to know that, if it came to blows, she would fight to win as quickly as possible and as savagely as she needed to. Ekaterina would damage him any way she could, and however stupid he was being, Kitty did not want that. He was her son, after all.

"What is more, don't you dare insult your father like that. You may have hated him, but I loved him as I love my own father and I will not hear him slandered by anyone. Do you hear?" Ekaterina looked from Garth to Andrew and back again.

Andrew still looked bewildered.

Garth subsided, nodding and mumbling.

"Good," she added. "Seeing as I am not welcome here, I shall leave now."

"Ekaterina…" Kitty reached out to take her arm, but Ekaterina slipped out of her mother-in-law's grasp and shook her head, before hurrying out of the room. They all watched her, then heard the front door slam shut.

"You really didn't know your father very well, did you, Garth?"

He turned to his mother, anger reignited in his eyes. "What do you mean?"

"You can't seriously suggest your father would pay any attention to a woman as high-maintenance as her, can you?" She stared at him for a while, then laughed and shook her head. Her daughter-in-law had much too much going on inside her head to attract Barry.

Garth evidently did not agree with her, as he stamped off out of the room and shortly afterwards slammed the front door even more vigorously than Ekaterina had.

Kitty looked at Andrew.

"I told Alison I wouldn't be long," he said, and made his way towards the door.

And you wouldn't want to annoy Alison, now would you, thought Kitty, smiling inwardly. She had little time for any of her other daughters-in-law, but least of all for Alison, who looked down that long nose of hers and was not nearly as clever as she believed she was. Anyone that clever wouldn't have put up with Andrew for very long. Once upon a time he had been a dear, sweet little boy. He had grown up to be a rather dull man with almost nothing about him that interested his mother any longer, especially his inability to provide her with any grandchildren, an inability he appeared to share with both his brothers.

Once upon a time Kitty would have been much more troubled by that than she was now. Time changed everything. Nobody needed her to put a plaster on their scraped knees or gentle them back to sleep after a nightmare had woken them. Their mere existence no longer gave her life meaning. As a girl, she'd been optimistic, convinced that life had a meaning, however hidden. The intervening years crammed full of the business of just being alive, the weekly church ritual, had left her empty inside.

It was to dispel that bleakness she poured herself a tumbler of Dancer's very best Talisker. He was the only one allowed to drink it, on high days and holidays. For anyone else to so much as touch the bottle would have had steam coming out of his ears.

"What have you got to say about it now, you old reprobate?" she asked aloud as the spirit burned its way down her gullet. She wasn't sure she liked the sensation but believed she could get used to it, given the opportunity she now had.

She took another mouthful of malt, allowing it to trickle slowly down into her stomach.

Chapter Twenty

Ekaterina drove to the cemetery and parked on double yellow lines outside the gates, her fury having dissipated as quickly as it had arisen. Even if she had noticed the lines she would not have cared. She always parked wherever she wanted to and if some lowly parking warden wanted to give her a ticket for that, well, good luck to them. She might not have diplomatic immunity or the notoriety she had in Moscow because of her father but somehow, she had not paid a parking fine all the time she had lived in England.

Getting out of the car, she became aware of the darkness gathering overhead, of the lateness in the day, and immediately worried that the chain might already be across the cemetery gates. In Moscow, a few roubles changing hands and possibly a bottle of cheap vodka would have seen a key appear. The jobsworths of Tyneside, who drove from gate to gate in anonymous vehicles, locked up then moved on somewhere they could not be found. Glancing at her wrist, Ekaterina was relieved it was only half past four, plenty of time to do what she needed to do. Even so, she hurried through the gates and along the winding gravel path until she reached the simple grey stone announcing the grave beneath to be the last resting place of William Barry Dance Junior, beloved husband and son, taken from us too soon.

As she stood there, head bowed, she wondered whether Barry Junior really had been a beloved husband

and son. Had he been beloved of her while he was alive and now he was dead? Certainly, she had enjoyed her time with him. He brought eccentricity and uncertainty to a life that had been conformist and rigid before she met him at the reception after they had presented him to the supporters of the football club in Moscow her father owned.

Not that anyone ever said in public that her father owned the club. He was too dark a figure for that, too deeply involved in the impenetrable shadows of a country and city where it might be said the sun never properly shone on public life.

Barry was as different to her father as it was possible to be, irreverent and seemingly carefree, always with a laugh on his lips that made Ekaterina laugh, too. He brought her flowers that did not bear the label of the most expensive florists, took her to unexpected places most Muscovites did not know, never mind an English footballer who had been there only a few weeks and whose command of the language sometimes seemed to be restricted to *do svidaniya*. Which was another lie he told about himself. He spoke Russian as well as she spoke English, especially when talking with her father, who had only two words of English – *Fuck* and *You*.

They got on well, her father and Barry, but it was only when the couple came to England after his football career was prematurely ended, that she met Barry Senior and realised their fathers were two peas from the same pod, alike in their outlook and business practices. None of which would have mattered at all had Barry Junior's first kiss not sent a jolt of what felt like electricity through her, making her realise she wanted this man as she had never wanted any other man, wanted him in ways she had not believed were real to her. She took him to her bed within hours of meeting him and when he left next morning she knew that all the poets and songwriters were only speaking the truth. Their life together after that had the same ups and downs, delights and angers, as any other couples had, but one factor remained constant; they knew ecstasy in bed.

But was that enough for him to be her beloved? Did that not require more of him, of them both? Or was that question just her bringing Russian gloom and existential angst to something that was much simpler than that, something to be valued for what it was rather than what it was not? Whatever the word meant, she had loved him and his absence left a bloody-edged emptiness inside her she did not believe would ever be filled, and which she suspected was expanding day by day, eventually to consume her.

"Did I do wrong?" she asked the gravestone. "Was I too impatient, too hasty?"

No answer came. If one had, she would not have been surprised. She knew there were more things in heaven and earth than she could imagine. Words from beyond the grave were the least of the possibilities. She knew that she would not have done what she had done if Barry was still alive. There would have been no need. For whatever reason, his father had taken notice of what he said in ways he did not regard what the others said, and Barry Junior had taken notice of what she said when it came to business, the need for there to be a firm hand on the tiller, one decisive voice to be heard. It was what her father had taught her and what his father taught him. Yes, it would all have been different had Barry lived, but in those last months of his life he had gone places she could not go for reasons she could not comprehend.

"I don't understand why it is so important to you," she had complained the only time he had tried to explain it to her. "You played football, you cannot play football any longer." It was a fact of life. There was nothing he could do about it. He should not waste time and effort on what was a lost cause. You did what you could and disregarded what you couldn't. But she had been unable to get through to him. He started to drink heavily, something he had never done when he had football – even though drinking seemed to be the pastime of choice for most footballers, drinking and golfing and gambling. One of his fellow players, before he moved to Moscow, had got himself into very serious trouble with his betting habit, got involved with people who would have given even the Dancer pause and ended up being excluded from the game. Barry Junior had joked the only thing he couldn't pass was the betting shop. Ekaterina had not laughed, and he never mentioned it again. As well as the drinking, he stopped looking after himself, putting on weight, wearing the same clothes for days at a time, not bathing or shaving; not in a designer stubble sort of way, just in a 'I really don't care anymore' sort of way. She didn't know which hurt more, what he was doing to himself or that there seemed to be nothing she could do about it.

Then there was no need to do anything. On a typically filthy night in February, he went out for a drive. She had said nothing because for the first time in weeks he was sober enough to drive, and driving was something he enjoyed. He might not have been a particularly good driver but it gave him pleasure, especially driving the Eau de Nil Baby Bentley – his last gift to himself for having been a footballer. She hadn't paid any attention to his not returning before she went to bed. He was a big boy and didn't need her permission to go out. It was only when she opened the front door to the two police officers who had been hammering on it for a good ten minutes at three in the morning that she realised something was really not right with Barry Junior. There had been a single-car accident on the Coast Road. He had collided with a lamp post. It looked as though he had been going faster than he should have been and lost control when he hit a pool of standing water. Maybe if he had been wearing his seat belt there might have been a chance.

She didn't tell them he had been obsessive about wearing his seat belt, even if he was only going to the local shops for a bottle of milk. She didn't tell anyone. Not his parents. Not her parents. Not his brothers. Not the police. An accident was one thing. Suicide was something else entirely, and she understood the term 'single-car accident' was the accepted code for suicide by car. Nobody spoke the truth of it. After all, there could be no formal Catholic funeral ceremony for a suicide and his parents appeared to put a lot of stock in the church. What they didn't need to know couldn't hurt them, and the truth was that Ekaterina hurt enough for all of them. She hurt so much she even told her mother not to bother when she said she would fly in for the funeral. Just then, she knew she did not have the strength to resist the efforts she knew her mother would make to take her back to Moscow, back home. Moscow was not home. Where Barry was, that was her home. This was her home even more than the house in which she lived, the house they had shared for so short a time.

"I'm in charge now." She waited for an answer, and when it came she nodded. He approved. She turned and walked away from the grave, then turned back. "You have not asked me why I did it," she said. She waited. When there was still no response, she shook her head. "I will tell you anyway. He was old. He was weak. Your brothers are just weak. They worry about what people think of them. The business needs someone who is strong, the way he used to be strong. I am strong." She stood and listened. A smile began to spread across her face, and she began to nod her head. She turned away again, and almost skipped along as she left the grave.

Chapter Twenty-One

Darling's long-lost friend, Paul Reid, rubbed his eyes, which hurt. Just because it was the twenty-first century and everyone was environmentally aware didn't mean that whenever and wherever gambling men got together in private to ply their trade, the air didn't instantly thicken with tobacco smoke and become rank with the reek of alcohol. He'd never smoked himself, except for a Havana cigar his father-in-law had pressed on him at his wedding reception, and the few puffs he had taken of it had only reassured him he was right to go without. He was not averse to booze or – unusually for an ex-copper – opposed to the consumption of less dangerous narcotics and hallucinogens as such, but he preferred to play cards sober. Cards were his business, his calling, his vocation. Any edge he could get, he would take.

The evening had been long and tedious. Sammy King, the game's host, was a more or less professional gambler like Reid, but the others around the table all had more money than sense and more sense than ability at cards. Not that they had the slightest idea of that. They had started playing just after ten. He and Sammy could have fleeced the four of them faster than it took them to smoke their first cigar and still have time to go out and find themselves a decent game. They had agreed ahead of time to go easy on the four punters, make them believe they had enjoyed a good evening with the cards, shown those two professionals a thing or two and go home with lighter wallets, but not so much lighter they would turn down Sammy's next invitation. It was a long-term business strategy.

Reid and Sammy sat back in their chairs once the punters had taken their leave and the paraphernalia of poker had been cleared off the table, although not its green baize cloth. Sammy had got out the good whisky and Reid enjoyed the warmth as it bit its way down into his stomach. He didn't approve of Sammy adulterating the malt with ginger ale and ice, having been taught his whisky drinking – as he had so much else – by the strict traditionalist, Joe Milburn, but he said nothing. Each to his own. He would stick to his diet cola for the time being.

"Did you hear about the Dancer?" Sammy enquired after taking a swallow of his whisky and a long pull on his cigar.

Being of the considered opinion that there was no such thing as an innocent question, even from a mate – especially from a mate – Reid made a noncommittal reply. "I could hardly have missed it, could I? Been all over the news."

"Funny business," Sammy observed.

"Not for the Dancer!"

They both laughed at that, but not for very long. They had both had their different encounters with Barry Dance, and both knew the kind of man he had been and the kind of man he appeared to have become. While he didn't know what Sammy thought, Reid agreed with Joe Milburn, that the veneer of genteel prosperity was just that, a façade, a thin cover on the backstreet thug Dance had been. Still, getting your head blown off with your own shotgun was hardly something to be celebrated.

"I hear it was a professional hit," said Sammy.

Reid snorted. "No such thing as a 'professional hit', not round here anyway." He laughed. "I never came across one and I met enough killers when I was a copper. They were all amateurs." He'd never made a secret of having been a copper. There was no point in a small place like Tyneside. He might not advertise the fact, but he believed it had its uses.

Even as he spoke, Reid could hear a doubt nagging at the back of his mind. Pen Darling had mentioned a professional killer, and she was even more of a straight-faced, straight-laced, straight-bat copper than Joe Milburn. Reid knew exactly what Milburn's response would have been to the suggestion that Dance had been murdered by a 'professional hitman'. You would have heard his laughter all over Tyneside. Yet here was a second mention, from someone who had nothing to do with either the police or the criminal world, other than lightening the wallets of members of either fraternity whenever the opportunity arose.

"I dunno," said Sammy, chewing at a flake of tobacco on his lower lip. "I heard something about maybe an ex-soldier, one who'd been a copper as well."

Once again Reid laughed. "Was this from someone who was trying to sell you a bridge he had in his back pocket?"

Sammy joined in laughing. "I suppose it does sound pretty ridiculous when I think about it."

Reid filled his empty glass with the malt Sammy was drinking and poured a good half of it straight down his throat without tasting it, rather luxuriating in the heat of it in his stomach, trying to hide that he was thinking about Sammy's remark. The more he thought about it, the less ridiculous it seemed.

"Got anyone in mind?" he asked, thinking even as he spoke this was a question too far, even for an acquaintance like Sammy.

Sammy shook his head. "God, no! How would I know a name?"

Reid laughed, nodding, and raised his glass. "Your continued health, wealth and prosperity, Sammy!"

Sammy joined in, oblivious of the fact that Reid did have a name that came to his mind, the name of another gambling man he had not liked the couple of times they had met, whose company neither he nor his wallet had enjoyed, a man who, if he never met him again, it would be much too soon.

"Here's to us!" Sammy laughed, raising his own glass to clink against Reid's. "There's none like us!"

"You can say that again," replied Reid before he swallowed the rest of the Scotch. It was probably just as well there weren't many like them. The small pool that was Tyneside could only support so many of their breed. "Time to go and get my beauty sleep," Reid said and laughed.

Sammy joined in, then he got up and escorted him to the front door, where he discovered it was hammering down with rain.

"You can stay if you like," Sammy offered, unenthusiastically.

Reid shook his head. Ordinarily the rain would not have bothered him. His coat had a hood, and there was a long-peaked cap in his pocket. "I'll call a cab." Reid would ordinarily have walked, especially with the clock scarcely past midnight as it was now, but tonight he couldn't resist the lure of a dry ride. It was not quite one o'clock when he closed his front door behind himself, not quite too late to ring Pen Darling and leave her a message.

Chapter Twenty-Two

When Darling opened the front door the first thing she saw was the winking red 'message' light of the phone on the hall table. Closing her eyes, she tossed her keys onto the table, where they made a heavy, jingly sound, dropped her bags, then walked into the lounge where she sat on the sofa, leaned back with her arms outstretched and relaxed.

The tension drained out of her now she was home and work had been left at the office. She never brought work home, ever. If it meant staying in the office or out on the streets until the early hours of the morning, as it had today, that was what she did. Home was where she was plain Penny Darling, a single woman who was content to remain single for the rest of her life, having tried marriage once and found it very much not to her taste. That could have been because the man-child she married turned out to be a completely self-absorbed mummy's boy, rather than any fundamental failing in the institution or herself; but once bitten and all that. She didn't need a man or want a boyfriend, or even a girl for laughs. It had taken a lot of hard work but she had got herself to the point where she could look in a mirror and like the woman looking back at her, where she was comfortable with herself.

Only when she had made and drunk a pot of Darjeeling tea and eaten a supper of cheese and pickled beetroot sandwich and two small, sour Cox's apples did she remember the blinking light she had seen on her way into the house. Could it wait until the morning? No, she decided, it couldn't.

"Pen, this is Paul Reid. I have a name. Give me a call and I'll give you it in person."

She cursed aloud. There was no one to hear her. Then she hit the redial button and had the satisfaction of hearing the sleep in Reid's voice when he answered.

Five minutes later, she had agreed to meet Reid outside the Laing at midday.

There, that wasn't so bad now, was it? she asked herself when she put down the phone. She was asleep before she could decide whether she believed it.

* * *

The next morning passed in its usual blizzard of paperwork and phone calls, all of which were designed to keep her from doing the job she had of discovering who killed Barry Dance. At ten minutes to twelve she got up and walked out of the office, ignoring all the looks, telling no one where she was going. Being an inspector had one or two perks, not many.

Reid was already sitting on one of the curved concrete seats on the pedestrian area called 'The Blue Carpet' outside the Laing Art Gallery with its now almost-colourless tiles, when she walked up into the square. They were of an age, in their late thirties. He was just under six feet tall, wirily built, still not running to fat, with thick, dark hair just over his collar and wearing the same uniform of leather bomber jacket, straight blue jeans and off-white Converse trainers he had worn for work since quitting the force. As she approached, he got to his feet and removed his dark glasses, putting them inside his jacket. She held out her hand as she came to him and he took it briefly. His grip was dry and firm with nothing of the test of strength coppers so often indulged themselves in.

They sat on the bench side by side. There was hardly room for the two of them before one would slide down the steeply curved edge of the bench. He made sure she had the safe end.

She was about to say it had been a long time when she remembered they would not be meeting now had they not encountered each other at the pool earlier that week.

"I'm sure you're busy, so I won't keep you," he began.

She realised he was nervous of her, of her position, her rank. When had that happened? When they'd been on the job together he had always been that one step ahead of her, until he crashed, burned and disappeared. He wasn't the first, and he hadn't been the last. She'd always thought of him as one of the good guys, not one of the Neanderthals like Morton. He hadn't been her type, any more than she was his, as they'd quickly discovered, but that – and his decision that the coppering life was not for him anymore – had never meant she didn't respect him. Yes, she was a detective inspector now and there were people who would do well to be afraid of her, of the hammer she could bring down on their lives, but there was something wrong if a man like Paul Reid was afraid of her.

"The name is Mark Wearing," he said.

She frowned. Was she supposed to know the name?

"Used to be a soldier, SAS or something like. That's what he says, anyway. After that, he was a copper for a bit. Now, who knows?"

"How do you know him?"

"I've played cards with him a couple of times. A right nasty piece of work, but that was just my first impression."

"And you thought of him why?"

He shook his head. "I didn't think of him. I'd put him completely out of my mind. You asked me to listen for whispers. That's the whisper I heard."

"Who was the whisperer?"

He laughed and shook his head. "Inspector, you know I wouldn't tell you that if I was still a sergeant and you were my guvnor. It's a whisper from these mean streets, nothing more."

She nodded. She had asked him for whispers and he had come up with the goods, the first of those she'd asked who had produced anything. She got to her feet, noting the disappointment in his eyes. "Thank you. Keep listening for whispers, will you?"

"Always." He grinned.

She felt his eyes following her as she walked away towards Forth Banks. Maybe she would have liked to linger a few minutes, catch up on what had happened in their lives, but as he said, she was a busy woman and this was the closest she had come to a lead in this important case. She had things to do. Maybe she would find time for Paul Reid in the future, maybe she wouldn't.

* * *

Back in the office, Darling laid a page from her notebook on Morton's desk as she walked past. "Everything you can find on him," she said without pausing.

When she sat down, the first thing Darling did was put in a call to Milburn. She didn't know the name Mark

Wearing, but if there was anyone in Forth Banks who would know it, that man was Joe Milburn. He was out, but Mrs Pye, his secretary, said she would give him the message as soon as he got back, unless Darling wanted her to disturb him wherever he was. Her tone was enough to convince her that disturbing Milburn was not the best idea. When he got in would be soon enough.

In the meantime, she opened the file on the Dancer's bank account to see whether there were any unusual payments made recently. Anything untoward would have been cash and Darling had no doubt at all the Dancer had had access to sources of cash buried away where only the most forensic of the accountants at the force's disposal would discover them. They would, eventually, but it would probably be too late to be of much use in tracing his murderer. She made a note to get the economic crime and fraud investigators to trawl through all the Dance companies' accounts. Doubtless the kids would scream blue murder but she had the irrefutable justification of needing to search out even the tiniest clue to his murder. Someone had murdered the Dancer. They had a reason for that, and that reason might be found in some business deal that had gone wrong, or even just gone astray. It might be too late to catch the Dancer but she knew she had the opportunity to do what Joe Milburn – at least – had wanted to do for years, turn the Dance empire upside down and give it a good shake to see what might fall out.

That done, she looked at his phones. There were three and she would not be surprised were there more. The contact lists were what interested her. She hadn't the time or the inclination to look through the calls. She had sergeants and constables to do scut work like that. The names she found were what she expected to find: the rich and connected of Tyneside and the whole North East; family members; some names she knew were dodgy and assumed they were his friends from way back when, before he made himself respectable. She had just started to scroll through the third list when she came across a name that rang an out-of-tune bell – Mrs Bainbridge. Mrs Bainbridge.

She was just tapping a pen on her teeth – a tic she had when she was searching through her memory – when Morton appeared by her desk, obviously waiting.

"Well?" she said.

"I've only been able to find one 'Mark Wearing' in this area. He lived at the decent end of Osborne Road, but that's all I can find for him on 192, and that is three years old. Other than that, nothing."

"But what?" It was obvious there was a 'but' from the way the sergeant shifted from foot to foot, like a child desperate to go to the toilet.

"You didn't say he might have been a copper once upon a time. I dare say I'm not the only one who remembers a Mark John Wearing who was on the job for a while. I didn't know him but I knew *of* him. Nasty piece of work. Very free with the physical incentives to cooperate, if you get my meaning."

Darling understood. She also knew that Morton had the selfsame reputation when he was in uniform. She nodded.

"Didn't stay long, and the grapevine has it that he left before he was pushed."

The 'grapevine' was part of the police canteen culture from which Darling was utterly excluded, both because she was now an inspector and the equivalent of management, if the station was a shop floor, and because she was a woman and therefore automatically beyond the pale. One of Morton's virtues was that he was firmly plugged into the grapevine and would tell her what he thought she needed to know, leaving her to imagine the rest.

"Odd thing, though," he continued, "he was military before he joined the force. Wouldn't say much about it, just hints that he'd been in the SAS or some special forces or other, jokes that he could tell us but he'd have to kill us afterwards with a way of laughing nobody else found funny at all. He could send shivers down the backs of some real hard types, could our Mr Wearing. All in all, he was a bit of a cunt by all accounts."

There were some female officers who would have taken distinct and immediate offence to that word, but Darling ignored it. He was just trying to get some reaction from her and she was not about to give him the satisfaction. "Thanks."

"Is he in the frame for the Dancer?"

She shook her head. "Nothing quite so formal as that. Just a whisper I heard, a one-time soldier and a copper, too. If this *is* a professional hit, he might be worth a look."

"You don't want to let Mr Milburn hear you say that." The sergeant laughed.

Darling let him laugh. She would be the judge of what she would let her boss hear. "Does the name 'Mrs Bainbridge' mean anything to you?"

It was clear to her from his physical reaction – a lift of the chin, a narrowing of the eyes, an intake of breath – that the name did mean something to him, and that he did not want to tell her what that was.

"Spit it out, Sergeant."

"She's a madam."

"And you know this, how?"

Morton tried to tell her that Mrs Bainbridge was non-stick, like Teflon, and that no charge had ever been proved against her, while trying to avoid saying that he had used Mrs Bainbridge's girls more than once, and that the lady would never permit him to forget. A person in her position could never have too many police favours in the bank.

"So, if the Dancer wanted some company he might go to Mrs Bainbridge to provide it."

"That's about the size of it," said Morton, his mouth dry with the possibility she might ask more questions. He wasn't the only copper on Forth Banks who owed Mrs Bainbridge a debt for services rendered.

"I think I need to have a word with Mrs Bainbridge. Get me her address."

She watched Morton walk back to his desk and knew exactly what he had struggled to avoid telling her. She made a mental note, something else to use when the inevitable confrontation came.

Just then, the telephone rang. "He's back," Mrs Pye told her and put down the phone without allowing her to reply. Darling stood up, took a deep breath and walked towards the stairs up to the next floor.

* * *

Milburn was sitting behind his desk with a pile of files to his left, one open in front of him and one more to his right, closed. He looked up as she entered. He was very obviously not in a good mood.

"Got something for me?" he growled.

Darling hesitated, then sat down. "I've heard a whisper."

He nodded.

"It's a name: Mark Wearing, possibly Mark John Wearing. He's an ex-copper, so I'm told, possibly an ex-soldier, too. I thought you might know more about him than anyone else."

Milburn glared at her, then closed the file, leaned forward and made a peak of his fingers pressing against each other.

Darling knew the gesture. This was not going to be a comfortable interview, but now she had started she had to continue.

"Is this part of your 'professional hitman' garbage?" he said.

She opened her mouth to argue the evidence showed a potential murderer skilled with firearms and capable of breaking and entering without leaving any trace or setting off the alarms, but then decided against it.

"It isn't 'my garbage', sir. We have to consider every possibility, and Wearing is the only name that has come up yet."

Milburn sat still for a moment, then leaned back in his chair and exhaled heavily. "I remember Wearing. Nasty piece of work, very nasty; not cut out to be a copper in the modern world. Suffered from delusions of adequacy, probably a result of the time he did in the army. Said he was SAS, but who knows? The SAS is a bit like Fight Club, you don't talk about it. If he was, then he probably knows more about killing than the average man in the street. He might have picked up breaking and entering skills there as well. Or on the job. He wouldn't be the first." He blew on the tips of his fingers again.

"Supposing," he continued, "just supposing this professional hitman theory is correct, Wearing might be on the list to have pulled the trigger. The more important question would be, who hired him to pull that trigger?"

Darling said nothing. As far as she was concerned the list of those who might be homicidally inclined towards Barry Dance was long and, so far, she had nothing to suggest she should remove anyone from the list.

"He always was the sort of man who could start a fight in an empty room," Milburn said. "Mind you, at the same time, he could knock a man to the ground, pick him up and go off to the pub together."

"So, he was bipolar?" Darling wondered aloud.

Milburn's brow furrowed. "More of an impulse-control problem, if you ask me," he said, staring past the still not-yet faded nicotine stains on his fingers.

It was more than five years since he dropped his twenty-a-day habit just like that, the coldest of cold turkeys, but not a day went by he didn't want the taste of tobacco in his mouth, want that hit of the nicotine to ease him through the next five minutes. Not that he would ever smoke again, whatever the craving. He shook his head and glared at Darling. "Is that it?" He tapped the pile of files on his desk. "I have some assessments to do."

Darling scrambled to her feet, not wanting to take up any more of his time than she needed to just in case her file was in the heap, reminded that she had assessments of her own to complete.

Back downstairs, she found a note on her desk from Morton.

> Mrs Bainbridge, 27 Loch Crescent, Jesmond.

She glanced at the clock above the door, wondering whether she could put off seeing the woman until tomorrow. While the day had not been particularly long or demanding, she could still feel a headache beginning to build behind her eyes. It was only just gone four. Why had she thought it was later than that? Had a wish been mother to the thought? Gathering up the note, she thought about taking Morton with her, just in case there was any monkey business from Mrs Bainbridge, but he was deep in conversation on the phone so she went on downstairs and took her car from the yard. What were the chances of the woman being there anyway?

Chapter Twenty-Three

The young woman sat in her Range Rover Vogue in the Tesco car park at Kingston Park, drumming her fingers on the steering wheel. According to the dashboard clock, he wasn't late yet, therefore she was early, which annoyed her. Being late was her prerogative, not his. The rattle-tap of fingernails on the window beside her brought her back to the moment. He grinned at her and blew a kiss. How had he got there without her seeing him?

"Exactly how stupid are you, calling me today?" she asked as she got out of the car.

He shrugged, a gesture that came close to annoying her. "You called me. Remember?" He raised an eyebrow, then stepped close, pinning her against the door, and kissed her so hard his teeth were grinding on her lips, forcing them apart.

She used her teeth to respond, watching over his shoulder as a middle-aged couple in shabby leisurewear pushed a full-to-overflowing trolley towards their car with expressions of 'Get a room, why don't you' disgust on their faces. She laughed inside, asking herself whether anyone had ever kissed either of them with such fervent, urgent need. They were just jealous.

"What can I say?" he whispered in her ear, making her shiver. "Killing someone always made me hot. Killing someone for you makes me... well..."

She quickly ducked her hand down his front and took hold of him. It was a good thing he was wearing fashionably loose trousers. She squeezed him hard enough to make him wince and step away.

"I thought we could have a good dinner," she chided.

"You can eat me here if you like." He grinned.

"You are an animal," she said, almost blushing.

"That's why you like me," he replied, walking back towards his car.

There was nothing she could say to that. It was just the truth.

She was positive the slot in which his Focus was parked had been empty when she arrived, and that no car had driven up anywhere near her while she was waiting. She got in the passenger side and sat silent as he drove out of the car park and up towards the roundabout over the A1, thinking about this, and was shocked when he spoke.

"Camouflage is an art. I'm an artist, don't you know?"

She turned to see him looking at her rather than the road, wearing that unreadable grin of his.

"Watch the road, you idiot," she told him, thinking, it's a dark art. Of course, there was a lot about him that was dark, that she really did not want to know.

"It's okay." He laughed. "I got fitted with radar in my head as part of my SAS training."

They talked of this and that on the way to the restaurant and throughout the meal, which was good, even if not quite as good as some meals she had eaten there in the past. When she asked, she was told Wednesday was Le Patron's day off, which was immediately followed by an enquiry whether there was anything amiss with the food.

"No" – she smiled – "it is delicious." Which it was, but she made a mental note not to eat there on a Monday in future.

They chatted inconsequentially, laughing and generally comfortable in each other's company until they got back in his car.

"Your place or mine?" he asked.

She had no doubt he knew where she lived, although she had never told him the address, but she did not want him there, and the one time she had been to the block of flats where he lived was one too many. Most of their times together had been in hotels, none that she had ever patronized before or would again. The house she took him to this time was one the Dance company estate agency was selling for a recently divorced friend of hers, who was taking a three-month holiday in Florida and New York on the settlement money. She had shown someone around that afternoon. They had shown just enough interest for her to know they wouldn't come back.

Once the door closed behind them, there was no more talking. There was a lot of panting and moaning, yelling and cursing, and when they eventually fell apart they could hear nothing but the thundering of their hearts, feel nothing but the delicious pain of intimate flesh that had been stroked and pounded, licked and bitten. Both thought the other was the best sexual partner they had ever had, the one who made them feel ecstasy in places no one else had ever touched. Neither would ever mention this to the other in case it spoiled the magic.

Eventually, he stirred and turned on the bedside lamp. "Bloody hell, what have you done?" Where he had been lying on his back, the bedding was striped with dried blood. He jumped off the bed and went to the wardrobe door, looking over his shoulder at his reflection, seeing the gouges all the way up his back where her fingernails had cut him. "You bitch, you've marked me!"

She stared at his reflection, and at him – at the perfection of his proportions and musculature, at the thick flaccid tube of flesh hanging between his thighs, at the adornment she had given him – and felt a sudden flush of wet heat between her own legs. Without thinking, she covered her groin with her left hand, fingers moving almost of their own volition.

"You like it," she growled. "Admit it, you like it."

"Let's see how much you like it when I do it to you," he snarled, flinging himself at her.

Eventually, she had to admit to herself that she did like it. She liked it a lot. She liked the beautiful pain he inflicted on her almost as much as he appeared to enjoy hurting her. Not that she was going to tell him that. Ever.

Chapter Twenty-Four

Loch Crescent was one of the many leafy side roads in Jesmond, the houses neat and well-kempt, much more so than the sprawling, teeming student quarter that was just a couple of roads away. Five-Series Beemers and assorted SUVs lined the road, along with several electric cars; strangely all of which were white. The door was coloured RAF-blue with floral-patterned stained glass in the panels, differentiating it from the other, white doors. Darling pressed the bell without hearing anything from inside and was about to press it again when the door opened revealing a tall, strongly built woman in her late thirties dressed in jeans and a Marilyn Monroe T-shirt. Her short, dark hair was pushed back behind her ears with white streaks on her temples from the flour on her hands.

"Yes? Can I help you?"

Darling held out her warrant card. "Mrs Bainbridge, I'm Detective Inspector Darling of the Northumbria Police. I have a couple of questions I'd like to ask."

The welcoming smile vanished from the woman's face, the light in her eyes being veiled by clouds of suspicion. "I'm in the middle of making my children's tea. They'll be home in a minute."

"This shouldn't take long."

They stood there for a long moment, waiting for the other to give ground.

"If you insist…"

"I do insist, Mrs Bainbridge. It concerns a murder investigation."

She stepped aside for Darling to enter and made sure the front door lock was secure, then turned around, nothing but shock and surprise on her face. "I don't know anything about any murder," she cried.

"I don't imagine you do, but I believe the victim was a customer of yours."

Mrs Bainbridge led Darling into the front room. It was high-ceilinged with heavy velvet curtains in the bay window, the colour of which matched the dark fawn upholstery of what looked like a very comfortable three-piece suite. Two walls were lined with books that looked to have actually been read, and the marble fireplace was topped with birthday cards for a twelve-year-old girl. There was no television in the room.

"Customer? I don't understand. I'm a widow with two young children. I don't have any customers."

Darling seated herself on the arm of the settee and looked at Mrs Bainbridge shuffling her feet and wringing her hands. Flakes of dried pastry showered the carpet.

"That is not what I hear, Mrs Bainbridge."

There was enough of a pause before she replied for Darling to almost believe she could hear the woman's brain working. Whatever, she was convinced Mrs Bainbridge was much more than the simple widow and hard-working mother she was trying to portray.

"What do you hear?" she said, eventually.

"That you run an escort agency – a rather exclusive, expensive escort agency for men who consider themselves gentlemen of taste and distinction. I'm sure my boss would think you live on immoral earnings but he is old school and that doesn't concern me, at the moment."

The woman stood where she was, still agitated, until she threw up her hands and shook her head. "Oh, what's the point? If you know, you know. How can I help?"

"Barry Dance, he was one of your clients."

Mrs Bainbridge's hands went to her mouth, her eyes wide open. "I heard about that. Shot, wasn't he? I didn't realise he was anything to do with me. I didn't put the name together with the man on my list. He called himself the Dancer. I'm not from around here so I didn't know the name. My husband is… was…"

Darling cut her off in mid-diversionary flow. "Did he hire one of your girls last Sunday night?"

Mrs Bainbridge hesitated, seemed to make one decision then changed her mind, got to her feet and went to an escritoire in the corner of the room, opened a laptop computer and switched it on. A few moments later she shook her head. "Not last Sunday. In fact, he hasn't done any business with me for the last three months."

"Three months?"

"I sent a girl to a room at the Hilton. It was on his account."

"Your clients have accounts?"

The two women stared at each other.

"Ever had any complaints from the girls you supplied to him?"

Mrs Bainbridge shook her head. "I have never heard anything other than he was a perfect gentleman, liked his action on the athletic side, the noisy side, but that was all. I insist my girls tell me about anything unacceptable, anything nasty, and I make it very clear to my customers that if they try anything unacceptable, anything nasty, they will not only never do business with me again, they will also get a visit from one of my business partners, my male business partners, who take a very dim view of our girls being treated with anything other than the utmost respect."

Darling chuckled. A prostitute was a prostitute was a prostitute. A madam was a madam was a madam. "Would I recognise the names of any of your business partners?"

Mrs Bainbridge shook her head. "I don't think so," she lied. Those business partners were mostly coppers of one sort or another, or had been.

"I don't suppose it is important… not now, anyway," said Darling. "It was just a thought."

"There is something else," said Mrs Bainbridge, turning back to her computer. "I have another customer by the name of 'Dance', a Katherine Dance."

"You have women customers!"

Mrs Bainbridge laughed. "This is the twenty-first century, you know. Sauce for the goose and all that."

"Most women I know would be more careful with their money than to use, well…"

"Girls just want to have fun, Inspector, and modern women are prepared to pay for the appropriate skills and expertise."

Darling did not doubt it but suddenly felt an inexplicable, urgent need to be elsewhere. She got to her feet and thanked Mrs Bainbridge for her time. Just as they got to the front door, it opened and two children piled in, a boy and a girl, both wearing the coloured blazer, collar and tie and grey trouser uniform of their school, the same fee-paying Royal Grammar School as the Dancer had sent his sons. They both saw Darling and stopped dead, staring at her.

"Go to your rooms, both of you. Get changed and start your homework. Dinner will be at six," said Mrs Bainbridge.

The children both regarded Darling for slightly too long a moment before dashing upstairs. The girl swung her bag at the boy. He almost avoided it.

"Children, where do they get their energy?" said Mrs Bainbridge.

Walking back to her car Darling thought that the 'escort' business must be very, very healthy for the commission Mrs Bainbridge took to pay for the house, two sets of school fees and everything else that was inside said house.

* * *

Mrs Bainbridge watched Darling drive away, shivered and went inside. That had been just about the least enjoyable encounter of her life, after watching the curtains close around Richard's coffin. She made a phone call to Jessica, wanting to know what she knew about the murder, only to remember she had called to report that the client was a no-show and to enquire if she had any other work on a Sunday night. Mrs Bainbridge was relieved when she had to leave a message, telling Jessica to give her a call as soon as possible without saying why. She knew she would not be able to keep the girl's visit to the Dancer's farm a secret for long, and she didn't want to do more than give her a warning that the police would want to talk to her. Trying to keep that secret would be a bad idea indeed, bad in every way she could imagine, and probably some she couldn't. She had no doubt that Detective Inspector Darling could close her down in no time at all, and she did not want that. She would give Jessica up in the morning, say she had made an administrative error. The girl had nothing to hide. She hoped.

Chapter Twenty-Five

Darling looked up, annoyed, when the phone rang. Another half-hour undisturbed and she would have finished the assessments and be able to get on with some real work.

"This is Inspector Darling."

"Inspector, this is Dorothy Bainbridge. I have just discovered that I may have inadvertently misled you when I said that Mr Dance did not book one of the girls on Sunday. Something was worrying me, and I checked the records this morning. He did book a girl for Sunday evening, at his property in Longhorsley, but when she got there Mr Dance was not to be found. It was a failed appointment. That was what confused me."

Darling listened to the woman describing a sexual transaction that was only borderline legal, if that, as though it was an appointment for someone to cut the Dancer's hair or shampoo his carpets. When Mrs Bainbridge was finished, she waited a long moment, then brusquely asked for the girl's name, address and telephone number. After she wrote them down, she read them back just to make sure.

"Thank you, Mrs Bainbridge. I may have more questions for you."

"Always delighted to help in any way I can."

Darling found herself staring at her disconnected phone, unsure whether she was furious with the woman or admired her for her self-possession. She had just spoken to a senior police officer who was conducting a murder investigation, told that officer she had misled them while running a business that might land her in jail one day, and she had behaved as though she was talking to one of her children's teachers about something that happened every day.

Darling put the phone down and almost got up to go and interview Miss Jessica Stearns straight away, but managed to catch herself. It might be much more interesting than completing the personnel assessments but those assessments would still be there when she returned, no matter how useful or useless anything Miss Stearns said might turn out to be. If she completed them beforehand she would be able to give the investigation her undivided attention, which was what it deserved.

* * *

Jessica Stearns lived in one of the slightly more upmarket streets off Chillingham Road. It was only when she got out of the car that Darling realised the next road along was Lesbury Road, where Lizzie Benton had lived. Once again, she was made aware of Newcastle being a very small city. There were three doorbells, she pressed the one labelled 'Stearns'. The speaker crackled.

"Yes, who is it? I'm busy."

Darling leaned forward towards the loudspeaker. "I'm Detective Inspector Darling and I need to ask you a few questions."

There was a short silence. "I'll be right down."

The woman who opened the door was almost six feet tall, and almost painfully slender. Blonde hair was raggedly tied behind her head and she was barefoot, dressed in jeans that were fashionably threadbare at the knees and a grey sweatshirt emblazoned with the legend 'Newcastle upon Tyne Medical School'. "I'm Jessica Stearns," she said.

Darling produced her warrant card. "I'm Detective Inspector Darling." She nodded towards Morton. "My colleague is Detective Sergeant Morton."

He flashed his warrant card.

Ms Stearns ignored both cards, and Morton, only looking into Darling's eyes.

"We are conducting a murder investigation and we believe you can help us with our inquiries," said Darling.

The young woman's face was pale to begin with, and without any make-up. The word 'murder' removed what little colour she had. "You'd better come in." She stood aside to let them enter, then pulled the front door closed, making sure the mortice lock was engaged. "In here," she said, indicating the door at the left-hand side of the short passageway, just opposite the stairs that led up to the other two flats.

The room was obviously used as a lounge and study, with books lining the alcoves either side of the fireplace; a battered two-seater sofa and matching armchair covered with throws and mismatched cushions faced the empty fireplace. The bay window was filled with an ancient dining table piled with textbooks, files and a large laptop computer, which Ms Stearns closed as soon as she could.

"I have my finals in six weeks," she said, as though that explained everything.

"What are you studying?" asked Morton.

She pointed to the logo on her sweatshirt.

Darling, nodded, smiled and sat on the sofa without being asked. She realised the answers to two questions that had been gnawing at her since Ms Stearns opened the door. The room was tidy, clean and smelled vaguely of lavender. She had never been in a student's room like it. Ms Stearns had seemed a little old for a student, a little too grown up. That she was a medical student would account for that.

"Who has been murdered?" Stearns asked.

"Don't you watch the news?" Morton said. "Read newspapers?"

Stearns gestured towards the table. "Not at the moment, no."

Darling took control. "Ms Stearns, we understand that last Sunday evening you attended an address outside Longhorsley with the intent of providing sexual services for a Mr Barry Dance." She saw the young woman's eyelids flutter. Tears were not far away and she trembled as she tried to keep them away. "Now believe me, I am not interested in any commercial transaction that may have taken place…"

"Nothing happened!" she wailed. "He wasn't there. I didn't meet him. There was no commercial transaction–"

"Slow down!" Darling snapped. "Start at the beginning. You were given his address by?"

"Mrs Bainbridge, yes."

The reply came out a little faster than she thought the girl had intended.

"What time did you get there?"

"Just after quarter past eight. I was supposed to be there at eight, but I misjudged the time. There was a hold-up on the A1…"

"There's always a hold-up on the A1," said Morton.

The girl's attention flicked to him, then back to Darling as she decided she was only going to take any notice of what the boss here said, and that certainly wasn't Sergeant Morton.

"I got there, but there was no sign of anyone there; no car, nothing."

"What did you do? Exactly?"

She opened her mouth to answer straight away, then closed it so she could think first, closing her eyes to review her memory more precisely. "I got out of the car and went to the front door, knocking on it using the flap on the letter box. I didn't see a bell or knocker or anything like that. I opened the letter box and called in. There was no reply, nothing. I tried again, in case he'd gone to the bathroom or something like that. No reply."

"What did you do then?" Darling asked.

"Got back in my car and drove back to Newcastle. I called Mrs Bainbridge in case she could get me another job."

"Did she?" asked Morton.

"No. All I got was my cancellation fee and my mileage."

"Cancellation fee! Mileage!" said Morton.

Darling waved him to silence.

"You did not see Mr Dance. You did not see anyone else. You did not see any vehicle at the property."

She nodded. "That's right."

"You drove there, you say?" asked Morton.

"Yes, I drove." She glared at Morton as though seeing him as a Cro-Magnon with no knowledge of how the modern world worked. "My parents bought me a car when I came up here. It's the Renault Clio parked outside."

Darling got to her feet, closing her notebook and slipping it back into her jacket pocket. "Thank you for your cooperation, Ms Stearns. We will need to take a formal statement from you. We'll be in touch."

She went towards the door, hustling Morton out before her. When he was out of the front door and going towards the car, she turned back to the girl. "As I said, I am not interested in how you keep body and soul together, but – a word to the wise and all that – you want to look for a different line of work."

"Such as?" The girl sighed.

"Oh, I don't know…"

The girl turned back into her room and re-emerged with her laptop, opening it and calling up a spreadsheet. "I'm a medical student, Inspector. My course is five years long. Do you have any idea how much I owe?" She showed Darling the computer screen. "That is my cumulative debt. Then I've got my overdraft for living expenses. Can you suggest a different line of work that will make any difference to that?"

The figure at the bottom of the sheet was more than twice what Darling earned in a year, a lot more, and that was before anything like tax or National Insurance was deducted.

"Thank you for your concern, but I'll look after myself, thank you very much."

Jessica Stearns did not exactly slam the door behind Darling, but closed it in such a way Darling knew that if she wanted to come back she would need a warrant.

Darling shrugged. There was something to be learned every day. Could she say for certain she would do anything different were she in the girl's position? She didn't think of herself as old, but the student world she had inhabited was very different to the one Jessica Stearns was experiencing, and Darling didn't think she could say things were better now.

The car parked outside the house was four years old, neat and tidy but clearly well-used. Morton was leaning towards the driver's door, hand shadowing his brow, peering inside.

"There'll be nothing in there to interest us," she said.

"She's a student. Of course there will be."

She thought of telling Morton to move into the twenty-first century, but just as she opened her mouth to speak she realised he might be taking the mickey, so she closed it and said nothing.

Chapter Twenty-Six

Morton's phone rang on the way back to the office. He answered it, listened and then swiped it off.

"Change of plan, boss."

"Oh?"

"We need to speak to Garth Dance. ANPR has him going north on the A1 on Sunday evening. Going straight home from the Dancer's house wouldn't take him anywhere near the A1. Nothing after the A697 turn–"

"To Longhorsely!"

"And Linden Lane."

"Why am I not surprised?" Darling muttered.

"Is that the sound of you jumping to conclusions, boss?"

Darling glared across at him, but only briefly because she had to keep her eyes on the road at all times. Besides which, he was right, She was jumping to conclusions. "Where is his office?"

"It's in Gosforth, in the town centre, opposite the library."

"In other words, we'll not get parked anywhere near it."

It turned out they found a parking spot in the cobbled back alley at the rear of the parade. There was a yard with a sign saying it was for Dance Enterprises staff and customers only, but there was no space left, so Darling parked where she could, with the passenger side hard up against a wall, and waited while Morton got out of the driver's side, and then they walked around the end of the street and down along the main road until they came to a four-storey, white-painted terrace house that had 'Dance Enterprises' in gold letters on an anthracite black sign.

"We're here to see Mr Dance," Darling announced to the woman sitting behind the reception desk.

"You haven't got an appointment, have you?" the woman said, her attention flicking between Darling and Morton. "Mr Dance only sees anyone by appointment."

"He'll see us," Darling insisted. "Now." Both she and Morton produced their warrant cards for her brief inspection. "Which way?"

The woman didn't really look at their cards but pointed to a glass-panelled door behind her that was marked 'Private'. Darling didn't bother to knock.

Garth's office was spartan, just a huge desk and a comfortable-looking chair. There were three large computer monitors on the desk and a large telephone console. An empty coffee cup was the only other item on the desk. Garth looked up from the monitors towards them, momentary bewilderment on his face.

"You can't just come in here…" he protested, getting to his feet.

"I just did," Darling replied. "I have some questions for you and I want you to answer them truthfully this time."

Garth hesitated, then bent forward and pressed a button on the telephone. "Avril, bring in a couple of chairs for our… guests. Oh, and some coffee, too."

"You needn't bother on our account," said Darling. "We're here for answers, not hospitality."

The receptionist brought in two metal folding chairs and left without a word.

"It's good coffee," said Garth, sitting down as they unfolded the chairs. "I live on coffee. Now, what are these answers you want?" He appeared to have regained his equilibrium.

Before Darling could answer, his phone rang, a cheap electronic rendition of *Ode to Joy*.

"Mind if I answer that? Time is money in my business."

"I'd rather you didn't. Time can cost a lot more than money in my business."

He touched another button. The Beethoven ceased.

"I asked you where you went after the family business meeting on Sunday."

"And I told you I went straight home to my family."

"Which I know isn't true. Your vehicle was captured on ANPR cameras heading north on the A1, which is not on the route you would have taken if you were hurrying home to your family. Unless you have another family we don't know about."

Garth opened his mouth to speak before subsiding back into his chair. "Not another family," he said. "Just a good friend."

"What is her name, this good friend of yours?" Morton asked, pen poised over his notebook. "Presumably she comes with benefits."

Garth sighed, then shook his head. "Her name is Alicia Dane. She lives on West Road in Longhorsley. I got there at about seven thirty and I left just after ten."

"What did you do while you were there?" Morton asked.

Garth's eyes widened. "You don't need to ask that."

"Presumably Miss Dane will be able to confirm your story," Darling interrupted.

"Of course she will, just be a bit discreet, will you? And it's Mrs Dane."

"Why should we be especially discreet?" Darling asked. "This is a murder inquiry, after all."

"Because Mr Dane would give you another murder to solve if he found out Alicia was having it off with me. She's his trophy wife, you see, twenty-odd years younger than him and a right looker. Edward Dane has a short temper."

Darling glanced at Morton, who nodded briefly. They had both heard of Edward Dane. "Very well, we'll try to be discreet. Where did you go after you left Mrs Dane?"

"Home. I mean it, I did go straight home this time. I arrived just before eleven."

"Your wife didn't ask where you'd been?" Morton enquired.

Dance shrugged. "She was asleep when I got in, flat out on the sofa with half a bottle of gin beside her. Not that she would have asked if she'd been awake. We don't have what you would call a close relationship these days."

"She will confirm all of this, will she?"

"I told you, she was passed out when I got home."

"You'll forgive me, Mr Dance, but I don't take anyone's word for anything without corroboration. When that person has already lied to me, that goes in spades."

Garth shrugged. "I can understand that."

Darling didn't smile. She wasn't concerned whether anyone on the other end of her questions understood why she did anything. "One more thing. What was the last thing you said to your father?"

Garth looked from one of them to the other and back again, his mouth flapping open and shut. When he replied his voice was a whisper barely strong enough to reach her. "I said I was going to kill him." He broke the silence that followed by loudly protesting that he hadn't meant it, that it was only a joke.

"I don't find jokes about killing people at all funny, Mr Dance," Darling said. "Especially when that person is murdered a short time afterwards."

"I didn't mean it," Garth insisted. "So I'm immature sometimes. So I've got a childish sense of humour sometimes. You can't hold that against me."

"Can't I? I'll be the judge of that. If you didn't mean it, why did you say it?"

Garth threw his hands up in the air. "How the hell should I know? I was angry with him. For the first time in my life I wanted the last word with him."

From what she knew of the man, Darling didn't expect many people got the last word in an argument with the Dancer. Whatever, Garth was going to have to live with it. With a bit of luck, it would disturb his sleep for a long time to come. She got to her feet just as Avril backed into the room with a large tray bearing coffee and biscuits. She could really do with a coffee, and she had never heard Pete Morton say no, but she wasn't about to give Dance the satisfaction of giving her hospitality.

"Thank you for your time, Mr Dance. You've been most helpful. We'll be in touch if we need to talk to you again."

"Try calling ahead," he called after her. "I can't guarantee being in."

Whereas if I *do* call, you can guarantee not being in, Darling thought. She said nothing, walking straight outside before halting and taking in deep breaths of air. However polluted it was, however many times it had been breathed before reaching her lungs, it still felt better to her than the air in Dance's office.

"Think he did it?" Morton asked.

She shook her head. "We'll know after we've spoken with Mrs Dane. But no, I don't think he did it. He was afraid of his father. That's why he wanted the last word. I don't think he's got the balls to kill anyone."

Morton sucked on his top lip. In his experience anyone was capable of killing. "This Mrs Dane must be something in bed for young Garth to risk bringing Eddie Dane's wrath down on his head. Now there's a man I know is capable of killing someone."

"Oh?" Darling asked, intrigued.

"You'll have to ask Mr Milburn about that. All I know is that when he was younger he was in the frame for a couple of murders, but nothing was ever proved. Anyone who knew anything wouldn't say a word about Eddie Dane. Bit like the Dancer, way back when, before our times. But Mr Milburn will know."

He would know because Joe Milburn knew everything about everyone who was up to no good on Tyneside. Not that she would ask him, not now. She had more immediate concerns than her boss's bucket list. Concerns like who killed the Dancer, who was one of the names on that list.

Chapter Twenty-Seven

The Dancer's funeral was a big affair, the service in St Mary's Cathedral packed out with Tyneside's great and good and some who didn't usually emerge before dark, all paying their respects to a man who had moved from the bloodstained backstreets of ducking, diving, hoping for the best and preparing for the worst, to the pristine, manicured suburbs where legitimate businessmen enjoyed the fine fruits of their endeavours behind high walls and cameras that always had someone paying attention to the feed. Hymns were sung, prayers said, and the archbishop delivered a brief eulogy that spoke of the devoted husband and father who had endured life's trials with a generous heart and an ever-open wallet when it came to charitable giving. Being an archbishop, he delivered it with such conviction that almost everyone there believed he meant it and the words were not cut-and-paste boilerplate phrases put together by the Dances' parish priest.

There had been times in his life when Milburn would have had to cough into his handkerchief to hide his laughter, but today he sat in the next pew to the back on the pulpit side of the church, and nobody who didn't already know him could have distinguished him from all the other middle-aged-going-on-elderly prosperous gentlemen who were beholden to the Dancer in one way or another.

The coffin was borne down the nave on the shoulders of half a dozen mourners, Garth and Andrew and four professionals who made sure they bore most of the weight. After it processed, the family came, Kitty on the arm of her brother Stanley, who needed her support more than she needed his, seeing as he couldn't enter any church without a quarter bottle of Scotch inside him.

Ekaterina walked alone, head high and wearing impenetrable dark glasses that hinted tears were not far away. Everyone was struck by her dignity and her strength, as well as her ever-so-slightly exotic beauty. She looked straight ahead, unlike the brothers, whose gazes roved about the congregation, seeking out those who owed and were owed favours alike, smiling and nodding equally briefly when they took someone's attention. Everyone else filed out as the ushers led them out of the pews, moving from front to back.

The family and close personal friends got into the cortège and were driven to the cemetery. All the rest had to scramble to cars parked out past the Life centre, in the Central Station car park, out by the Discovery Museum, and anywhere and everywhere in between. The prepared few knew where they would park when they got there. Certainly, the cemetery car park could not accommodate such an impressively large cortège.

The graveside service was brief, almost perfunctory compared to the celebration in the cathedral. Nobody minded. Nothing anyone could say would ever bring the Dancer back. Besides which, there was a nip in the air. Stanley might be too well-oiled to notice but everyone else did. When the prayers were said, the flowers and the earth thrown atop the coffin, quite a few of those who had come to mourn filed past the family, paying their respects, offering their condolences.

Ekaterina did not so much as acknowledge a single one, staring directly ahead, her eyes invisible behind her shades. One or two looked at her for a moment as though they were inclined to take offence at her indifference, only to remember she was Russian and, therefore, probably mourned differently. Nobody wanted weeping and wailing, gnashing of teeth and rending of garments like they saw on television news clips from foreign funerals. A few noticed the golden inscription on the night-black marble stone next to the grave, 'William Barry Dance Jnr' and remembered she was Barry Junior's wife, so had good reason to be distracted.

Eventually, though, all that needed to be seen to be done had been done, and it was time for even the family to go home for the wake. The immediate family went in the funeral director's Daimler limousine, the men sitting on jump seats facing backwards, towards the ladies.

"You could have tried a bit harder," muttered Andrew, once they were moving and the driver had raised the smoked-glass partition that divided him from his passengers. "Those people are our friends, our partners. You owe them to be more civil than that."

Ekaterina turned towards him almost glacially slowly, stared at him, then removed her glasses to reveal her teary, bloodshot eyes.

Both men started. Even their mother hadn't shed any tears.

"I owe those people nothing." Ekaterina reached out and put her hands on Kitty's, which were clenched together on her lap, but directed her voice at Andrew and Garth. "I am here to honour my father, whom I loved as a daughter, even if you did not love him as dutiful sons. I am here to honour my mother." She squeezed Kitty's hands and was rewarded with her mother-in-law's equivalent of a brief, brave-in-tragic-times smile. "My mother who has never done anything but make me feel welcome and loved, a stranger in a strange land."

The two women embraced, then turned defiantly towards the men, chins up, ready for anything that might come next.

"Oh, by the way…" began Andrew before having to grab the sides of his seat to prevent himself sliding off as the driver took a curve a little too quickly. "By the way, that idea of you taking over the companies, you can forget that."

"That was what your father wanted! It was in his will!"

"In the codicil, actually," continued Andrew, as unctuous and disturbing as any lawyer could be in a room full of enemies, much less a car carrying family members. "I've given that my professional scrutiny and I find it unenforceable. Sinclair agrees with me."

"Of course he agrees with you," Kitty sneered. "He's paid to agree with you."

"You're wrong," Andrew said. "I took another second opinion."

* * *

Ekaterina zoned out of the discussion, pursuing her own thoughts. So far as she could tell, she had two choices. She could take control of everything, as was her wish and, she knew now, her father-in-law's. If she did that, as was her first instinct, she would face a fight with Garth and Andrew over every single step. That, in itself, was no great dissuasion. She was as confident in her ability to see off any and every challenge from them as she was about every other challenge in life. She won. Life really was as simple as that. She could just give up on her plans and go back to Moscow. Father would be disappointed, to be sure, but she would talk him round to understanding that liaising with the Dancer was one thing, with his sons was a very different, much less attractive proposition.

Reaching between the two men, she tapped on the screen. It slid silently out of sight.

"Stop here and let me out," she ordered.

"I can't!" the driver told her. "I'm on the Central Motorway."

"Well, get off it as soon as you can and let me out of this car!" Her tone told him that not doing as she told him would probably be the most unwise decision of his life.

He stopped the limousine between the University and the RVI. Ekaterina got out without bothering to close the door and walked away without turning to see the limousine leave. The afternoon was very much darker now, almost night, with the street lights beginning to illuminate. The wind drove a thin, bitter rain into her face and she was forced to hold her coat closed at her throat. She began to laugh. Being Moscow born and bred, she was certain she knew everything there was to know about bad winter weather, certainly by comparison to the temperate weather of even North East England. Now it appeared she was wrong in that as well. When the wind off the sea carried rain in its teeth, Tyneside could be just as unpleasant as Moscow, in its own, insidious sort of way. She shivered and hurried on. There was bound to be a taxi she could hail nearby. The boys could say whatever they pleased. She was going to take control of the businesses, and if that meant dealing with their objections she was content to deal with them any way that was required.

Chapter Twenty-Eight

Elders Club was a very conscious physical facsimile of a gentleman's club in London, Boodle's or White's or any of the many others that required not only deep pockets of their members but also a public-school education and a double-barrelled name. Comfort and discretion were the watchwords in Elders even if the standards Elders required weren't quite as onerous. To be a member, all anyone had to do was have a recommendation from an existing member and the folding money for their stake at any of the tables in the gambling rooms that were kept very much separate from the public rooms of the club. That was not necessary nowadays, but when it was first opened, gambling anywhere that was not the racetrack was illegal. While that had never prevented gentlemen losing their shirts over a hand of whist or something as exotic as the spin of a roulette wheel, the various groups who had owned the club over the years had never been inclined to flaunt their facilities, even now, for fear the hoi polloi might want to play their games. There were any number of establishments where they might pretend they were James Bond playing baccarat or poker for high stakes.

Quite how Mark Wearing did not qualify as a member of the hoi polloi, he neither knew nor cared. A member of Elders he was, and that meant he could take advantage of the tables there, and the punters who habituated them. He was more circumspect in his gambling there than he sometimes was elsewhere, winning consistently, but not so big that anyone might suggest he take his Pool Hall Richard attitude elsewhere. The only professionals supposed to inhabit Elders were the croupiers and some of the very attractive, well-dressed single women who nursed weak drinks throughout the evening or until they struck up a meaningful conversation with one of the customers, after which the champagne could flow like water.

One such young lady sat beside Wearing, making polite, entertaining conversation, sipping on her gin and tonic and being very careful never to look at his hand. She had dark auburn hair she wore in waves to her shoulders and tucked behind one ear in a conscious imitation of an old-time movie actress whose name he could not remember. Her blue silk dress fitted her where it touched, and that was just about everywhere.

He turned towards her and if he hadn't managed to swing his head backwards just a fraction at the very last moment, he would have kissed her full on the lips, lips that looked as though they should be kissed very often.

"I must tell you, Miss…"

"Rebecca," she purred, "my name is Rebecca Fitzgerald."

"That's a very beautiful name for a very beautiful woman," he found himself saying, wondering why he was saying it. He never complimented a woman, much less a working girl. He smiled and brought the conversation round to what he wanted to say. "I must tell you that I never pay for it."

She leant backwards, eyes opening wide and mouth opening even wider. "How can you say such a thing?" she demanded, an expression of outrage on her face, that was replaced by a mischievous smile as she dipped her head towards him and whispered in his ear, "Who says you have to pay?" Her tongue followed her words, making him shiver from head to toe as though he had just touched something electric. "Maybe it's like the song says."

"What song?"

"*Girls just wanna have fun*!"

A moment later they were both laughing, laughing so much the croupier asked whether he was in or out.

Wearing got to his feet, leaving his chips behind, and allowed her to take him by the hand and upstairs to a room that was even more discreet than the gambling rooms, furnished with a very large chaise longue upholstered in deep-burgundy velvet. There was an occasional table on which sat an ice bucket holding a bottle of champagne, and two glasses.

"Make yourself at home," she invited as she opened the champagne with a loud pop that made even Wearing start, and he thought himself used to sudden loud noises.

He had just managed to remove his jacket when she approached him carrying two flutes. Just then his phone rang.

"Going to answer that?" she asked, tracing her lower lip with her tongue.

"No."

She dribbled a fine white powder into the one then took a glug from the other. "What's the matter?" She laughed. "You're so slow. It's only something to make the evening go with a swing. I had some as well!" She took another mouthful of wine, and laughed.

Wearing drained his glass, then set to unbuttoning his shirt as he watched her reach behind her back and tug on something that must have been a zip, because a moment later the blue silk dress was in waves at her feet. She wore nothing beneath it.

He reached for her, but she slapped his hand aside. "At least take your shoes off!" She laughed, and tugged down the zip on his trousers.

* * *

Wearing had no memory of what happened after that, but sometime later in the evening, he found himself not so much walking as floating through the centre of Newcastle to where he had parked his car on Grey Street. There was no doubt about it. There was absolutely nothing like an energetic bout of meaningless sex to make a man feel good about himself, about life, about everything. He stood for a moment and closed his eyes. He had felt like a fucking god! It was only when he got behind the wheel of his car that he realised he couldn't remember her name.

What the hell? Names didn't matter. She didn't matter. She was in the past, enjoyed but forgotten. All that mattered now was the card game he had to get to, the game where nobody would mind if he was the shark in the water. "Dear God, life is good!" he shouted as he reversed out of his parking space.

A Mercedes G-Wagon almost drove into the back of him. He began to laugh, not stopping when a middle-aged woman dressed as a much younger girl tottered over from the Mercedes on six-inch heels, and hammered on his window, screaming something he didn't need to hear to understand. He looked up at her still laughing while she became more enraged by the second. Eventually, he blew her a slobbery kiss, raised the middle finger of his right hand and pulled away, tyres squealing on the cobbles.

When he only just made the right-hand turn into High Bridge Street without hitting the stage lorry parked alongside the Theatre Royal, he realised that quite possibly he wasn't driving with the control he usually tried to exert. Stunts like that would attract attention, if not that of the coppers, then whoever was sitting in a darkened room somewhere keeping tabs on the screens attached to all the cameras that littered the town centre. By the time he turned onto Pilgrim Street and went down towards the Central Motorway, he believed he was in control of himself. Even so, when he merged onto the motorway the driver behind him flashed his lights and sounded his horn, making Wearing jump. He hadn't seen the car when he checked to his right. Shaking his head, he cursed inwardly, and tried to remember where he was supposed to be playing cards that night.

Chapter Twenty-Nine

Reid followed his host into the dining room that had been transformed into a games room by draping a green baize cloth over the table. He saw the four men seated around the table and almost turned straight around. The only reason he didn't was his being a guest there; that and Puncheon's reputation for holding high-stakes games where a man with skills could make himself some serious money. Reid did not want to prejudice any future invitation. Even so, it was a shock to see Wearing sitting there looking like he thought he was George Clooney in *Ocean's Whatever*. He did think asking whether his host knew of Wearing's reputation as a card sharp, but said nothing because card sharp was exactly what he was. He went to the chair Puncheon indicated was his. At least he was sitting as far away from Wearing as he could.

Puncheon introduced the players to each other. Despite shaking hands, even with Wearing, Reid had forgotten the three punters' names before he sat down. Their names weren't important to him. What was important to him was studying their play, picking up their tics and tells, in order to empty their wallets as the game went on. By the time the deck was back in Puncheon's hands for the fourth time, it was clear to Reid that one of his opponents would not look at his hand once he believed it was a winner, while another could not keep himself from looking at his cards every five seconds if he thought he was going to win. Puncheon's habit was blowing through teeth while the other punter was a compulsive spectacle cleaner.

Wearing, on the other hand, appeared to be totally unpredictable. He had chased hands that had no chance of winning while at the same time throwing in hands that would have won. He had drunk half a bottle of Scotch in that time, and while he was nowhere near falling-down drunk, Reid was sure he had been drinking beforehand and was the worse for wear. Reid didn't know anyone who regarded themselves as a serious card player who would play in that condition, and he tried to bail out early on any hand Wearing looked like he might chase.

Then came the time he found himself with a hand he could not bear to throw away, a full house of aces and eights. Later, he told himself he should have remembered it was the dead man's hand, the one Doc Holliday held when he was shot, but that was after the event. Anyone could be wise after the event. When he saw the cards, all he knew was that it was almost impossible for any of the other players to have a hand to beat him. Even so, he played cautiously, not raising the stakes so that he might frighten anyone off.

One after another, however, they dropped out as the pot grew way beyond anything they had seen that evening, until only he and Wearing were left in. By then, Wearing had drunk more than even he could handle, and he grew more agitated as he got closer to what he thought would be his pot. His eyes flared. His cheeks turned red. Spittle collected in the corners of his mouth. Whatever the antithesis of a poker face was, Wearing's was it. Eventually, he had only sufficient chips left to shove them all into the pot and hiss, "See you!"

Reid took a deep breath and wondered whether it was too late for him to throw away his hand and let Wearing have the money. There was something unsettling about the man's expression, his attitude. He could almost imagine steam coming out of his ears.

"Didn't you hear me?" Wearing snarled. "I said I'll see you!" He leaned forward and stretched out as though he intended to take the cards out of Reid's hand.

The other men around the table took a collective deep breath and leaned backwards in their chairs. You didn't behave like that at the card table.

"Very well," said Reid, and turned over the first two of his cards, the eights of spades and hearts.

Wearing cackled. In that moment, Reid knew what Wearing had in his hand, two pairs, both higher than eights. He turned over his three remaining cards singly and exquisitely slowly, the ace of hearts followed by the ace of diamonds followed by the ace of spades. Wearing would only beat that if he had a royal flush, and it was obvious from the way the colour left his face that he didn't.

"You're a cheat," he hissed at Reid.

"I'll not have talk like that at my table," said Puncheon, getting to his feet.

Wearing ignored him, leaning over the table towards Reid, supporting himself with his hands on the chips piled up. "You are a fucking cheat. You better sleep with one eye open in future. I'll be coming for you. You won't know where or when, but I'll get you."

"Oh, for God's sake…" Puncheon gasped.

Wearing climbed even closer. His breath in Reid's face.

The acetone sweetness mixed with the alcoholic sourness – suggesting that booze wasn't the only substance scrambling his mind – almost made Reid fall backwards off his chair.

"I'm a killer, me, and don't you fucking forget it. I've killed men!" He tried to grab hold of Reid's shirt, who didn't have to slap Wearing's hand aside very hard to make him lose his balance and fall heavily onto the table.

The impact was accompanied by the screech of wood tearing loose from its fastenings. The nearest table leg collapsed inwards. The table itself suddenly tilted down, causing the cloth and everything on it – cards, chips, glasses, ashtrays and Wearing – to slide off and onto the floor in a heap of confusion.

Reid jumped to his feet to avoid being crushed and then stood where he was, watching Wearing thrash around on his back trying to get to his feet, flinging cards and chips everywhere. Reid was hard put to keep from laughing out loud but managed it because he had a good idea how the man would react to his laughter. While he had done enough backstreet brawling as a copper to have little fear of any unarmed combat he might be faced with almost anywhere, he knew enough about Wearing's background, and about the unpredictability of the effects of combining unknown narcotics with alcohol, to want to avoid the risk. There were some drugs he had encountered on the streets that could give a junkie amazing strength or – worse – convince them they were that strong, that invulnerable.

Wearing got to his feet eventually, playing chips in both hands, looking at each of the other players who were regarding him with incredulity. Nobody appeared to know what to do, until Puncheon stepped forward.

"Take the chips if you want them. They're worthless and I'm not going to change them for you. Take them and go, and I won't call the police."

Wearing pushed out his chest, thumping it above his heart with a clenched right fist that leaked chips. "I'm not frightened of fucking coppers. Call 'em if you like. See if I care. I shit coppers, me, shit 'em. I'm a dangerous man. I kill people, I do. Kill people."

Puncheon shook his head. "Just get out, man. Get out."

Puncheon was twenty years older than Wearing. Even in his prime he'd never been the physical specimen Wearing was, and that prime was a long, long time ago. If push came to shove it would be no contest, and everyone knew it. Even so, he had something it appeared the drunk lacked, which was pride. They were in his home. This game had been his idea. He was responsible. He took another step closer. "Leave. Leave before you make things worse than they are."

They stood there for a long moment, not quite head-to-head, not quite locking antlers, but each playing the alpha male in their different ways. Reid had no idea which way it would go. His right hand went into his jacket pocket where he had that roll of pound coins in a cash bag taped together in an innocent cosh he had been shown in his first week out of Police College, on the streets. If necessary, he would put it upside Wearing's head and knock him senseless. It wouldn't be the first time he'd used it.

Then the big man seemed to shrink in on himself, the bluster and defiance evaporating. He threw the chips onto the floor and made for the door, stumbling on some obstruction covered by the table cloth and almost falling down, catching hold of the door jamb and just managing to stay upright. In the doorway, he turned around and pointed at Reid.

"You needn't think I'm going to forget you, either."

Then he was gone, leaving the others to relax, take a deep breath, and begin to make a start repairing the room, only for Puncheon to stop them.

"Let's call it a night. I don't think I can deal with this right now." He gestured at the debris in the room. "That table cost five grand when we bought it. God only knows how I'm going to explain to Gladys how it got broken."

Reid presumed Gladys was Mrs Puncheon, a lady he had never met or wanted to meet.

Puncheon took hold of his arm. "Can you remember how much was in that last pot? I'll give you your money."

Without thinking, Reid shook his head. "There's no need. Just give me what I came with. Give everyone what they came with. Give the idiot's money to charity. I think that would burn his bum even more than me walking away with it." He smiled, trying to convince his host that his idea was the only decent way of resolving the chaos around their feet.

"Are you sure?"

"It's only money," Reid said, again without thinking, only realising as he saw the others stare at him in astonishment that he had just spoken heresy. To them 'only' and 'money' were never words to be associated.

"One last drink before you leave!" proposed Puncheon.

They all accepted but Reid declined. With the unpredictable Wearing somewhere out there in the darkness promising to rain down vengeance and violence on him, he thought it good policy to stay sober and drive home as quickly as he could.

Which was what he did, seeing no sign of Wearing on his way, and he looked as carefully as he could while still watching the road and other traffic. At that time of night, Wearing was by no means the only alcohol-fuelled danger out there.

Chapter Thirty

Wearing woke to find himself curled up on the back seat of his car, aching in places he'd forgotten he had, with his tongue welded to the roof of his mouth, drool dried on his chin, and feeling as though his head would explode at any moment. What the fuck had happened? He'd been drunk often enough, but never like this. This feeling wasn't a hungover, it was sickness. Just moving his head made his eyeballs feel as though they were about to fall out.

Moving as slowly and smoothly as he could, he extricated himself from the car. The sudden blast of cold air on his face when he exposed it was both refreshing and enervating. If he hadn't held on to the car roof, he would have certainly fallen over. Standing there, trembling, the world seemed to move in and out of focus. The longer he stood there – looking straight ahead, breathing as deeply and evenly as he could – the more what passed for normality reasserted itself. The muscles of his chest and back and neck ceased to feel as though they were bowstrings about to snap at any moment. His knees ceased trembling and he felt as though he could probably stand unsupported, not that he put the theory to the test.

Just as his body restored itself, so did his memory, in flashes as though he was watching an old movie in which the film sometimes came off the projector sprockets, moving along the timeline in random jumps that could have been as mystifying as the scenes he saw, about a card game, at which selected Tyneside gambling men were given the opportunity to lighten the wallets of some of Wally's card-playing friends who had more money than sense. Every gambling man in Toon wanted to be invited and yet, when he was invited he went along feeling distinctly under the weather and had attempted self-medication with some of Wally's Scotch. After which things had got much worse. He'd lost all his winnings and even his stake money, busted up the place and ended up threatening that dickhead Paul Reid.

Why had he lost it with Reid? The guy was another ex-copper, for fuck's sake. He could obviously handle himself, and those two missing fingers on his left hand were downright creepy. Wearing had heard he'd lost them in a showdown with some Triad soldiers, a showdown Reid had walked away from, which meant he had won it. Those Chinks were stone killers.

Wearing got behind the wheel and reached to put the key in the ignition. He missed, and again when he tried another time. "Fuck, fuck, fucking fuck!" His yell was loud enough to attract the attention of a young woman wearing an army-surplus hooded parka, faded jeans and half-laced boots, who glared at him and gave him the finger. He had to laugh. It was either that or weep, and he couldn't remember ever weeping in his entire life. Getting out of the car, he set off to walk home. At least he hadn't pissed himself while he was out of it.

At home, Wearing filled a tall glass with lukewarm water before adding three tablespoons of salt. He took the glass into the bathroom, poured the water down his throat and then voided the contents of his stomach into the toilet bow, which made him feel a little more like himself. He went into his bedroom, stripped off and put himself through a double dose of his normal morning calisthenics, telling himself repeatedly it was only pain and that the sweat was worth it.

After that he got into the shower, scrubbing himself raw with a towelling mitt under water as hot as he could tolerate. Then he dressed, went to the nearby Magpie Café and ordered himself exactly the breakfast he had dreamed about.

While he was eating breakfast, he reviewed the last twenty-four hours to try and decide who had Mickey-Finned him.

Then he remembered. That bitch at Elders had put something in his drink. Well, she was going to pay for that.

Chapter Thirty-One

Ekaterina surveyed the office, making sure that everything was exactly as she wanted it before she told Janice, her PA, to let the visitors in. The room was almost empty, save for

Ekaterina's large, blonde-wood desk with only her closed laptop on its gleaming surface, her sizeable leather wing-backed chair on one side of it, and a couple of altogether less grandiose chairs on the other. Austere was the word to describe it, and she liked austere, even if it was contrary to her Russian upbringing. Austere was so very different from the fussy 'if you've got it then flaunt it' style the Dancer had preferred. Not for her, the raised dais under the chair. It wouldn't fool her, so why should it fool anyone else? She wasn't nearly two metres tall. Nothing she could do would make anyone believe she was physically bigger than them. She had other tricks she could play.

Ekaterina sat down and pressed a button hidden underneath the desktop. A few moments later, Janice opened the door and ushered two men into the office. One was tall, with a mane of flowing, dark hair swept back at the temples and streaked with grey, wearing an obviously expensive three-piece suit on top of a crisp white shirt that was open at the collar, which showed a gold six-pointed star hanging on a thick gold chain, on top of a finer gold chain from which hung a shark's tooth. Ekaterina's first impression was that he was not as young or handsome as he believed himself to be, and probably never had been. The other man was older, in his early middle age, anonymous. He carried a briefcase.

Both men stared at Ekaterina as they walked the few steps between the door and the desk. It was obvious they had been expecting someone else to be filling the Dancer's shoes, Garth in all likelihood. She suppressed a small smile of satisfaction.

"I'm Frank Geddes–" began the younger man.

"I know who you are." She glanced at the other man. "Both of you." She saw a shiver of discomfort run through him. "You may be seated." She gestured towards the chairs.

They hesitated, looking at each other, before sitting down.

"You may know who we are," Geddes said, "we don't know who *you* are."

Ekaterina looked at him levelly long enough for him to become uncomfortable. "Who I am is immaterial. What I am is important."

Geddes glanced at his partner, who shrugged, opened the briefcase and produced a small blue Dictaphone, which he put on the desk in front of himself, switching it on.

"What are you, then?" Geddes asked. "Important?"

Once again, Ekaterina did not answer immediately, glaring at him the way a teacher whose patience was already exhausted might glare at a student who had just said something they believed was cuttingly clever, but wasn't.

"I am in charge, that is what I am," she said, eventually.

The two men smirked at each other.

"If you say so." Geddes shrugged.

"Oh, it isn't just me who says so," Ekaterina assured him. "Barry Dance says so. My late father-in-law left me in control of all Dance Enterprises."

Geddes looked as though he had something to say about this, but his companion put his hand on his forearm and shook his head.

"I understand you are here to discuss terms for the renewal of your lease for Elders Club."

Geddes nodded. "That was the business we had hoped to discuss…"

She produced a slim file from a desk drawer and pushed it over the expanse of the desktop towards them.

The older man caught hold of it before it could shoot off the desk and, when Geddes nodded at him, opened it and began to read. Moments later, his eyes opened wide and his mouth fell open, revealing a lot of expensive gold dentistry. He closed his mouth, glanced at Geddes and then looked at her.

"You can't—" he began to say, only for his voice to dry up. He coughed into his hand and began again. "You cannot be serious."

She stared at him, once again for an uncomfortably long time. "This is business. When it comes to business, I am always serious; very, very serious."

He shook his head and then read the first page of the file again before handing it towards Geddes, who pushed it back to him. "I forgot my reading glasses."

She knew then that the information in the file the Dancer had kept on Geddes was correct. The man was illiterate, and almost paranoid about anyone outside his immediate circle knowing it. His accountant shook his head.

"You can't double the rent," he said.

"Can't I?" she asked. "I believe you will find I can."

"What gives you the right?" demanded Geddes. The prospect of paying twice as much rent had got his attention.

"Market forces, that's what," she replied. "Your club occupies a prime site that has the attention of many of your competitors."

"We don't have competitors," sneered Geddes. "Imitators, maybe, but not competitors. Doubling the rent would make the club unprofitable."

Ekaterina laughed. It was a brief, bitter sound, utterly lacking in humour. "Just because I am a woman, and new in my position, don't imagine I am a fool who knows nothing. Your original lease from my father-in-law was at a less than commercial rate because he gave you help to get started, help he believed he had to give you because of an obligation he owed to your father. He made it perfectly clear from the beginning that the rent would go up to a commercial level on renewal. You knew that. You agreed to it."

"That's a lie," snarled Geddes.

"Is it?" She smiled, and nodded at the recorder. "You are not the only one who records all your business conversations. I listened to that conversation before you arrived. It is very clear in my memory."

Geddes sank back in his chair. His memory, too, was clear. There was silence in the room, until the other man gasped. He had been reading through the other terms.

"You can't make us buy all our drink and food from Dance companies!"

She shrugged. "Can't I? I am not making you do anything. If you want a new lease on those premises you will sign that agreement, and that will be why you will buy all your supplies from Dance companies, as well as hiring all new staff from us."

"That will cost us half our profits!"

Once again, she shrugged. "But you will still make profits."

"The Dancer didn't do business this way," Geddes protested.

Ekaterina regarded him so intently that he seemed to shrink in his chair. "The Dancer is dead," she said calmly. "He grew soft as he grew older. I do business the way he did when he was young and vigorous."

Geddes had not known the Dancer when he was young and vigorous. His accountant, however, had, and he quietly closed the file, putting it in his briefcase. "We will have to read this very carefully," he said, picking up the Dictaphone and dropping it into his briefcase as well.

"Read it as carefully as you wish," she said. "It is non-negotiable. You take it or you leave it."

The two men got up and went towards the door, nothing like as cocky as they had been when they entered. Geddes was reaching for the door handle when Ekaterina said, "One more thing."

They turned back towards her.

"We will also take fifty percent of the profits you make on the drugs you supply in your club and the girls you pimp."

"That is outrageous," began the accountant, whose face had suffused a deep red almost beetroot colour. Geddes took hold of his arm, shaking his head.

"You can just fuck off, you cunt," Geddes snarled.

"Which do you mean?" Ekaterina asked, mildly. "If I am a 'cunt' I can hardly 'fuck off' now, can I?"

Geddes snatched the case out of the other man's hands, ripped it open and took out the file, tearing it in two and flinging the pieces away in a shower of paper.

"You can always be provided with another copy," she said and smiled.

Geddes swore, long and vividly in a language Ekaterina did not recognise but did not need to speak to understand the meaning of the words. Then he caught hold of his accountant's arm and dragged him out of the office, even as the man was trying to catch the pieces of paper as they fluttered down. The door slammed shut behind them.

In the silence that echoed behind them, Ekaterina wondered whether, in fact, the accountant had known of that side of the club's business. Possibly not. After all, they weren't income streams that would be declared on any tax return. She smiled to herself as she sat back in her chair, luxuriating in the moment. For a first business meeting, that had gone tolerably well, and if further negotiations were needed with Mr Geddes, well… she had a few more persuasive tricks at her disposal, tricks that had worked for her father in Moscow. She expected they would work for her in Newcastle.

Chapter Thirty-Two

Darling knocked on the door of Milburn's office feeling a degree of trepidation. That she was not trembling as she was that first time all those years ago did not make her feel any better.

"Come in, Inspector!" he replied almost before she had finished knocking.

She opened the door, slipped inside and closed it behind herself as though nervous about who might be observing her. Even after the time of being an inspector, and in charge of important, sensitive investigations, she still felt as though she was going to see the headmaster, the expert in all things police and detecting, when she went to see the superintendent. She fancied she would always feel that way, even when *she* was the superintendent in the big chair – as she intended to be in the fullness of time – and Joe Milburn was feeding the seagulls chips on Seaham front.

"Take a seat, Penny," he invited, gesturing her to the chair in front of his desk. She felt a tightening about her chest at his using the diminutive of her name. It was never a good sign when Joe Milburn used first names. Civilians got 'Mr X' or 'Mrs Y', occasionally 'Ms Y' if he remembered he was living in the post-feminist twenty-first century. First names meant he was going to be friendly, which was disturbing to anyone, and *seriously* disturbing to anyone who believed they knew him well. She could only have felt more uncomfortable had he addressed her as 'Penelope'.

"You'll know what I'm going to say…" he began, an almost apologetic smile of sympathy on his face. "I've sat in that chair often enough and had it said to me, what I have to say to you."

She nodded.

"I have to have a word in your shell-like because Mr Pattison has had a word in my ear as a result of the chief constable calling him at home. You'll know why the chief constable called Mr Pattison at home."

"Because Kitty Dance has the chief's mobile number on speed dial," she muttered, just loud enough for him to hear and splutter with laughter.

"Not Mrs Dance. I understand her personal sky has not exactly fallen on her head because of her loss. The youngest son, however..." He shook his head trying to remember the name. "The lawyer?"

"Andrew."

"That's him!" Milburn laughed again. His contempt for the legal profession was legendary. "Seems he is not entirely satisfied with the progress of the investigation into his father's murder."

She shook her head. "Given that we haven't arrested anyone yet," she said, "there is a very dangerous man still loose; I'd say that means at least two of us aren't satisfied with the progress of the investigation." She was surprised at the harsh conviction in her voice, the realisation that she really was uneasy at the murderer still being free.

Milburn shook his head. "I know how you look at these things, Pen. I know you take it personally, in a way I never did. I always told myself it was just another piece of dead meat, whether it was some pretty kid who'd been raped to death by a pervert or some old lag who would never be missed." He looked into her eyes and nodded his head this time. "That makes me sound like some bitter old man, doesn't it? Well, I may be old but I'm not bitter. It is just that when I moved over to CID, the greenest DC you ever did see, so wet behind the ears I had to wear a towel on my shoulders to keep from rotting away my one-and-only work suit..."

Darling did not know how she was expected to respond to this, whether she should laugh or just keep a straight face.

"…there was this grizzled old DS, Bill Holder. He was about six weeks from retirement when I joined, and he took me under his wing. He taught me that a copper cannot identify with a murder victim, *must* not because nothing you can do is ever going to bring them back, no matter how hard you try. As a detective that isn't your job. You leave that to the priests and the head-shrinkers. Your job is to find the bastard and make sure they don't do it again. That is the extent of your obligation to the victim and their family. Find the bastard and make sure they don't do it again."

Darling nodded. She understood. Milburn had told her all this during the course of the first murder investigation to which they had both been assigned.

"The best way of finding Dancer's murderer is by being the best, most professional detective you can be, and making sure your team are as good and professional as they can be. Don't concern yourself about the lawyer phoning the chief constable. He knows how this game is played. He's been playing it long enough. So has Mr Pattison. So have I. You're not a player in that game. Leave it to me. I'll catch the flak for you just so long as you are doing your job."

Darling nodded. "Thank you, sir."

"And don't think I won't come down on you like a ton of bricks if I suspect you aren't giving it your best."

"Of course not, sir. I don't expect any favours."

Milburn laughed, shaking his head. "There's never been a female copper born who was ever done any favours. Just go and find the bastard before he kills anyone else."

Darling scrambled to her feet. "Sir."

She cursed herself for allowing him to make her feel clumsy, to forget she was a detective inspector because she was twice as good as the male competition she'd had before her promotion, whatever was said in the canteen. She didn't say anything more as she left his office. Rather than going back to her own desk she went straight to the toilet, sat down in a stall and listened to her heart rate slow down, cursing herself for behaving like some weak, giddy female. She might be female, but she was not weak, or giddy, and she had work that wouldn't get done if she didn't do it.

Chapter Thirty-Three

Wearing did not feel comfortable in a suit and tie in daylight, but it was a uniform like the others he had worn – a disguise, something necessary no matter how he felt. What mattered was the mission, and this mission was to search out and destroy the bitch who had doped him and cost him so much money. Search and destroy. It was that simple.

Elders Club was behind a discreet, anonymous doorway in the sandstone old architectural finery that was Grainger Town in the heart of the city. Wearing knocked on the door. When it was opened slightly, he handed in a plain white membership card. A flash of blue light came from within and the door was fully opened, allowing him to step inside and retrieve his card from a tall, bored-looking blonde woman with a long nose down which she looked at Wearing, her cold eyes telling him that even if he was interested she never would be. He could have cared less, but not much.

The entrance hall was all highly polished wood that was reddish-brown in colour, the panelling and the floorboards alike giving the impression they had been lovingly polished every day for the past two hundred years – high days, holidays and world wars not excluded. His footsteps echoed in the hallway as he marched down its length and turned into the room at the right-hand end. This room was also decked out in polished wood, although there was a deep green carpet flecked with gold fleurs-de-lis on which were several round tables with matching chairs. Wearing believed they were Louis-XV style, but he wasn't sure of anything except they hadn't been made to make a man of his size feel comfortable. He went to the bar, leaned on it and beckoned the bartender over.

The bartender was a tall, slender young man with finely etched good looks, long fingers and polished nails. He wore black trousers that a tango dancer might have considered a little on the tight side, and a black waistcoat, on top of a shirt so white it almost glowed in the bright lighting behind the bar; a stark contrast to the subdued, almost dim lighting on the customers' side.

"You are early, Mr Charters," the barman said in a melodious baritone voice guaranteed to put anyone at their ease. "The tables don't open for another two hours."

Wearing, whose membership at Elders was in the name of Malcolm Charters – a man who genuinely did live at the address in the club records but had no idea Elders or anything like it existed – shook his head. "I'm not here to play."

"Can I get you anything to drink?"

Wearing shook his head. "You were in last night?"

The barman nodded.

"You remember the woman I was with?"

He did, and breathing was suddenly more of an effort than it had been before. "Ms Fitzgerald, you mean?"

"If that's her name." Despite their intimacy of the previous evening, and the bodily fluids they had exchanged in one of the club's private rooms, Wearing had not taken any interest in anything about her that might signify her as another human being, like her name. "Is she here now?"

"No, she is not."

"When do you expect her?"

"No idea."

Wearing could tell she was a subject the barman did not want to discuss.

"Come on, she's just a working girl, a whore like all the others."

The barman stiffened as though he had just been punched, then leaned forward across the bar so he was speaking virtually straight into Wearing's ear. "A word to the wise. Don't use words like that about Ms Fitzgerald, sir. Not within these walls, at least."

"Oh, and why not?" Wearing asked in a voice loud enough to be heard by everyone else in the room; then he looked around, and saw there were other people in the bar who were not there when he entered.

Three men walked towards him, all tall, all well-built, all wearing anonymous suits and ties. The middle of the three looked directly at him, a smile on his lips. The other two had one eye on him and one on the guy in the middle. They might as well have had 'muscle' tattooed on their foreheads. He was well acquainted with men like that. He'd served with enough of them. The three came to a halt before him, just more than an arm's length away. The barman was at the very far end of the bar, suddenly polishing a glass with studious intensity. The middle of the three looked Wearing up and down, slowly. When he spoke, it was in a voice so neutral and modulated it could have been artificial.

"The reason for that is Ms Fitzgerald is Mr Geddes's fiancée."

Wearing shrugged. "Who is Mr Geddes when he's fucked?"

The man smiled. There was a hint of condescending pity in the expression. "He is your host." He turned to look at the other two men, whose attention was now wholly fixed on Wearing. "Our employer. I think it is only reasonable to advise you that everyone here is, to a greater or lesser extent, in love with Ms Fitzgerald, and we take a very dim view of anyone insulting her."

Wearing shrugged, calculating how he would beat the three of them. "You might like to tell Mr Geddes what his fiancée did with me in one of your back rooms yesterday evening."

The man shook his head. "I expect he already knows. After all, everything that occurs anywhere on the premises is recorded for his subsequent viewing pleasure. And before you say anything more, Mr Geddes is so enamoured of Ms Fitzgerald, he is quite prepared to forgive her little lapses. You weren't the first." He shook his head again, someone lamenting the latest waywardness of a stubborn child. "I very much doubt you will be the last."

Even though he knew his position was hopeless from a combat point of view, Wearing decided the break the first lesson of war, and give his enemy what he wanted. He stood up and swung a roundhouse right hand towards the man's face. His wrist was caught by the muscle on that side before he made contact, although he managed to pivot around his trapped hand and drive a straight left into the man's nose. His hand was released at the same time as he felt bone and cartilage crunch underneath the knuckles of his left hand, and heard a muffled howl of pain as the man raised his hands to his face in a cup, as though to catch the spurting blood coming from his nose.

Before anything else could happen, something solid struck him on the back of his neck. The universe exploded into the light of the Big Bang momentarily and then, just as quickly, faded into blackness. In that final instant, he felt something slam into his stomach, sending a jag of pain up his spine towards his head. Then the darkness took him.

When Wearing regained consciousness, he was curled up on the cobbles of a back lane, cobbles that were slick and blue with the rain that had fallen on his face and roused him. For a long while he did not move, methodically appraising his body, determining what had been injured and what had not. The second list was not very long at all. He had been beaten up before but never like this. Everywhere hurt, although so far as he could tell nothing was broken. Which was not going to prevent him waking up in the morning with an all-over body tattoo of bruising. Slowly he forced himself to move, until he was sitting upright with his back supported by wall. When he managed to open his eyes, he saw the young man who wasn't muscle, squatting against the opposite side of the lane, a hooded coat draped over his head and shoulders to keep the rain off.

"Back with us, are you? Mr Charters, or whatever your name is?"

Wearing turned his head and spat. At least, there wasn't any blood in his spittle.

"I will only say this once. It would be most unwise of you ever to show your face around here again, most unwise. Do you understand?"

Wearing smiled and nodded, immediately wishing he hadn't. "You'll never see me again," he promised. *Because if you do, I'll be the last thing you see before you die.* "I can take a hint."

The man nodded, smiled, got to his feet and walked away, opening a door further down the lane and stepping inside, out of sight. Wearing got to his feet without screaming out loud or falling over, congratulating himself that his fitness regime and all that army training so long ago had left him able to take a professional beating and walk away, albeit slowly and with a pronounced limp.

As he walked, the pain and discomfort eased, and by the time he emerged onto Grainger Street he could walk more or less upright without wincing with every step. He had to walk much more slowly than was his habit, but at least he did not attract attention to himself from the few others who were braving the darkness and the rain. As he walked in the general direction of where his car was still parked following last night's debacle, he mulled over his next action. He had disregarded the first law of war. He would not disregard the second. Rather than getting mad, he would get even, very, very even.

Chapter Thirty-Four

Ekaterina followed her morning regime of half an hour's calisthenics to tone her muscles, followed by a shower, then a breakfast of grains and fruit, and black tea sent especially from Russia by her mother. She might not brew it in a samovar but neither did she defile it with milk or sugar the way the English did. Once she was perched on her high chair in the kitchen, she switched on the television to watch the local news bulletin.

Halfway through, she saw footage of a fire in the centre of Newcastle overnight, smoke and flames billowing into the night sky, steam rising as three fire engines poured water onto the flames to no obvious effect. Footage in daylight showed the shell of a building, stonework blackened, roof gone, with just charcoaled joists remaining, and there were gaps there, too. According to the journalist standing a safe distance away behind a blue-and-white tape, occasionally glancing over her shoulder, the fire brigade could not say for certain whether the building was repairable, and would not be able to decide until damping down was finished and an expert examination could be carried out. She asked an obviously weary senior fireman with smuts on his cheek and deep, dark rings around his eyes whether he could comment on the cause of the fire.

"It's much too early to tell," he assured her. "A lot of these old buildings have wiring that isn't yet up to modern standards, and clubs like Elders very often have lighting and heating that place severe demands on the wiring…"

At the name 'Elders' she sat bolt upright, spilling tea on her fingers and having to put down her glass so she could suck them dry of the sudden scalding pain. She was sure the club's wiring had been exactly up to modern specification. She knew the Dancer had supervised the renovations himself, and he had never cut corners. The Dancer also knew enough about the building trade, having been something of a builder himself amongst his other businesses, to take a hands-on attitude with his developments to ensure any contractor did exactly what he had been contracted to do; what the Dancer paid him to do. The club had not gone up in flames because somebody had overloaded a multiplug.

"There have been rumours that the fire was not accidental…" the journalist began. The fireman took half a step backwards, shaking his head and waving his right hand between them.

"I couldn't possibly comment on that," he replied. "It is much too early to come to any conclusions."

Behind them, a baulk of blackened timber gave up the fight and fell from what was left of the second floor into the piled-up debris inside the remaining walls. Flame and sparks billowed up, together with a black cloud of soot and ash. Immediately, the firemen played their hoses on the area, quenching the flames, sending steam plumes hissing up into the lightening sky.

"As you can see, it is still much too dangerous for anyone to go in there and make an inspection. As soon as we know anything, we will make an announcement."

With that he turned away and hurried back to the nearest fire engine. The reporter handed back to the studio, where the anchorwoman immediately gave way to the weather girl, who predicted rain and a sharp onshore breeze keeping temperatures down below the seasonal average.

Ekaterina switched off the television and sipped at her tea. She was not overly concerned about the loss of the premises. That was why they paid insurance premiums. The loss of the extra income stream that would have flowed from Elders once the new lease was in place was something of a disappointment, but nothing more. The demand supplied by and within the club was not going to go away just because it had burned down, and it would have to be satisfied elsewhere. What thrilled her was the possibility of turning the fire to her advantage. Ekaterina doubted there was anyone in the present-day Dance organisation who would have set the match. The Dance Enterprises wasn't that sort of organisation any longer. Geddes, however, did not know that.

Going through into the room she used as an office, she quickly turned up Geddes's private mobile number and called it. The phone rang long enough for her to be on the verge of ending the call when he answered.

"Wha' the fuck d'you want? Doncha know wha' the fucking time is?"

"I take it you haven't seen the local news this morning, Mr Geddes."

"The fuck d'ya mean?"

"Look at the local news, Mr Geddes, and ponder the wisdom of believing you can outplay me."

She put the phone down and slowly peeled an orange. Being tough in business was one thing, and she would have sanctioned the torching of the club at some time in the future if the dog had not come to heel. Taking advantage of someone else's handiwork and convincing your opponents that it was yours, well, that was the sweet opportunism of someone who recognised opportunity when it presented itself.

She was still smiling when she got to her office, earlier than everyone else, as usual. It was half past nine when Geddes came storming into her office unannounced, very much less well-kempt than he had been the previous day.

"If you think you're going to get away with this, you mad bitch, you are wrong. You are very, very wrong. I'll get you for this, I promise I will."

For a long while, she sat back in her chair looking up at Geddes leaning over her desk, his fists planted as firmly on it as his feet were on the carpet.

"Get away with what, Mr Geddes? What do you think I have done?"

"You as good as told me you torched my fucking club!"

She shook her head. "I did no such thing. Believe me, I had nothing to do with your misfortune. Why should I wish to damage something I own, something from which I profit, something which I intended to profit from even more?"

She let him stand there a while to let him think about what she had just said, try to reconcile it with what she had said on the phone. With what he believed she had said on the phone.

"Mr Geddes, what has happened to our club is a bad business, and bad for business, yours and mine. Believe you me, I am all about business, pounds and pence in my purse. Now my buildings insurance will pay for the rebuilding of the club, eventually, but in the meantime, you are going to be out of business. You will not pay me the rent you pay me now, much less the rent under the new lease. Then there is all the other money you are not going to be paying me. What have I got to gain from your loss? Mmmm?"

She could see him thinking, or doing whatever passed for thinking inside that thick skull. Fooling him was not much of an effort, and she was not entirely convinced it was worth the effort.

"We had a disagreement, that is all. Such things happen daily in business life, and it is just business. Besides, as you say, this is not Moscow." *If it was Moscow you and that whore of yours would have woken up this morning with a bullet through the back of each of your necks.* "No, if you have been the victim of arson, I assure you I was not responsible. It makes no sense."

He was nodding in agreement. She could hardly keep from laughing.

"If you are looking for a culprit you would do well to consider other enemies you may have made. I am sure they must make a long list, considering your diplomatic skills."

Questions flickered across his face as the frown deepened into a scowl, and she wondered whether she might have gone too far.

"You're right," he said, standing back from her desk. "You're right." He walked towards the door. "There's a few people with questions to answer."

Then he was gone and she sat there a long while, staring at the door.

What was the English saying? 'It is an ill wind that blows no good.' Or, as her father put it, 'What is important is not what you do but what your enemies believe you might do.'

Chapter Thirty-Five

"Park away from the flats," Darling told Morton.

He glanced at her with questions in his eyes, but did as he was told. The street was typical of Jesmond, prosperous houses with pricey cars parked outside and well-established trees dividing the carriageway from the pavement, roots forcing the paving stones out of alignment here and there. The houses had been built for families and most were still single-family residences, unlike some of the nearby streets that had all been divided up. Thame House was a purpose-built block of flats, red brick with parking for six vehicles in the courtyard divided by white lines that looked as though they had been repainted recently. There were only two cars there, a dark-grey Ford Focus and a Ferrari-red Fiat 500 that stood taller than the Focus, nothing like the minicar the model had once been. There were six doorbells, each with a carefully printed name behind the transparent plastic next to the button. The top button was labelled 'Wearing'. Darling pressed it without hesitation, and then again when there was no reply.

"Whaddya want?" asked a slurred voice coming from the speaker grilled.

"Are you Mark Wearing?"

She heard coughing. "What wants to know?"

"I am Detective Inspector Darling of the Northumbria Police…"

"Well, you can fuck right off, then, can't you?"

She paused.

"You still there, copper?"

"…and I have reason to believe you can help me with an investigation I am conducting, into a murder."

The reply was more silence. Morton leaned forward towards the microphone.

"If you're the Mark Wearing we think you are, you'll probably remember me. I'm Peter Morton…"

"And you can fuck right off."

"…and I'm telling you we can do this one of two ways. You can let us in and we can have a friendly little chat, grown-up to grown-up. Or we can break down the door and take you down the nick in handcuffs."

"I'd like to see you fucking well try, Morton!"

Morton laughed. "The pleasure would be all mine, believe you me. While you're cooling in a detention cell, I'll have a scenes-of-crime team turn your place over. I'm sure they'll find something you don't want found." Whether you put it there or not, he muttered with a grin Darling did not like one little bit. "So, what's it going to be, boy, yes or no?"

There was a further silence, then the lock buzzed and the door swung open onto a moss-green-tiled vestibule that would have been fashionable in the mid-seventies. Here and there the tiles were cracked. The steps leading upwards were bare concrete with pronounced well-worn yellow-and-black non-slip treads. Darling guessed that the landlords had been hit with an insurance claim from someone who had slipped sometime in the past.

"I'll go first, ma… guv," said Morton, pushing past her. "If he is our culprit we don't know how he's going to react. He may be armed."

That's very chivalrous of you, thought Darling, and followed him up the steps without comment.

Morton was about to knock on the right-hand door of the two on the second floor when it opened. He looked at the man standing in the doorway, someone tall and strongly built, wearing well-worn jeans, a Marine-Corps grey sweatshirt, bare feet and what he imagined were reading glasses pushed up just above his hairline. His eyes were bloodshot. "Been a long time, boy," Morton said, grinning.

"Not nearly long enough." Wearing looked past Morton at Darling, who felt him looking her up and down the way he would any woman.

She did not like the way that made her feel one little bit. It was time to remind him she was a police officer. She stepped past Morton. "You are Mark John Wearing?"

He nodded.

"If I can step inside we can do this where we will not be overheard."

"And if I say no?"

She laughed. It was the dismissive laugh of a woman who had been getting the better of men who considered themselves real tough guys all her working life. In the right-hand pocket of her trousers, she carried an extendable metal truncheon with which she could break any bone in his body. Strictly speaking, it wasn't legal, but who expected an inspector to get into a situation where she needed to subdue anyone? She had not used it in a long time because she had the likes of Sergeant Morton to do the rough stuff for her.

"If you say 'no', Sergeant Morton will do as he promised and put you in cuffs, drag you down those stairs and we will do this in Forth Banks."

Wearing glared at her then shrugged and stepped aside.

If she hadn't known he was ex-army before, one glance at his lounge would have been enough to convince her. Except for the plasma screen on the wall opposite the window, the walls were bare. There was an expensive leather recliner facing the television, and an empty glass and whisky bottle on the occasional table next to the chair. Other than that, there was no indication that anyone actually lived there.

"Don't do much entertaining, eh?" Morton observed, looking around for somewhere to sit.

Wearing opened a cupboard door and produced two folding metal chairs, which he opened and set before them. Then he sat in the recliner. "Whaddya want?"

"Where were you last Sunday evening?" asked Morton, leaning forward towards Wearing. "Specifically, between the hours of five and eight."

Wearing snorted. "I was here, watching a box set."

"Can anyone confirm that?"

"I was alone, if that's what you mean." He paused a moment. "Mind you, the old guy downstairs gave me a right earful on Monday. Told me if I didn't turn it down he'd get the council in. I gave him a bottle of wine for his trouble."

"His name?" asked Darling.

Wearing snorted again. "He's the old guy who lives downstairs. How am I expected to know his fucking name? Ask him yourself."

"Oh, we will, we will." Darling smiled. "What were you watching?"

"*Breaking Bad*. What else is there?"

Darling and Morton glanced at each other. Why were they not surprised?

Darling got to her feet.

Wearing's gaze followed her. "You said you were investigating a murder. Whose?"

She shook her head. "You don't need to know that."

"Why pick on me, then?"

"Because you fit the profile, sunshine. That's why." Morton seemed intent on provoking Wearing. "We're all into profiling these days."

"We may have some more questions, later," Darling said, walking to the door.

Wearing shrugged. "I'm not going anywhere."

"Good. We'll see ourselves out."

Morton turned in the doorway and glared at Wearing, who did not look in the least bit intimidated. On the way down the stairs Darling told him to go and speak to the downstairs neighbour before the sergeant could say anything. Wearing was lying, although whether that was about Sunday evening or just on general principle she did not yet know. Leaving Morton behind, Darling walked out of the building and went to the car without turning back. She was sure at least one pair of eyes were following her, almost certainly from the top flat. That was not exactly new, even in this relatively affluent area of town.

Sitting in the car, she made a couple of routine phone calls while she allowed her subconscious to process what little she had learned from the meeting with Wearing; it hadn't been an interview, more of a shot across his bows letting him know he was on their radar, hopefully shaking him into doing something that might provide then with more evidence. *More* evidence? *Any* real evidence at all would be a good start.

Morton returned and got in behind the steering wheel, started the car and drove off without saying anything. When he turned the corner and they were out of sight of anyone who might be watching them, she told him to stop.

"Find anything?"

"Mr Kolchak confirmed that Wearing's TV was playing very loud on Sunday evening. He said he went upstairs to complain but Mr Wearing did not open the door, even when Mr Kolchak took off his shoe and hammered on the door with his heel. He also said that Wearing's car was not in the car park at the time."

Darling nodded, giving no sign of the satisfaction this gave her. This might well be the evidence she needed that Wearing was lying. If anyone had a dedicated parking space around there, they would not leave their car somewhere else. That Wearing's car was not in its space at the time was not proof of anything, but it was evidence that having a hard look at him might pay dividends. Wherever it had been, it would not have escaped the attention of the city's traffic cameras.

"I want our Mr Wearing watched."

"Think he's our man?"

Darling shook her head. Another lesson ground into her by Joe Milburn was 'never jump to conclusions'. "I want him watched. That's all."

Morton got out of the car.

"Before you go, Sergeant, have a good look for any CCTV cameras in the area."

He nodded and walked away. Darling got out and went around to the driver's side. Had they made a breakthrough? Milburn would be pleased to hear it if they had.

Chapter Thirty-Six

Darling woke up slowly, knowing it was Saturday because her alarm clock had not gone off to drag her, kicking and screaming at least metaphorically from sleep. She didn't have to go into the office, not strictly anyway, and could luxuriate in the snuggly-bug warmth of her bed, the pillows, the duvet. She could even switch on the electric underblanket if she really wanted to cook. She didn't, so she didn't, although she did switch on the television to find it was already time for the cooking shows.

All her feelings of comfort and satisfaction evaporated in an instant. She disliked cookery programmes with an intensity that bordered on hatred, and what sort of idiot wasted their time and energy on hating anything as unreal and ephemeral as a television cookery show, even one that made a celebrity out of a professional Yorkshireman? She disliked the breed. Her father had been a Yorkshireman, her ex-husband too. Right tykes the pair of them, and she was heartily glad they were both out of her life.

Her mother, Pamela, however, was still in her life, and today was her birthday. They had an understanding that, no matter what, they would lunch together on her mother's birthday and pretend to be civilised human beings. Neither of her parents had agreed with her decision to join the police after university, and her father had gone to his grave having taken every chance that presented itself to tell her what a wasteful choice it was, no matter the progress she made in her chosen career. He had liked Robert, liked him a lot, probably more than she had herself, if the truth were told, and her kicking him out had been another source of discord between them, so much so that she had stormed out of their house vowing never to return if he kept on taking Robert's side. Just over two years later, her father died without any reconciliation, and there was enough of him in Darling for her not to regret it, at least not much. When it came to bearing grudges, she had inherited his genes.

She had planned on a slow, relaxed morning. As it was, she had time to shower and take a rushed breakfast before climbing into her car and driving north to Craster, where her mother had moved after her father had died, freeing her from any obligation to live in Yorkshire. The village itself was dominated by the ruins of Dunstanburgh Castle to the north, one of the castles built along the coastline to discourage Vikings, just as the castles and mottes in the marches had been built to ward off cattle raids from Border Reivers. None had been particularly successful. Her mother lived in a cottage on the Dunstanburgh Road, built by a fisherman close to the ground to endure the raging winter storms that came in off the North Sea and did their best to tear the house off its foundations. Darling had been in the cottage during one such storm and didn't care to repeat the experience. Her mother had just maintained a degree of inebriation that allowed her to ignore the wind and rain, except when it disrupted her television reception.

"You're late," was Pamela's greeting when she opened the door.

Darling had her own key but would not have dreamt of using it while her mother was in the house.

"There was an accident," she lied. "I was held up." She handed over the bunch of lilies that were the real reason she was half an hour later than the agreed time.

Her mother looked at the flowers as though trying to decide whether she should eat them or just throw them in the bin. Eventually she smiled. "Thank you, sweetheart. You know how I love lilies."

That's why I bought them, Darling thought, but said nothing. She smiled, a smile of relief. At least she had remembered that about her mother. She made to enter the house, but her mother stood in her way and reached for her coat, which hung on the pegs in the hallway.

"We haven't got time for idle chit-chat," she said, doing up the buttons. "You know what The Jolly Fisherman is like. If you aren't there at the time your table is booked for, they give it to the first in the queue, and you go to the back."

Darling had no idea if this was true, but couldn't be bothered to argue. There was nothing to be gained. She just walked alongside her mother as they negotiated the cobbles and weather-crazed pavement into the heart of the small village, making small talk and wishing she had worn a scarf. The breeze might not be strong but it still sent a chill through to the marrow of her bones, as it always did when it came in off the North Sea.

The landlord greeted Pamela as though she was one of his best customers, which she might well be for all Darling knew, and showed them to a table in the bay window looking out over the harbour. It might not be as bustling as it had been when her mother's cottage was built, but there were a couple of working fishing boats tied up beneath the breakwater, idle on a Saturday, meaning it was one of the few working harbours still left on the North-East coast. Mother ordered a steak and chips, rarely done, and a bottle of house red to wash it down. Pen settled for haddock and chips, with sparkling water.

"You never have anything but the fish when you come here," her mother complained.

Darling shrugged. "What is the point of coming to a fishing port and not eating the local fish?"

"It probably comes from Grimsby," observed her mother, tearing apart a roll and reaching for a knife to plaster it with butter.

Darling did not reply. The board outside the pub proclaimed all fish was locally caught, unless otherwise indicated. She was prepared to believe it. The local trading standards crew were hot on false advertising.

"Why not have some wine?" her mother asked with just a hint of reproach in her voice. Wine was her literal solution to just about everything.

"Mother, I'm driving. I can't run the risk of some woodentop who doesn't know who I am stopping me and making me take a breathalyzer. I could lose my job."

Her mother shook her head. She was of a generation that believed police officers and bank managers had to be able to hold their drink. Her daughter's virtual teetotalism of late was not something she could understand, neither was she prepared to try to understand it. Even so, they ate their way through the meal making polite conversation and managed not to disagree about anything. Whether this was by luck or judgement, Darling did not know, or whether she had just managed to avoid mentioning any relative who was in her mother's bad books for the first time in her memory. She even ate the apple pie with pecan ice cream and cream, and finished the meal with an Irish coffee, much to Pamela's approval, although she had managed to tell the waitress to show the glass the bottle rather than put any into the coffee while her mother was 'powdering her nose', as she put it.

"We don't take cards," the landlord told her when she offered to pay for the meal. "Not now. Nobody round here does. We all got badly burned by a couple of con artists."

"That's a shame," she muttered as she took all the notes from her purse and put them on the bar. "Keep the change," she told him, though it was nearly a tenner and the food hadn't been that good. It was worth it not to hear him run down the police because of their losses. She was sure he knew she was a police officer, even if not a particularly local one.

Outside, her mother slipped her arm through hers as they walked back to the cottage.

"Let's sit here," she said, as they came to a couple of bench seats just below the road, on the slope above the harbour.

Darling would much rather have gone straight back to the warmth of the cottage. The sky had clouded over while they had been eating, the wind picked up a little more, and it felt a good five degrees colder than it had been.

"Of course." She smiled, and sat down on the chilly green bench slats.

They sat there for a while, in silence, until Darling turned towards her mother, and saw her mouth opening, as if to say something she had really wanted to say for a long, long time, something that evaporated and blew away on the breeze, as though it had never been. She was looking at herself in thirty-something years' time, the grey in her hair kept at bay by subtle use of dark-auburn hair dye, the wrinkles around the corners of her eyes and mouth covered over by make-up, her thin lips plumped and reddened. Only the tears in her eyes weren't hidden.

"Why do you do it, Penny?" She shook her head as she asked the question. "I saw you on the television. Why do you do it?"

There it was. The question her mother has never actually asked, 'Why are you a police officer?' It was a question she had never asked herself, in so many words. Nobody she had known at school or college had become a policeman, except for Guy Crosby, who had gone back to South Africa in the crazy expectation of being made a colonel in the anti-terror brigade, and being allowed to torture black people. He'd consumed far too many drugs at college and she had no idea whether he had succeeded in his ambition, and didn't much care either.

Hers had been an emotional decision, more than anything else. A couple of college friends had been attacked in the street one Saturday night on the way home from a disco. One had taken a kicking. The other had her purse and her leather jacket stolen. Everyone she knew had agreed that something had to be done, that someone had to do something, although nobody knew what.

Some vowed they would never speak to her again when she said she was applying to join the police – the fuzz, the filth, the pigs and all the other names they had for the force. She hadn't joined with any great ambitions or even any belief she could so something other people couldn't. It was only when she finished her training and had been on the streets that she realised she enjoyed what she did; whether it was helping people – some of whom were victims of crime, some of whom were criminals who didn't want to be criminals, some of whom had been caught up in incidents and accidents way beyond their control – or catching those who believed they could prey on everyone else. She seemed to have some insight into such people, even if she told herself that they were dumber and slower and less intelligent than most people, and it was only their lack of inhibitions that allowed them to commit their offences in the first place.

Only when she transferred to the CID and came within the orbit of Joe Milburn did she discover the truth of it. At her second personal-development review with him, he had observed, out of the blue, "You're good at this, Darling. I don't think you know how good you are."

Which was what she told her mother. "I do it because I am good at it, better than I am at anything else. I do it because I can make a contribution."

Her mother looked at her with incomprehension in her eyes.

Her father had been a solicitor all his life, with a sideline in property development. Her mother had been a housewife and an active member of various charitable organisations, as well as a keen golfer. As far as Darling could tell, the idea of 'making a contribution' to society was alien to them. Mrs Thatcher had voiced their unspoken belief when she said there was no such thing as society. Darling disagreed with that. She lived in society. She saw its good side and its dark, rotten underbelly. Sometimes it wasn't very nice to look at. Sometimes its reek was poison. But not always.

"But searching for murderers… it's so dangerous."

"What can I say? Nobody has ever lifted a finger to me," she said, which was a lie.

More times than she cared to remember, a lot more than a finger had been raised against her, as was the case for every copper she'd known, but after the first time, Darling realised the truth of the lesson on her second day in Police College. "Forget rules," the sergeant said. "Forget fairness. When it comes to a fight, it is your duty to end it as quickly as possible. If that involves putting your boot into Johnny's balls, so be it. You put an end to it as quick as you can, any which way you can. That's the way you keep others from getting hurt. Understand?" They had all understood.

"It is what I'm good at," Darling repeated.

The two women had stared at each other for a long while until her mother shivered and got to her feet. "Let's get home and get something hot to drink," she said, brightly, slipping her arm through Darling's and all but dragging her off the seat.

She was snoring gently on the sofa when Darling got up to leave. Darling didn't need to smell her mother's breath to know she had laced her coffee with brandy. Was it any concern of hers? Mum is a grown woman, she thought.

Darling bent over and kissed her mother's forehead as she left, seeing a face that seemed more at peace than she could remember for a long, long time.

On the drive back to Newcastle, Darling kept the driver's side window open so that cold air whipped into her face and she could convince herself it was the wind that brought the tears into her eyes.

Chapter Thirty-Seven

"Katy, darling, this is a surprise seeing you here."

Ekaterina looked up into the face of a blonde woman of about her age, who was dressed a decade younger without having the figure to carry it off. Her make-up must have taken her the better part of two hours to apply. That, or she had had it done professionally. It was a lot more than she had worn the last time Ekaterina had seen her. Stephanie had been an annoyance then, and Ekaterina had had no more time for her then than she had now – a stupid English bitch who did not realise how insulting it was not to use her given name. After all, she was English while Ekaterina was merely Russian. The man accompanying Stephanie tonight was also a lot younger than any of her previous escorts. He appeared young enough to be skipping homework to be with her.

"Stephanie, it's been too long!" Getting up from the table, she kissed the air by the side of the other woman's cheeks, smiling thinly.

The last time they had met had been at a gallery opening in Gateshead, given by Frank Bonner – a rather difficult artist and an even more difficult human being, especially when he had been drinking, which was most of the time. Ekaterina had bought several of his pieces.

Stephanie's male companion from the night in Gateshead was now sitting across the table from Ekaterina, and had already told her several of Stephanie's secrets in the few moments they had engaged in pillow talk.

Stephanie held her hand out to him.

He reached forward and bent over to kiss a millimetre above her knuckles while gazing directly into her eyes.

"Wade, I can't say I expected to meet you here," she said.

The man gave no sign of being distracted by being called by a name he did not use very often, merely turning up the wattage on his smile.

"You're looking well," he said, relaxing back into his chair but still fixing Stephanie with his eyes.

Suddenly enraged by what was going on, Ekaterina raised her hand above her head and snapped her fingers. "Bill!" she said to a waitress passing by, who promised to bring it right away.

"You've not even finished your dessert!" said Stephanie.

"I have eaten as much as I want to eat here tonight," Ekaterina replied, getting to her feet.

"Have I said something to offend you?" asked Stephanie. The concern on her face was very obviously false to anyone who knew either of them.

Ekaterina turned very slowly towards her 'friend', who took an involuntary half-step backwards.

"Stephanie, darling," she said, ladling on the oily, 'friendly' charm. "If you live to be a hundred, I assure you that nothing you say will ever be anything near important enough to offend me."

She smiled at the other woman's confusion, then walked out of the restaurant, head high, looking neither right nor left, and most definitely not backwards. Her partner for the night, raised his glass to her and looked around the restaurant for anyone who might share the rest of his evening.

Stephanie watched her go and then turned towards Wade.

"Wade, darling, what is going on?"

He got to his feet. "I am sure I don't know," he said.

"But you must know!" Stephanie wailed.

He stepped close and spoke into her ear. "I know nothing about her. All I do is fuck her." He stepped away and began to follow, only to turn around. "By the way, my name isn't Wade and she's a lot better than you; a lot, lot better."

His voice was audible to everyone sitting nearby, all of whom had the good manners not to turn and look but just giggled into their suddenly raised napkins. Then he strode out of the restaurant, leaving Stephanie open-mouthed and with nothing to say.

She went back to her table, where her young escort for the night – who called himself Philippe and had just the slightest French accent – had watched the encounter with amused interest. He smiled broadly at Stephanie, scrambling up to get her into her chair.

"A friend of yours?"

"She was, I thought," said Stephanie, attacking her pepper steak with a ferocity that suggested she had no real need of cutlery.

* * *

Outside the restaurant, Ekaterina tapped her foot in annoyance until she heard the locks click. She got into the passenger seat and waited for her man to arrive. After a short while, she turned her head to look for him. He was strolling towards her with a huge grin on his face. He stopped and raised his hand, waggling his fingers at her, and for a moment she thought the top was coming off her head, steam coming out of her ears, until she began to laugh. In a moment she was laughing uncontrollably, tears streaming down her face, hiccoughing and choking. He sat beside her and stared at her, unmoving. Eventually she calmed down, got some wipes out of her bag and removed all her smeared make-up, checking her face in the passenger side mirror.

"I called you. You didn't answer."

He shrugged. "I'm not at your back and call twenty-four hours a day."

"I didn't know you are called 'Wade'."

He shrugged. "I'm not."

"Should I call you Wade?"

He shrugged. "If you pay, you can call me anything you like, Wade, Dumbo, Richard the Lionheart."

"Dumbo it is, then. Take me somewhere quiet and fuck me till I can't walk straight."

He grinned. "Your wish is my command."

"You had better fucking well believe it!" She spoke in Russian, one of the many languages he did not understand, but her voice was cold enough to drip ice water down his spine, and her expression sent a thrill of apprehension through him. He hadn't met many people who scared him, and wondered whether he should, perhaps, add Ekaterina Dance to that list.

He drove into the country, up the A1 and west past Morpeth where there were few other cars on the road, following her directions. Only when they turned off the road and into the farmyard did he realise where she had taken him. He hadn't come this way since the last time he was there. For a moment, he thought of stopping the car and telling her this was too perverse, even for him, but he didn't. Partly because she was employing him to do this and he had always been a firm believer in doing his job to the best of his ability, no matter what, and partly because her perversity was a turn-on, her determination to do what she wanted, the way she wanted to do it.

He parked in the farmyard and followed her towards the door, which she opened with a key, quickly opening the alarm cover and resetting it. "Don't bother trying," she said. "I've changed the code."

"Who said I was going to try anything?" he asked, following her into the front room. There was still a taped outline of the corpse on the parquet floor.

She turned towards him, put her hands behind her head and unzipped her dress, letting it fall to the floor. Other than a flimsy, almost immaterial thong, she was naked. Her nipples were more engorged than he had ever seen them before.

"Here?" he asked.

"Here," she replied, reaching for him.

He took her in his arms, bending his head to suck on her breasts, at the same time putting his right hand between her legs as she wrenched open his trousers. He bit her nipple as hard as he could without actually severing it. There was nothing sensuous about it, just the desire to hurt her as much as he could. She screamed and his hand between her legs was suddenly drenched. He picked her up and slammed her down onto the floor as though it was a wrestling match. Her head bounced off the wood but that did not prevent her taking his balls in her hand and yanking them upwards, her nails digging into his flesh. It was his turn to scream in pain. After that the beast in both of them took over. Anyone who described what they did to each other as 'making love' would be a fool. To call their savagery 'lust' was to dignify it altogether undeservedly. By the time they were done with each other, they fell apart and lay where they were, inert, their heads pounding, their senses scrambled.

Eventually, the numbness faded to awareness. They dressed without looking at each other, as though ashamed of what they had done, what they had allowed themselves to become. Neither had ever experienced anything quite like that before, or had come away feeling so bruised and even torn. Both knew that some time, somewhere, they wanted to do that again, perhaps not now, perhaps not soon, but that need was there in their futures, the need and the possibility that one or both of them would not walk away from it at all.

* * *

"I had a visit," he said when they were back on the main road into town, the first words either of them had spoken since the savagery began.

"Oh?" she said, disinterested, staring out into the gathering darkness with the orange lights of Tyneside ahead. "Who from?"

"The police."

Her attention bored between his eyes like a drill. "What did you tell them?"

"Nothing. What else was there to say?"

"What did they want?"

"They wanted to know where I was the evening I killed your father-in-law."

Suddenly, there was a metal band being tightened around Ekaterina's head. It was a novel sensation and she didn't like it one bit.

"What did you say?"

He laughed.

She almost slapped his face but managed to restrain herself.

"I told them I was at home, watching a box set."

They drove on in silence for a while.

"Look, I'm good at what I do," he said. "I plan. I prepare. I cover every eventuality. They have no evidence it was me. All the physical evidence is gone. What they did is draw up some profile for a killer who could have done that the way I did it, and someone came up with my name. That's all."

Ekaterina said nothing in reply. There was nothing to say. What he had just told her was all she needed to hear.

Chapter Thirty-Eight

Morton sat at his desk trying to make sense of his thoughts. Like the boss, he believed Wearing was far and away the best candidate they had for the Dancer's murderer. He was the only candidate now Garth had been eliminated, and Morton didn't believe he was allowing his personal antipathy towards the man colour his view. After all, he hadn't even thought about him since the day Wearing quit the job, so he couldn't be that important to him. Even so, he could not escape that missing piece, the gap in their thesis. Why had Wearing murdered the Dancer? Who had persuaded him to commit murder? After all, in real life murder was always a big deal, whatever it might be like in books or films. How much had they paid him to do it? What was their motivation? Wearing might be the smoking gun, but who had pulled his trigger? As far as Morton could see, they were nowhere near answering that question.

He reached into his jacket pocket and brought out a tub of chewing gum, flicking open the cap and tossing two breath mints into his mouth. What he really wanted was a cigarette. He wanted a cigarette and a half of bitter with a chaser of Scotch – it could be a blend, he wasn't proud. It was years since 'they' had allowed smoking inside the station, those non-smoking, smug, superior fascists who had no idea at all what it was like to be an addict, to be in need. He could go out under the shelter in the station yard if he really couldn't manage without his fix, but he would be damned if he would give them the satisfaction of seeing him out there, greedily sucking on a tab. He'd give up before giving them that satisfaction. Come to that, he'd die before giving them that.

He became aware of a uniform standing by his desk. Looking up, he recognised one of the latest intake of probationary constables, one who even now could not hide his ambition to sit in a chair in the CID room. "Yes, Simon lad, what can I do for you?"

The constable said nothing for a moment, shifting his feet.

"Out with it. I haven't got all day."

The constable nodded towards the glass wall with its photos and chinagraph pencil, writing and connecting lines.

"I saw him last night," he said, pointing at Wearing's face.

"So what? I saw him yesterday, too."

The lad shook his head. "It wasn't just him I saw." He stepped to the wall and tapped Ekaterina's photo. "He was with her."

"What?" Morton started to get to his feet. "Where?"

"They were at the Jesmond Dene House, having a meal together. She got into it with some other woman and they left together."

"You were having dinner at The Dene?" Morton shook his head, almost laughing. "Since when did a constable get paid enough to afford to eat at The Dene?"

Philip shuffled his feet again, then took a deep breath and shook his head. "I wasn't paying."

Morton laughed. "You've got a girlfriend who can afford those prices? Jammy bugger."

The constable took another deep breath, obviously wishing he hadn't started this conversation. "She isn't exactly my girlfriend…" His voice petered out.

Morton relaxed back into his chair, reached over and tapped the other chair at the side of his desk. "Why you were there isn't important. What is important is what you saw. Take the weight off your feet, lad. Tell me all about it." There was a mixture of invitation and command in his voice, a tone he had developed working as a detective to get people to tell him things they didn't want to tell him at the same time as they needed to tell him.

Simon sat down and, once Morton had brought them both paper cups of filthy coffee from the machine seeing as the canteen hadn't opened yet, he told him the story. When he was finished, Morton sat still for a moment, then tossed his cup into the waste bin, the dregs of coffee emerging in droplets as it flew through the air.

"You're going to have to tell the boss," he said.

"Do I have to?" the constable wailed.

"Don't worry, she won't bite," Morton said. "But this is evidence you've collected about her case. You have to tell her."

Five minutes later, they were both standing in Darling's cubicle as the constable recounted his story.

"You are sure he was with Ekaterina Dance?"

The constable coloured and nodded. "When I was a lad, Barry Dance Junior, the footballer, was my hero and I kept a scrapbook about him, including his wedding. She's not a face you forget."

Darling nodded. "True enough. Well, Constable, you go off and write a report of the incident. You wait here, Sergeant."

Morton did as he was told, waiting while the inspector sorted the papers she had left on her desk and logged out of her computer.

Then she got up. "Come with me, Sergeant," she said and walked out of her office.

"Where are we going, boss?" he asked as they got into her car.

"Somewhere we can talk where nobody can hear us."

They went down to the back door of the station, out to the car park, only to discover it was hammering down with rain. They ran to the shelter of the decrepit bike rack and then waited until Darling spoke. "How confident are you Wearing is our man?"

Morton shrugged. "We got nobody else. For all we know, it could have been someone flown in from New York who was back home sleeping in his own bed before we even knew the Dancer was dead."

Darling snorted. "And it might have been a little green man from Mars."

"Boss, we can't say for sure it wasn't a little green man."

They stared at each other for a few seconds before she began to laugh. He joined in, until the moment had run its course.

"Let's go with it being him for the moment, in the lounge, with the Dancer's own gun. Why did he do it? There must be a reason. So far as we've found, there was no connection at all between the two men except his daughter-in-law making use of his services as a gigolo."

"That is what Mr Milburn won't accept. That he was 'contracted' to do it, either for money or as a favour."

Darling pursed her lips.

Morton knew she didn't like the professional hit idea any more than Joe Milburn did, but he also knew she would at least consider it if there was any evidence. "Who? Who got him to do it?"

Darling shook her head. "Oh, for goodness' sake, it's what we were taught in our first criminology lecture. *Cui bono?* Who benefits from an action? Who benefits from the Dancer not being around?"

Morton scratched the palm of his left hand. "They were rowing about the business before he stormed out, just before he was killed. Him and the kids."

"Now there are some delicate questions I've got to ask."

"I'm not a betting man," Morton lied. He had an account with a local bookmaker. His losses were one of the bones of contention with Mrs Morton. "But if I was, two to one says it's the daughter-in-law."

"She did strike me as being more dynamic than either of the sons."

"The lad at Wayfarer Security struck me as being scared shitless of her." He quickly reminded her about his visit to Wayfarer and what he had found there.

"Before I go charging in there I want to know more about her, her background," said Darling.

They were both startled to find Joe Milburn standing behind them.

"I might be able to help you on that score," Milburn said, tapping the Newcastle crest that was in his lapel.

"I've been a United fan as long as I can remember. My dad took me onto the Leazes End when I was a lad. I've been a season-ticket holder as long as I could afford it. It has been a long era of gloom punctuated by isolated bursts of blinding light. Anyway, the only hobby I have, other than nicking villains, is the history of Newcastle United. I know facts that identify me as being a total Toon anorak. I took a particular interest in Barry Dance Junior, for obvious reasons. Other than Gazza, he was the most naturally gifted player from around here in my time. When he came back from Moscow, I called in a favour with a police captain from there. I'd met him at the only international conference I ever attended, when Hughie

Pattison was having his gall bladder operation and couldn't go himself."

"It turns out that Ekaterina Irina Simeonova is the only child of Vladimir Petrovich Simeonov. He's the head of what might be called the Simeonov criminal family, a very rich man with fingers in just about every pie in Moscow, in the good books of politicians up to and almost certainly including Comrade Putin – either that, or he had something incriminating on all of them – and he has definitely not put his criminal past behind him the way the Dancer had. Why should he? Nobody can prove anything, and anyone who was prepared to be a witness against him would end up face down in the Moskva River. He's the man Al Capone wanted to be, and Ekaterina, being his only child, was raised to take his place when the time came."

Darling and Morton stared at Milburn. Neither had even suspected that of Ekaterina. She might be a tough businesswoman, but they weren't as unusual as they had been only a few short years ago. A mafiosa was a horse of an entirely different colour.

"Of course," he continued, "all I have to back this up is a telephone conversation with a Moscow copper who will deny he ever met me, and I wouldn't tell you his name anyway, in case it got back there. Like I say, Ekaterina's daddy is the great white in that ocean, and he has a hard-earned reputation for getting even in a permanent, irreversible way."

"So, what you need is proof, proof that there is a connection between Mrs Dance and your man Wearing," said Darling.

Morton opened his mouth to say they were just talking about that, only to close it on seeing Darling's quick shake of the head.

"Thanks, boss," she said. "That does show things in a different light."

Milburn began to walk away, before turning around in true Columbo style. "Just a thought, but I wouldn't interview Mrs Dance on your own, either of them, but especially the younger one." Then he left.

Morton looked at Darling, almost certain she was thinking exactly what he was thinking.

Darling got to her feet. "Oh well," she said, "questioning her won't get any easier if we leave it to stew, will it?"

Chapter Thirty-Nine

Ekaterina sat behind her desk, impassively looking from one police officer to the other and wondering why they were there. Did they know something she did not know they knew?

"Mrs Dance—" began Darling.

"Call me Ekaterina," she said. "It will distinguish me from the other Mrs Dances in the family."

She briefly switched on her megawatt smile, directing it almost entirely at Morton. As a policeman, he should be immune to it but few men could entirely resist that smile and the unspoken promises behind it. Morton's ears went red and he looked away.

Darling spoke. "Ekaterina, I have to admit that we are making very little progress in our investigation. Our most promising line is that the murder was the result of a business deal that went wrong."

Ekaterina shrugged. "This is not Moscow, Inspector. You people do not kill each other over business deals."

"You were privy to all Mr Dance's business dealings?" Darling enquired, watching Ekaterina consider her response to that. The circuits inside her head were glowing.

"Not before his death, no. Before his death, I concerned myself only with those areas of the business that were my responsibility."

"Which areas would they be?" Morton asked, pen poised over his notebook.

He was treated to that smile again, very, very briefly. Ekaterina saw him shift from cheek to cheek, his discomfort not caused by the chair.

"That would be the security company and our estate agents."

Morton frowned. "I didn't know there were any Dance estate agents."

"We retained the original trading names when we bought the agencies. What would be the profit in throwing away all the goodwill the original owners had built up over the years?"

Okay, so you're a good business woman, Darling thought. *That don't impress me much.* "You said you only had limited access to the family companies before Mr Dance's death. That suggests his death changed things," she said.

She considered Ekaterina's eyes and watched a thoughtful shadow come down over them. Darling had no doubt the woman had rehearsed this conversation. Ekaterina must have known it would be coming, and sooner rather than later. Rehearsal was all very well. Darling indulged in it herself, but never to the extent that she forgot the first rule of good questioning, which was 'active, intense listening': to listen to the answers and be prepared to ask a question following on from what was said.

Looking at Ekaterina, Darling could almost hear the alternatives being weighed in the balance.

"In his will, my father-in-law gave me his control over the family businesses," she said.

"I bet that pleased your brothers-in-law," Morton said.

"You will have to ask them about that," Ekaterina replied, her icily neutral tone making it very clear she did not care much about the reaction of Garth and Andrew.

"Neither of them strike me as the sort who would keep his views to himself on the direction the business should take."

Ekaterina leaned forward. "Inspector, we have not had any discussion about the businesses," she lied. "My brothers-in-law have only just buried their father. They are in mourning. I cannot burden them with business matters now. I think we Russians understand the necessity for mourning much more than you British."

Darling put that remark behind her ear for later consideration. It might even be true. Not that she believed any son of the Dancer would let such a minor thing as their father's murder get in the way of taking care of business.

"I must ask you this question, Mrs Dance… Ekaterina. It would be unprofessional of me if I did not," said Darling.

Her response was a languid shrug of the shoulders. "Ask whatever questions you want to ask, if you believe my answer can help you find my father-in-law's murderer."

"Did you know he was going to put you in charge of the business?"

"Did I know?" She shook her head. "You didn't know my father-in-law very well, did you?"

"I never met him. I only knew him by reputation." Darling wondered whether Ekaterina knew what the Dancer's reputation was, especially when he was a younger man, and decided she probably did. They came from similar backgrounds.

"He kept his own counsel," Ekaterina said. "If he sounded out anyone about anything they would not know it. His decisions were like those of God, brought down on tablets of stone from the mountain, not to be questioned by anyone. I knew nothing of his intention until Kitty read his will. Ask either of the boys, or Kitty."

Darling recalled that the family meeting the Dancer had quit with a show of temper had been about family business, but decided this was not the time to mention it.

"How did your brothers-in-law react to the news?" Morton asked.

Ekaterina just stared at him in reply, as if challenging him to justify asking such a stupid question.

"How do you think they took it?" she asked, eventually.

"Not well?" Morton suggested.

Ekaterina's laugh was so bitter it almost made the air about her face smoke.

Darling nodded. One of the advantages of asking a lot of questions was the understanding that someone might be telling the truth even when everything they said was questionable because there was no advantage in telling anything but the truth. "I believe you," she said, and caught the sudden, brief widening of the sergeant's eyes. You never told the subject that you believed them, at least not until you plunged the hook into their jaw and reeled them in to shore.

"Thank you," said Ekaterina. "They did not behave like the gentlemen they pretend to be."

Compared to their father, they don't have to pretend, Darling thought. Instead of saying anything, however, she got to her feet. "I don't think we need to take up any more of your time today," she said, smiling and holding out her hand for Ekaterina to take. "What you've told us today has been very useful."

Morton had the good sense to follow her lead, shaking Ekaterina's hand, too. He looked almost disappointed that she didn't flirt with him this time, her indifference making it clear that her hand was all of Ekaterina Dance he would ever get to touch.

"We may need to speak to you again," he said.

"One more question," Darling said from the doorway. "Do you know a man by the name of Mark John Wearing?"

* * *

So, there it was, the question the police inspector had come to ask. Ekaterina recalled what her father had told her about policemen asking questions, or policewomen for that matter. A good detective virtually only ever asked questions to which they already knew the answer. The most effective way of answering was to tell the truth, or as nearly as you could.

"Yes, I do know Mark Wearing," she said, in what she believed was a convincingly measured tone. "I know him socially, that is."

"Well," said Darling, "I wasn't asking if you knew him biblically."

She laughed, briefly, then shook her head and rearranged her face into her customarily neutral expression.

Ekaterina wondered exactly what Wearing had told the police in his encounter with them, before assuring herself she had made a very wise decision about him. He had his uses, of course, but that utility was at an end.

"Thank you, Mrs Dance. You won't mind answering any further questions that might arise?" asked Darling.

"Of course, I am happy to speak with you at any time, any time at all," she replied, and watched them leave.

What had she told them that was 'very useful'? What was the purpose of their questions anyway? What were they trying to discover? Ekaterina's head was aching when she gave up trying to answer those questions. The police bitch was a lot cleverer than she had given her credit for, and she was going to need to be even more cautious about everything she said to her. But not too cautious. She remembered another lesson her father had taught her – one of the many – that a police officer could interpret as much from what you didn't say as what you did, putting both together with what they knew, which you could never be sure was more or less than you thought they knew.

Aching or not, she made a decision. Taking out her laptop, she went online and searched for a flight to Moscow, giving herself two days to complete the business she still had on Tyneside. She would fly from Heathrow to Sheremetyevo. The website asked whether she wanted a return flight. She hesitated about this before leaving the box blank. There would be enough time to think about returning when she was at home with her mother and father. Her father would understand, she was certain.

Chapter Forty

Morton opened his mouth to speak as they walked towards the car, only to close it as he saw her brief shake of the head and turning of her eyes in the direction of the CCTV camera, which he saw panning to follow them. He held open the rear door for Darling to get in and then got behind the steering wheel to drive them back to the station.

"If you're going to take the piss, I'll get you a driver's cap," she said.

He laughed. "I bet Russian detective inspectors get driven around everywhere!"

She shook her head. "I hope she's a lot more frightened of me than she would be of any Russian copper, given who her father is."

Morton said nothing. Darling did not frighten him most of the time, which was hardly surprising seeing as they were both coppers. Every so often, though, he saw a glint of steel in her and he could understand how she might frighten bad guys.

"What do you think?" she asked.

"If she's telling the truth and she didn't know the Dancer was giving her the companies, that means she's not very likely to have got Wearing to off him."

"You think so?"

He was still thinking about his answer when she suddenly shook her head. "Taking the Dancer's place is not the reason she did it. It is just a pleasant by-product, that's all – like getting plastic when you crack oil to make petrol. She had him killed because she'd decided he was a weak old man who needed to be got out of the way."

Morton sat for a moment, looking at his hands on the steering wheel. "That would make her one cold, calculating bitch," he eventually said.

Darling laughed. "Didn't you know? Supercomputers are kept chilled by liquid nitrogen."

He turned towards her, tilting his head questioningly. *What the fuck was she talking about now?*

"That's because they do their best calculating when they are frigidly cold, like our Russian ice princess."

Oh! It was a joke. He laughed, more because he thought he was supposed to than because he found what she said funny. "What do we do now?" he asked.

"I'm surprised you need to ask that question. We think we know what happened, even if we don't know why…" She allowed her voice to trail away into silence, a silence he eventually could not bear to allow to continue.

"So we find out why," he volunteered.

"No, Sergeant. Finding out 'why' would be useful, but not essential. We must find proof of what happened, evidence that Wearing shot the Dancer that we can take into court and use to convince a jury that he did it. Remember, he's a copper."

"Ex-copper!"

"There's a lot of them around," Darling said. "And juries still tend to place trust in what coppers say, even ex-coppers, although God alone knows why. We need proof.

Now my impression of Mrs Dance is that she's not just clever, she's competent. I doubt she'll be giving herself away to us any time soon."

"That could be because she doesn't think she's done anything wrong," Morton said. "She's a sociopath." He'd encountered enough sociopaths in his time as a policeman, cleared up the messes they made.

"Wearing, on the other hand, struck me as the sort of man who is neither as clever nor as competent as he believes himself to be," Darling continued. "He confuses having been lucky with having been good. He will give us our proof. Which is why you are going to follow him everywhere he goes."

Morton said nothing but kept on driving. He thought Wearing was just as much a sociopath as the woman. Both needed to be exposed.

Chapter Forty-One

The house Ekaterina chose for her liaison was another owned by a friend whose marriage had disintegrated. Some people might have questioned themselves if as many of their circle couldn't stay married. Not Ekaterina. She could no more conceive of staying married than she could conceive the grandchild she had so far failed to give her mother, who never missed an opportunity to remind her of that sad fact. Her marriage had not lasted long enough to fail. Maybe it was just that the whole idea of marriage now offended her, or that since Barry died, she had not met a man, or woman, she could contemplate the prospect of waking up next to for the following week, never mind her whole life. Ekaterina was a decidedly single lady and could not be bothered to try to understand the dynamics of her friends' failed relationships. As long as they didn't cry on her shoulder, or expect her to mop up their tears, she just ignored their alarms as much as she could and got on with her own life.

Glenda had taken her kids to live with her recently retired and emigrated parents on Australia's Gold Coast while things got sorted out with Derek. From what Ekaterina had heard, the kids were having a whale of a time out there, and Glenda was getting hot and bothered about their dentist, who owned a chain of surgeries and was already richer than Derek could ever hope of being. Which she took to mean Glenda would not be coming back to her house any time soon.

She had spent the afternoon in town taking care of business and so allowed him to pick her up from outside the library. So far as she could tell, nobody noticed her waiting at the top of the steps up to Lisle Street, until she saw his car come along Market Street and turn right up John Dobson Street and out of sight. Sauntering, she made her way down the steps and around the library, and got into the passenger seat of his car, taking a Berkeley menthol cigarette out of her bag and lighting up.

"I didn't know you smoked," he said.

She inhaled deeply, held the breath and then exhaled. "The better you get to know me the more you will realise you actually know nothing about me."

"If you say so." He shook his head and pulled away from the kerb, only to have to stop at a red light a few metres on. "Fuck it!" He reached over and plucked the cigarette from her mouth, dropping it into a mostly empty plastic coffee cup in the holder on the central binnacle. "Nobody smokes in my car. It's unhealthy."

That is why I do it, she thought.

"Of course," she said and smiled, reaching over and stroking his cheek in a way that would have been a tender gesture in most women's hands, only she didn't do tender, nor did she care whether he knew that or not. Your body is a temple at which I must worship and not defile in any way, she thought, and settled back into the seat. If she had entertained any doubts about her plans for tonight, they all evaporated away, leaving her calm and strong.

During the journey, she glanced in the wing mirror occasionally, and after the third or fourth time she lay back in her chair, brow furrowed.

"That blue car behind us," she said. "It has been there since we left town."

He glanced into his rear-view mirror. "What blue car? That's a purple Peugeot 108." She bent forward and stared into the wing mirror. The car behind was, indeed, purple, and a lot smaller than the car she had imagined was following them.

"Forget it," she said, drawing a deep breath. "Just drive."

Once they were inside Glenda's house, she did a great deal of worshipping his body, the body he used to worship hers. They played a dominance game they had started a few bouts previously at his request, where she would have her eyes blindfolded and her hands tied to the bedposts, leaving him free to make her scream in any way he chose. At first she had been suspicious of being restrained, unsure whether she could trust him, but when she discovered the scalding heat he could make flow through her when she was tied up, she quickly forgot her suspicions. Today, it was probably a good thing the house was detached and some way removed from its neighbours, because he made her scream and writhe and thrash to such an extent she was genuinely afraid her heart might give up and she would die then and there. All her life, she had been as much of a control freak in bed as she was elsewhere, scarcely able to permit herself to orgasm because she feared that loss of control. Tonight, however, she came as never before and the tristesse that followed in the wake of that release was caused by her regret of not having let go before now.

Eventually, though, even that tide of passion ebbed and she became herself again. "Release me," she said, and he did. She found him lying beside her on the bed, regarding her with what she could only describe as a proprietary grin. His body was as slicked with drying sweat as hers, his pubic hair was dark and tangled with semen and her juices.

"Bloody hell, they never taught me anything like that in school." He laughed. "You are a fucking animal, you know. An animal."

She sprang up to lie on top of him, feeling his cock enlarge and move on the bruised lips of her vagina. She moved her hips to ensure his attention was exactly where she wanted it to be. Then she took hold of the scarves that had bound her and used them to tie his wrists to the bedposts.

"What're you doing?"

"Sauce for the goose," she said, stirring her hips and feeling him all but erupt into her. She bit her lip to keep from voicing an animal reaction, almost changing her mind as the pleasure shot through her like lightning. "Is sauce for the gander," she eventually added, tying a third scarf over his eyes and around his head, before sitting backwards and gasping with disappointment as his cock came out of her. For a moment she stared at it, reaching towards it, asking herself whether she really did want to do without that. Then she stepped off the bed.

"Where are you going?" he cried.

"You'll see," she said, reaching out and giving him such a hard squeeze he all but jumped off the bed. "I have some new games in mind for us."

"That'll be good," he grinned. "I wouldn't want to think of you getting bored."

While she thought of several replies, she said nothing, just took some toys out of her bag. Using two plum-coloured cords that looked as though they could be used as tiebacks for very large, heavy curtains, she tied his ankles to the bottom of the bed. At first, he shrugged, but she flicked out her hand and clipped his cock in a way that was at once playful and remonstrative. "Behave yourself or you won't get to play," she said as coldly as she could, and he obediently relaxed so she could finish the job. While she had never been in the scouts, she was pleased with the knots. He was not going to extricate himself from them.

Standing up, she moved towards his head, tracing her fingernails over his flesh, watching him writhe and hold his breath as she did so. His cock seemed to grow even bigger. Taking a device of straps and a ball she had bought in a London sex shop specialising in S&M and bondage, she quickly lifted his head, stuffed the ball into his mouth and fastened the Velcro straps behind his head, then stood back. Looking at her handiwork, she was satisfied, then turned away and dressed herself before looking at him again. From the noises escaping around the ball, she guessed he was demanding to know what was going on and what the fuck she was playing at, accompanied by some less-than-polite demands to release him. She said nothing. She did think of sucking him off one last time but shook her head even though the thought was pleasurable, turned off the light and closed the door behind her as she left.

Taking his car keys from the jacket he had draped over the banister, she left the house, making sure it was all locked up and the alarms activated. She had no idea when anyone might find him and cared even less. It would be too late for him whenever it was.

As she drove to the airport, she considered how calm and efficient she had been. After all, she had never actually killed anyone before. Perhaps it was a talent she had inherited from her father. He had never denied in the family that he had personally killed at least one man, when he was a lot younger than she was now.

At the airport, she parked in the long-stay area, paying with five twenty-pound notes that bought a week of trouble-free parking, which she would have considered cheap at twice the price. Then, she made her way to the arrivals lounge and waited for the last flight to arrive from London, the one she had previously bought a ticket for and would have the printed receipts to prove it, should anyone ask. When it arrived, she joined the arriving passengers, a business woman returning after a busy day in the capital wearing an ever-so-slightly crumpled business suit and carrying a heavy-looking attaché case.

The taxi driver glanced at her in the rear-view mirror as she gave him her address and probably decided she did not want to hear his line in small talk. She wasn't interested in the Toon anyway, although she was a dead ringer for that stupid twat Barry Dance's missus. Even so, she tipped him lavishly when he dropped her outside the house.

Above her head, in a sky so dark it was almost black, a silver moon glared down, two days from full, and high, wispy clouds were driven across it on winds she did not feel on the ground. She felt so invigorated she almost began to sing and dance, but she controlled herself and went into her house, yawning. It had, after all, been a long and demanding day.

Chapter Forty-Two

Paul Reid parked his Peugeot 108 under branches that escaped over a brick garden wall and hung over almost half the road. He had watched the Russian woman drive away alone in Wearing's car but had resisted the temptation to go to the house and see why Wearing had not left with her. He knew he did not live there because there was no way a low-life loser like Wearing could afford a house out here. This was a place for not-so-young-anymore executives and their families. The only reason it wasn't a gated community was because the people who lived there weren't yet quite rich enough to believe they needed to live in one. Wearing must be doing something in there, although Reid could not imagine what that might be.

The tapping on his window startled him, and he was even more startled to see Sergeant Morton standing there, smiling at him with that 'boy, are you in trouble' smile of his. He wound the window down.

"Good evening, Pete, my old friend. What can I do for you?"

Reid's agreeableness did nothing to soften the detective sergeant's glare.

"I was just wondering what you're doing here," he said.

'Your job,' Reid almost said, reflexively, but managed to keep the words in. Having been on the job might buy him a moment's goodwill from the sergeant, but those words would have burned it to the finest of ash in an instant. His being a private detective had never earned him any brownie points from those who still wore the uniform. Reid quickly outlined why he was watching Wearing after their encounter at the card table.

"You follow everyone who threatens you?" Morton asked.

"Only people I think are murderers," Reid answered, quickly and brightly, without believing he convinced the policeman. Coppers didn't like civilians getting in their way, disliking them even more than they disliked the con men and felons, thieves and murderers who were their normal stock in trade.

"And you haven't seen our Mr Wearing emerge from the house he entered in the company of Mrs Ekaterina Dance, whom we have both just seen drive away unaccompanied?"

"He could have been in the boot."

Morton snorted. "Wearing is bigger than me. I don't think the ice princess would be able to get him into the boot without him or someone else helping. Even if she had the help, we would have seen her, don't you think?"

Reid said nothing, there being nothing he could say to contradict this very obviously true statement. Instead he wondered how he could have been so preoccupied he had not noticed Morton's arrival, or his presence if he had been there before him. But that was impossible. He had followed the car here. Morton could not have been there before them, unless he had known they were going there, and how could he have known that? It did not seem at all likely that Mrs Dance or Wearing would have advertised this clandestine liaison. Which meant Morton had followed him, driving his car from the Forth Banks pool, and he had not noticed him. He shivered and then tried to open his door.

"We'd better go and find out what he is doing," said Reid.

Morton did not move, preventing him from opening the car door wide enough to allow him to get out. "There is no 'we' in this, Paul, my old mate. I'm a copper. You're a civilian. I have the right to do more or less what I like, go more or less where I please to detect or prevent a criminal offence. You have the right to remain silent, and not much else. Now I am going to go into that house and apprehend a man I believe to be a very dangerous criminal. You, on the other hand, are going to stay exactly where you are. If you enter that house I will arrest you as well. Do I make myself clear?"

"Crystal. Only, shouldn't you be following *her*, make sure she doesn't, oh, I don't know, flee the country?"

Morton shook his head. "My orders are to follow Wearing, not Mrs Dance. We think he is the murderer. We'll worry about Mrs Dance later."

Reid slumped back in his seat, saying nothing, wondering whether Morton had called Darling to get backup, whether she had told him to wait where he was until that backup arrived. If Wearing was what they both believed him to be, Morton's going in there alone was about as sensible as Clarice Starling going into the Tooth Fairy's house alone in *Silence of the Lambs*. Not that Morton would listen to him if he said anything like that. So he watched Morton walk briskly to the house, stand in front of the door, busy with what Reid assumed was the standard-issue copper's lock picks and then step inside.

* * *

Morton's first impression on entering the house was that everything looked as though it should still be wrapped in its delivery cellophane. Did anyone live there? Everything was so perfectly in its place – the umbrella stand with its two multi-coloured golf umbrellas and one tightly furled black gents' one, the blonde-wood cabinet with the telephone base unit that could drive phones in every other room in the house, the silver dish containing half a dozen wrapped mints, the rural prints on the walls. He half-expected to see a photographer from *Ideal Home* following him inside. He almost called out just to see if his voice would echo, but managed to prevent himself, remembering that Wearing was almost certainly a murderer; a murderer who had killed a man like the Dancer. He probably wouldn't hesitate to off a mere detective sergeant.

Moving as stealthily as he could, he looked through the downstairs rooms, the kitchen, the dining room, the lounge, the music room and the study. All of them were empty of life, everything in its place, untouched by a human hand in who knew how long, covered with an even patina of dust that had to be at least two months old. You would have thought anyone who could afford a house like this would be able to run to a cleaner.

Morton tiptoed up the stairs as though he was a youth creeping in two hours after the deadline set by stern parents after a breathless exchange of bodily fluids with a surprisingly willing girlfriend. Even this did not prevent a riser squealing loud enough to rouse the dead in the churchyard a mile away. Morton froze, staring around in near panic, listening for a response.

He heard a muffled moaning from upstairs, a thumping like someone jumping up and down on a bed. They were not the sounds of someone lying in wait to do him harm, and they went right through his professional caution to that atavistic need to help someone in trouble, which was the reason he had become a policeman in the first place. He took the remaining stairs two at a time. The first door he opened was the bathroom, the second revealed a single child's room that was bigger than the room he had shared with his wife most of his married life. He opened the third door and stopped in the doorway, holding the doorknob with one hand and the door jamb with the other. His jaw dropped open at the sight of Wearing, spread-eagled, naked on the bed, wrists and ankles tied securely to the bed frame, with something out of a torture dungeon about his mouth. Morton began to laugh.

"Well, this is a sight you don't expect to see on a working day," he said. He reached over and undid the scarf around Wearing's head.

The man's eyes flared and he repeatedly smacked his head against the bed in his rage and frustration.

"Looks like you're pleased to see me" – Morton moved to stand at the bottom of the bed – "but maybe not that pleased."

Wearing's semi-tumescent cock shrank under his gaze, as embarrassment and hatred added themselves to his expression.

Morton took out his mobile phone and took half a dozen photos of the outstretched figure. "You certainly do keep yourself buff, I have to give you that. The ladies like that, I suppose." Morton briefly wondered whether he should join a gym himself. He held up his phone. "How much will you give me not to put these on Instagram?" Then he laughed, and put the phone away. "Not that I do social media, you understand."

Putting his hands on his hips, Morton looked at Wearing critically. "She left you here. You know that, don't you? She's gone. I watched her leave. I don't imagine she's coming back any time soon, if ever. What do you think that means for you? How long do you think it would take you to die of dehydration, do you think? I'd think an ex-SAS man like yourself would know that. That is what you say you are, isn't it, ex-SAS? Bit cruel, if you ask me, just leaving you here to die very, very slowly, inch by inch, in agony, knowing what is happening to you and that there is sod all you can do about it. Now I think about it, that must be the very worst of it for an action man like you, that you've been reduced to impotence by a woman. By a woman. That must bite your bum so bad." He shook his head, laughing.

"Oh, the lads at the station will appreciate these photos," Morton continued, "some of the lasses, too. What does that song say, inviting public critique? Now I might not be able to prove it, yet, but I know you murdered the Dancer. Yeah, that's right. We know it was you. It seems to me that you've got a choice. You can confess to it and I'll release you. Or you can keep shtum and I'll just leave you where you are for a day or two, let you think it over, let you shit yourself, let you begin to eat yourself away from the inside. Nobody else knows you're here. I could walk out and tell the boss that I lost you. Only other person who knows you're here is Mrs Dance, and she isn't coming back, is she. What do you say?"

The two men stared at each other until Wearing nodded, briefly.

Morton laughed. "I knew you'd see sense."

Pulling on a pair of purple rubber gloves he took from his jacket pocket, Morton bent over and released Wearing's feet, hearing the man sigh with relief as he did so. Next, he undid the gag, standing up and examining it. He had seen these while working Vice in the Met buy never actually seen one in use. Tossing it aside, he undid Wearing's right hand and then his left. "She knows how to tie a knot, doesn't she?" he said as he stood up, aware of Wearing relaxing on the bed. "You can get dressed in your own time. I'll just call this into the station."

The next thing Morton knew was that he had an arm across his throat, as implacable as an iron bar, choking and choking, no matter how he tugged on it.

"Dumb fucking copper," Wearing hissed in his ear. "If nobody knows you're here what's to stop me killing you and getting away with it like I got away with the Dancer?"

"That's a confession," Morton wheezed, or thought he did. He couldn't be sure any words got past the constriction in his throat, where Wearing's arm felt as though it would be pressing against his spine very soon. His vision had gone from red around the edges to being almost totally black. He could feel his blood pounding more and more slowly in his head as lassitude took away even the pain. Was this what death felt like?

There was a dull, cracking noise close behind Morton's head, and he was released, falling forward, gasping aloud as pain surged back through him at the same time as he gulped in lungsful of air. Pain meant he was alive, so he welcomed it even as he fought it. Fighting was good. To feel pain was to be a living human being.

He turned over onto his back as his vision cleared, and saw Wearing slumped, unconscious on the bed with a dribble of bright red blood coming out of his right ear. Reid stood over him, grimacing, his right hand tucked into the warmth of his left armpit.

"Good job for you I don't take notice of stupid orders," Reid said, then lifted his right hand in front of his face and waggled his fingers, wincing and almost crying aloud in pain. "I think I broke my hand. Oh shit, it hurts."

Morton levered himself to his knees, then to his hands and knees and finally to his feet. "What did you do?"

Putting his hand back into his armpit, Reid glanced at Wearing, then bent over him to study his face close-up. "Still breathing. Thought for a moment there, I might have killed him." Stepping away, he turned to Morton. "I followed you inside, and found him choking you. So, I punched him in the side of the head."

"No wonder you broke something if you hit him in the head with your bare hand!" Didn't everyone know that skull bones were more resistant than finger bones? thought Morton. Finger bones were delicate.

Reid bent down and picked something off the bed, handing it to Morton, who almost dropped it, surprised by how heavy it was. It was a roll of what he guessed were coins, wrapped in grey woven duct tape and then wound with clear adhesive tape. From the weight of it, Morton guessed the coins were pounds and the roll fitted nicely inside his clenched right fist – he remembered being shown something like it by a grizzled old uniformed sergeant back in his first days as a young copper, being told that sometimes a policeman had need of a weapon that couldn't get you into trouble if a superior found it in your possession and wasn't your truncheon.

"What was his name, the guy who showed us this, Anderson?" he asked.

"Alderson, Sergeant Alderson," replied Reid.

"Nasty piece of work he was," Morton said, unable to keep the nostalgic admiration out of his voice. "It was probably this that hurt you." He dropped the roll back onto the bed, where it came to rest against Wearing's unresisting flesh. "I'm going to call this in, then I'll tell you everything that happened." He began to walk towards the door, just managing to catch hold of the bed frame and stay upright when his right knee suddenly gave way beneath him. He took out the Dictaphone from his breast pocket. "He gave me a confession, you know."

Reid nodded. Of course he had.

Chapter Forty-Three

Wearing sat on one side of a scarred table in a dimly lit interview room in Forth Banks Station, with Darling and Morton on the other side. He wore a grey sweatsuit that was a couple of sizes too big because his clothes had been removed for forensic examination. He slumped in the chair looking as though he wanted to kill someone, or die, he didn't much care which. His eyes were bloodshot, his face devoid of colour, his lips cracked. They'd offered him a drink but he'd declined and now was clearly regretting it.

"Mr Wearing, you are aware that you can have legal representation present, aren't you?"

He glanced at Darling, then looked away, staring up at the camera in the corner between the walls and the ceiling. A red light showed on it. "Used to be a copper, didn't I? Course I know. Still don't want one."

"Just have to make sure," she said.

Like most police officers, Darling didn't have much time for defence lawyers, although she understood the necessity for them. She also believed that a man who refused counsel and defended himself had a fool for a client, even if he was as self-possessed and competent as Wearing evidently believed he was. She reached over the table and depressed the 'record' buttons on the tape recorders. She spoke the date and time, then introduced herself and Morton, then Wearing, reminding him to say his answers aloud for the recording.

His expression said, 'Do you take me for an imbecile?'

"We'll start with today's escapade, shall we? What were you doing in a house belonging to someone you don't know?" asked Darling.

Wearing shrugged. "I was taken there by a friend to have some rough sex."

Morton coughed into his fist. Given the photographic evidence that was still on his phone, there was not much mileage in denying what he knew so clearly to be true.

"What is your friend's name?"

"You don't need to know."

It was Darling's turn to laugh. "Let me be the judge of what I do or don't need to know. Who were you with?"

"She's a married woman. I don't want to embarrass her."

"That's very chivalrous of you, Mr Wearing. From what my sergeant tells me, she wasn't overly concerned about embarrassing you."

He glanced at Morton, seeming to make a mental note of something else in the minus column of the sergeant's ledger with him.

"Her name?"

"Not going to tell you."

"She left you tied up to die slowly, horribly, and you want to protect her?" Morton said.

"What can I say? I'm a gentleman."

Darling shook her head and opened one of the files she had brought into the room with her. She produced four prints of images Morton had taken at the house. The quality wasn't good, Northumbria Police didn't have the budget for decent photographic printers, but the images were still decipherable. The first was of a dark-grey Ford Focus stopped on the driveway with two people inside. The registration plate was clear, 'CX164JUD', which a quick check with the DVLA before the interview had confirmed it as registered to Wearing. The second showed the car again with driver and passenger outside. The driver was clearly Wearing. Darling tapped the image.

"You will agree that is you," she said.

"Can't deny it, can I?"

"What about her?" She tapped the photo of Ekaterina. He shook his head. "For the record, I have just shown Mr Wearing a photograph of Mrs Ekaterina Dance standing with him beside a car that is registered in his name. Mr Wearing has continued to refuse to identify that person." She looked at him, inviting a comment on what she had said.

His reply was a thin-lipped smile entirely devoid of mirth.

She showed him the third image, which was of him following Ekaterina into the house. A raised eyebrow got no response from him, and neither did the fourth image, which was of the Focus driving away from the house with just one occupant, Ekaterina, behind the wheel.

Wearing shrugged. "I can play this game all night long. It's the SAS training, you know."

For a moment, she wondered what Milburn would make of her trying some 'extreme interrogation techniques' on Wearing but allowed that thought to fade. If the man really did have SAS training it probably wouldn't do any good, and anything he did say wouldn't be admissible anyway. She wondered why the man was annoying her enough to even make her think of anything so stupid. She took a deep breath, and changed tack.

"Then let us talk about your attempted murder of Sergeant Morton here."

Wearing shook his head. "I didn't try to murder him."

"That's not how it felt to me," Morton said, leaning over the table towards Wearing as though about to take things into his own hands.

Darling rapped the table with her knuckles, not letting on how it hurt. "Sergeant!" she said. "If you can't control yourself I'll have you replaced."

A momentary glance was enough to convince Morton she was serious. He leaned back in his chair.

"You say you didn't try to kill him. That's not what our witness says. Our witness says he found you with your arm barred across Sergeant Morton's throat with him losing consciousness."

Wearing leaned forward. "I don't try to kill people. Like Yoda says, do or do not, there is no try."

"So you say. In this case, you were disturbed before you could succeed. That's why you've got that bandage around your head and a throbbing headache."

Wearing automatically reached up and touched the bandage at his right temple and couldn't prevent himself from wincing. Even with the painkillers he'd been given, that was going to hurt for quite some time.

Darling continued. "The question is not whether you kill people but why. Why, for instance, did you kill Barry Dance?"

He shrugged again. "Who says I did?"

"You do, sunshine," said Morton, smiling. "You confessed to me."

"Prove it!"

Morton produced the Dictaphone from an evidence wallet, placed it on the desk and pressed the 'Play' button. The recording was thin and tinny, but distinct. "Dumb fucking copper. If nobody knows you're here what's to stop me killing you and getting away with it like I got away with the Dancer?"

Wearing snarled and lashed out with his hand, knocking the machine off the table and onto the floor, where it bounced a couple of times and then slid across the lino, coming to a stop against the wall.

Morton laughed, got out of his chair and picked it up before placing it back on the table, where he pressed 'Play' again, and they all heard his words again. "Modern technology," he said. "Takes more than falling a couple of feet onto the floor to damage this."

"Added to which, it is part of the recording of this interview." Darling gestured towards the recorders. "So, what's it going to be? We have your confession to killing the Dancer. We have witnesses to your attempting to kill

Sergeant Morton. We have photographic evidence of you arriving at the house in your car with Mrs Dance. Now, we could go on playing this tedious game until we're all sick and tired of it, or you could just accept the inevitable – that we have your arse for two crimes that are going to have you working on your prison tan for a long, long time – and fill us in on the details we don't know yet. You have nothing to lose by cooperating with us, nothing at all."

Wearing sat back in his chair, arms folded across his chest, gaze fixed on a spot on the wall behind Darling about eighteen inches above her head.

"Get us some coffee, Sergeant. I think we're in for a long night," said Darling.

Morton glanced at Wearing, raising an eyebrow.

"Fuck no," said Wearing. "I remember the muck they serve in these places."

"Suit yourself," she said.

Darling switched off the recorders as Morton walked out of the room, leaving the door open so that nobody could ever claim she was alone in the room with Wearing to contaminate any evidence, or for him to attack her. In a way, she half-hoped he would try it on. She was confident she could handle anything he could bring to the physical table of conflict, and she would not mind hurting him – just a bit – for what he had done to Morton. But she was annoyed with her colleague for putting himself in a position where he could be attacked. From what she had seen of his photo gallery there was absolutely no need for him to have released Wearing before calling for backup. The man was not in any danger, and Morton should have realised he was a dangerous man. As it was, they both sat there, occasionally glancing at each other and plotting their next moves.

Morton returned bearing a tray with two tall, steaming mugs and a plate of muffins. Wearing's eyes widened. He said nothing but it was clear he thought the police station canteens had moved on since his time.

"Americano for you, Inspector?" Morton placed a delicately pale pink mug in front of Darling and a slightly more boyish blue mug in front of his chair. "And a caffè latte for me." He smiled at Wearing; he didn't drink coffee very often but when he did he liked to feel he was endangering the enamel of his teeth. "Help yourself to a muffin," he invited. "There's blueberry, triple chocolate and cranberry."

Wearing shook his head again, his eyes filled with disgust as they drank their coffee and demolished their baked goods. "You can only hold me for twenty-four hours," he said, eventually. "You might want to get on with the interrogation."

"Actually, it is thirty-six hours for an indictable offence like murder. I'd have thought that an ex-copper would know that. As for interrogation? Is that what you call this?" Darling said, licking chocolate crumbs off her fingers. "Oh, well, if you really want to be interrogated." She turned to Morton. "Sergeant, you'd better go–"

"And fetch the comfy chair!" he finished for her.

They both laughed until they allowed themselves to be aware of Wearing's stony face.

"Oh, come on." Darling giggled. "You must know it. It's Monty Python!"

When Wearing did not reply, she nodded to Morton, who picked up the tray and put it on the floor behind them, where Wearing would be able to see the two remaining pastries if he looked. Darling pressed the 'Record' buttons and recommenced the interview, stating the time and the names of those present, asking Wearing again whether he still wished to forgo his entitlement to legal representation. After that, she asked him a series of simple questions about his whereabouts at the time of the Dancer's murder.

"I already answered those questions" – Wearing yawned – "and the old guy downstairs confirmed what I told you."

"How do you know that?" Darling wondered.

"Because I fucking well asked him, that's how I know."

"Yes, he did confirm that your television was playing very loudly during that time." She touched a printed sheet of paper in a plastic wallet. "He was good enough to give us a formal statement to that effect." She smiled at him, that tight-lipped, hard-eyed smile of someone who was about to show they knew something their antagonist believed they did not know. "He also told us that your car was not in your parking space at any time during those hours." She watched Wearing very closely as she said this and saw a momentary flicker at the corner of his right eye, a tightening of his lips.

Everyone but the most pathological sociopath had some sort of tell that spoke to their lying, some physical or verbal tic. Investigative textbooks were full of them – crossing or uncrossing legs, touching a finger to the corner of an eye or to the lips, leaning forward or leaning back. She'd read most of the lists and knew they were by no means comprehensive or exhaustive. Were those two tiny gestures Wearing's tell?

"Where was your car?" she asked. "Parking isn't easy around your place."

He shrugged. "Honestly?"

That one word told her what he was about to say was a lie. Words like 'honestly' were a dead giveaway. Proficient liars never used them. They were as skilled at answering questions as Darling was at asking them. They knew what was on the lists. They practised. They rehearsed.

"Honestly, I don't recall where I'd left it. I'd gone out on the town Saturday night, had a skinful. I was probably still over the limit the next afternoon. I don't drive when I've had a drink. I got a taxi home."

Morton took a deep breath and was about to launch into questions when Darling shook her head briefly and waved her left hand while producing a photograph from the file. It was a still taken from a CCTV traffic camera.

Nobody could have described it as high definition but it was still a clear picture of a dark-grey Ford Focus. The front number plate was legible and the driver was clearly Wearing.

The man's brow furrowed as he looked.

"That's your car?" she asked.

He nodded.

"For the record," said Darling, "Mr Wearing agrees that the photograph I have shown him is of his car."

Wearing leaned forward to study the photograph, reaching out to trace the date and time that were printed semi-legibly in yellow dots at the top right-hand corner. Then he suddenly leaned back, seeming to sigh and shrink in on himself.

"The driver," Darling said. "He looks a lot like you."

"He doesn't look a lot like me," he muttered.

"Oh, why not?"

"Because it is me." Wearing threw up his hands. "Look, you're right. You've got my arse. Just give me a bit to think and I'll tell you everything."

He closed his eyes and began to breathe deeply and rhythmically. Then, just as suddenly, he opened his eyes and began to talk as rapidly as a machine gun. He told them in graphic detail how he had laid in wait at the farmhouse for the Dancer, waiting long enough to decide that killing him with his own shotgun was a better idea than using the Glock 17 pistol he had liberated when leaving the army. "Just seemed appropriate. Of course, I didn't have a key to his gun cabinet, but I found a paper clip and picked the lock in no time at all. Lovely piece of work, it was, twenty-gauge, over-and-under. Must have cost him a fortune."

"How did you get into the house?"

"She gave me a key, didn't she? A key and the code for the alarm."

"*She?* Ekaterina Dance?"

Wearing snorted. "Who else do you think it was? Of course it was her."

"And you'd arranged this execution some time before you actually killed him?"

He nodded. "Weeks. I'd been there a couple of times to recce the place, you know. That's what the SAS taught me, thorough preparation."

"Why did you do it?" Darling asked eventually.

"Because she asked me to. She asked me, and I fancied a bit of meaningless violence, if you see what I mean."

They didn't, but chose to say nothing about it.

"Why did she want you to kill him?"

He shook his head. "You'll have to ask her that yourself. Most women are hard enough to comprehend, but that frigid Russian cunt is impossible."

"What did she promise you, for killing him?" Morton asked.

Wearing regarded him steadily, then laughed. "That's just it. She didn't promise me anything. Not a penny. She didn't have to. I did it for kicks." He looked first at Darling, then at Morton, then back to Darling before beginning to sing a tuneless version of Johnny Cash. "I shot a man in Reno, just to watch him die." He laughed again.

Darling held up her hand. "I just want to be sure I've got this right. Ekaterina Dance asked you to murder her father-in-law some weeks before you actually did. Is that the truth?"

He nodded.

"Why should she ask you?"

Wearing grinned. "The lady and I had a… how should I put it? Business relationship. It began sometime after her husband planted his Bentley into that lamp post."

"How did you meet?"

"We were introduced by a mutual acquaintance."

"By the name of Bainbridge, perhaps?"

Wearing shook his head. "That would be indelicate. But no, actually. I was recommended by a friend of the lady."

Morton leaned forward. "So, let's see if we've got this right. You're fucking Mrs Dance. She asks you to kill the Dancer. You do it. And a few days later she gags you, and ties you to a bed where nobody is going to find you before you die a horrible death. Am I right?"

Wearing nodded. "You always did have a gift for getting right to the meat of a situation, didn't you?"

"Why did she try to kill you?"

He shrugged. "Dunno."

"It seems like an extreme reaction to me," Darling said.

"Like I say, she's a crazy bitch." Wearing looked directly into Darling's eyes when he used the word.

She did not react at all.

He shrugged. "I'm well shot of her." He closed his eyes again, sat back in his chair with his hands clasped behind his head and wearing the expression of a cat about to dive head first into a barrel of cream.

Chapter Forty-Four

While Wearing was being questioned, charged and taken to the cells to await his court appearance in the morning, Detective Constables Cope and Matthews drove to Ekaterina's house to arrest her for conspiracy to murder and attempted murder, of Barry Dance Senior and Mark Wearing respectively, having called her office to be told she had not gone in to work that day and that nobody had any idea where she was. They turned onto her drive to discover it empty, with the curtains drawn shut at every window and the garage door locked. Cope peered inside the garage.

"It's empty."

"They did tell her not to leave town without informing us, didn't they?" Matthews said.

Cope nodded. "Standard operational procedure. Mind you, I don't think Mrs Dance sets much store by keeping her word to anyone, much less to us."

Matthews strode to the front door, rang the doorbell, hammered on the door with his fist, then rang the doorbell again. There was no sound from inside, although the door was made of such solid dark polished wood that it was entirely possible they just couldn't hear what was going on.

"There really is nobody in there," Matthews muttered, knocking on the door again. He gave it one more try, then turned away.

"She's planned this, hasn't she, to the last detail."

"That is a bit of a presumption," Cope observed. "For all we know, she might just have gone off for a spa and some retail therapy with her girlfriends."

Matthews stepped back so he could see the entire front elevation of the house, which could be worth seven figures. "Did she strike you as the sort of woman who goes off for a girly weekend?"

Cope shook his head. "How would I know? I never met her."

They both turned around as a dark-blue Mondeo pulled up on the drive beside their Focus. Morton got out from behind the wheel, Darling emerging from the passenger side.

"Let me guess," she said. "Nobody home."

The constables nodded. Morton looked away. The drive out there had been mostly silent after she ripped him a new one for not having followed Mrs Dance, not calling for backup to deal with Wearing, and whatever had happened in the house.

"Let's assume she knows we are on to her. That's the only reason to kill Wearing, isn't it? He told her we'd spoken to him and she put two and two together," said Darling.

To Morton, that sounded very much like Darling putting two and two together to make five, or six, anything but four. He said nothing, however. This sort of out-loud brainstorming was a technique she'd picked up from Joe Milburn and it had worked damned well for him over the years.

"Where would she go?"

Morton looked at his boss as though wondering why she should ask him. While she kept on looking at him, he suggested, "Home?"

"This is her home!"

"This is her house, right enough, but I meant 'home' as in where she comes from. Moscow."

Darling stiffened, as though she had just completed an electric circuit with her hands. "Of course, where else would she go? Even if we did charge her, Daddy could make her just disappear for ever and he's got the contacts to divert any official claims on her." She strode towards the car, then turned back towards Morton. "You're staying here. Get a locksmith to get you into that house without having to break any windows. When you're in, go through it with a fine-tooth comb. I'll get some help sent over."

Cope looked at Matthews wearing an expression that suggested he was wondering whether they were experienced detectives or woodentops.

"You two, I want you to go to her business premises – all of them – and check whether she has been into work today."

"We could do that on the phone," Cope complained.

"You could, but you wouldn't see anything, would you?"

"Yes, boss, of course," said Matthews, catching hold of Cope's arm and dragging him towards their car. If his colleague could not see the thunder in Darling's eyes, he could.

Morton fished in his pocket for his telephone. "You got it, boss. Any chance of some overtime for this?" That last sentence was spoken very much *sotto voce*, not intending her to hear him. She stopped very suddenly and turned around.

"You've got a point there, Sergeant. No guarantees, but I'll speak to Mr Milburn."

Who will speak to Mr Pattison who will speak to the chief constable who will be very sorry, Morton thought, as he nodded his gratitude towards the boss. *Yes, Massa. No, Massa. Three bags full, Massa.* He looked at his phone and called up the locksmith the constabulary used when discretion was required to gain entry, rather than a smash 'em down taking the front door off its hinges for the benefit of the media when they were raiding some druggie's crib.

* * *

Using her Bluetooth as she drove back to the station, Darling told Milburn's secretary that she wanted the boarding manifests of every commercial flight leaving Britain for Moscow in the next twenty-four hours. "If the name Ekaterina Dance or Ekaterina Simeonova is on any of those lists, have our friends arrest her and take her off the flight. Tell them she is dangerous, well-connected, and is a person of interest in two murder cases."

"Two?"

"Just tell them, Mary. I'll explain everything when I get there."

She cut the connection, confident that Mary would do as she asked, or would know someone who could. Mary Pye knew just about everyone in the country who might be able to help with an investigation, and more than a few outside the country. To the best of Darling's knowledge, Mary Pye did not keep all those details on Rolodex or in a computer file anywhere; everything was in her head. Darling made a mental note to have Mrs Pye write down everything on that list before she retired on her next birthday.

Try as she might, Darling just could not get back into town nearly as quickly as she wanted to. There were three major roadworks in the northern, eastern and western approaches to the city that were causing gridlock almost everywhere. Once the day-to-day accidents, bad parking and idiotic driving were added to the mix, she would probably have been quicker walking when she got to the Western Bypass.

"Any news?" she asked as she hurried into the office.

Mrs Pye waved a sheaf of yellow telephone notes at her and said, "She is booked onto a flight from Heathrow to Moscow Sheremetyevo due to depart at 17.45. There is a Detective Inspector Pickering of the Met who is prepared to haul her off if you can give her a good reason to create a diplomatic incident."

Darling wanted to say she wasn't surprised Ekaterina had connections with the government is Moscow, and that yes, she thought apprehending a murderer was a good reason for getting up diplomatic nostrils. Instead, she took the notes and went into her office where she dialled the mobile number of DI Pickering.

"Pickering here." The woman's voice was faint and distorted.

"Inspector, this is DI Darling in Newcastle. I want Ekaterina Dance pulled off that flight so I can charge her with conspiracy to murder and attempted murder. Do they seem like good enough reasons to you?"

The laugh that came down the line could have belonged to a mountain troll. "I'll have her apprehended before she checks in and held at the Heathrow nick until you come to collect her. I have to say, she's a good-looking woman."

"How do you know that?"

"You PA emailed a photo."

Darling had not asked Mrs Pye to do that. There would certainly be some extra Brownie points on her annual review. "I'm on my way."

With that she put down the phone and went to knock on Milburn's door. He told her to enter. He did not look up from the small mountains of paper on his desk.

"Mr Milburn, I need someone to accompany me to Heathrow and bring back Mrs Dance for charging."

He closed the open file and put it on the 'dealt with' pile. "I know just the man."

"Who?"

He got to his feet. "Me." He went to the coat stand in the corner of the room, behind the door, and took down the ankle-length Burberry coat he had taken to wearing since Mrs Milburn had given it to him as a Christmas present to replace the disreputable tweed overcoat he had worn for twenty years. "We'll take my car. It's much more comfortable for a six-hundred-plus-mile round trip than yours. I'll see you in the car park."

Darling had expected to take thirty minutes to clear her desk and tell Morton what she was doing and organise help for him at Ekaterina's house. She made it down to the car park in fifteen.

Milburn's car was a 5-Series BMW, sleek, black and looking like it was breaking the speed limit standing still.

"Put your things in the boot and get in," he ordered, and she did as she was told.

He had almost pulled out of the car park before she had closed the door and definitely before she put on her seat belt. It was only when she settled down and looked around that she noticed he was not wearing one.

"Don't even think about it," he said, not looking at her as he negotiated the Swan House roundabout to get down onto the Tyne Bridge.

So, she didn't. Neither of them said anything until the *Angel of the North* was in his rear-view mirror and he had settled down to doing a smooth, constant 80mph in the outside lane.

"Tell me about it," he said, eventually.

They had driven past Leeds and onto the M1 before he was satisfied she had told him everything he needed to know.

"So, the tough guy's tough guy cried like a baby. Why?"

She did not answer for a while, having thought about that question a lot. It was only when she was given Wearing's army record and discovered his SAS story was just that, a story, that she concluded he was all mouth and no trousers, all talk and no action. Yes, he'd read all the manuals and knew how to plan a 'mission' but killing the Dancer must have been as much of a shock to him as it was to everyone else. He'd confessed because that was his way of waving his arms in the air and telling people, 'look at me, I did that!'

"Very psychological," Milburn observed, "and probably true. You don't mention your bit of luck, though."

"Luck?"

"That he boasted to Paul Reid. Reid and you were an item, weren't you?"

Did the boss ever forget anything?

"For about five minutes, and that was a long, long time ago, before I introduced him to Marianne Marshall."

Milburn drove on in silence.

"You've done good work, Detective Inspector. Good work. You and that sergeant of yours."

"Morton isn't mine!"

Milburn laughed, derisively. "If he wasn't, he certainly is now!"

Chapter Forty-Five

It was gone ten in the evening when Milburn drove into the car park at the police station at Heathrow Airport. Even so, the roar of activity almost knocked Darling backwards when she got out of the car. She'd always thought of Newcastle as being pretty much a twenty-four-hour city but had to admit that, compared to the energy of the busiest airport in the world, her home city was a sleepy backwater. Their warrant cards got them inside and taken up to a small office, where DI Pickering tried to crush both their hands with a handshake that could have belonged to The Hulk. Darling was pleased to see the woman looked exactly as she had imagined – as big as most men, solidly built with close-cropped dark-blonde hair, and wearing a grey three-piece suit with a silk tie and highly polished Oxford shoes. Darling wondered whether a man or woman put the diamond engagement ring and the wedding band on the third finger of her left hand. Pleasantries over and done with, Pickering had Ekaterina brought through.

If looks could kill, Darling would have fallen to the floor with two smoking holes in her forehead.

"This is outrageous," Ekaterina said. "You have no right to prevent me going home, no right to arrest me, to detain me in this" – she looked around the office, which was spartan with a distinctly temporary air about it than any of the thousands of other offices in the airport – "this hovel."

"I have every right to do all of that, and a lot more besides, Mrs Dance," said Darling.

Ekaterina glared at her as though she had just insulted her. She half-expected her to say, 'Don't use my slave name', but she said nothing.

"Take a seat, please." Darling gestured towards the seats on the other side of the chipped Formica-topped table, scarred and scorched by countless cigarettes.

After a defiant moment, Ekaterina did as she was told. Darling and Pickering sat on their side of the table. Darling switched on the recorders and introduced the three of them for the tape.

"Mrs Dance, this interview will be formally recorded. You are entitled to have a copy of that recording. I must tell you that you are entitled to legal representation in this interview. You can call your own representation or one will be provided for you. Do you understand?"

Ekaterina glared at her, but said nothing.

"Mrs Dance has declined to answer. You do not have to say anything, but it may harm your defence if you do not mention when questioned something which you later rely on in court. Anything you do say may be given in evidence. Do you understand what I have just said?"

Ekaterina's silence continued.

"Now I wish to discuss with you several offences. The first is the murder of Mr Barry Dance Senior, your father-in-law."

She looked across the table. Experience told her that using the word 'murder' in the direction of a suspect usually elicited some sort of reaction. Ekaterina did not flinch or change her expression, nor give any indication she had heard the word.

"The other is the attempted murder of Mr Mark John Wearing, which offence took place at number five, The Larches in Hazlerigg. This property is owned by Mrs Glenda Reardon. The sale is being handled by Wycliffe Properties. Wycliffe Properties is a wholly owned subsidiary of Dance Enterprises, of which you are the managing director. Do you have anything to tell me about either of these offences?"

Ekaterina gave no indication of having heard the question, and even less of any inclination to volunteer an answer.

"Mrs Dance has refused to answer the question."

Darling glanced at Pickering, who shrugged. Ekaterina wouldn't be the first person who had imagined saying nothing to questions would gain them everything they wanted, as though by not answering they could negate anything and everything the interviewer already knew and, in the case of a police officer, prove to a court's satisfaction. Milburn had taught her that, while an interview could produce useful, even vital, information, the best position to be in was to already know everything an interviewee could tell you and so not be disappointed if you didn't get what you wanted.

The interview proceeded strictly along the lines of Darling asking a question, Ekaterina remaining silent and Darling confirming her silence for the recording. Eventually, Darling sat back in her chair and closed the file. "I believe we have made all the progress we are going to make. Mrs Dance, I have to tell you that you are going to be charged with conspiracy to commit the murder of William Barry Dance Senior and with the attempted murder of Mark John Wearing. You will be returned to Newcastle where further investigations will take place. They may lead to further charges. Do you understand?"

"Of course I understand, you stupid woman," Ekaterina said, her voice sounding like a diamondback's rattle in the instant before it struck. "Do you think I am an idiot?"

Darling formally terminated the interview and switched off the recorders before turning back to Ekaterina. "No, Mrs Dance, I do not think you are an idiot. I think you are a very clever, very able woman who also happens to be a murderer and a sociopath. That last is only my opinion as an educated layperson, by the way, I'll have to leave the definitive opinion about that to my colleagues in that profession. That you are a murderer is my professional opinion as a police officer with more than fifteen years' experience, and on the evidence I have at my disposal I'm confident the charge will stand up in court. You might like to think about that in your cell."

Ekaterina's sneer only became more pronounced. "My opinion that you are stupid is confirmed by your imagining you will ever get me in court."

Darling could not keep herself from chuckling, and Pickering joined in.

"Now I know that Russian 'entrepreneurs' have been buying up places in London to the extent there are whole districts known as Moscow-on-Thames, but I remind you that this is England, not Russia." Darling paused for a moment, then continued, "There your father might have the ear of powerful people who can make things happen for you. Here, though, I am the one with friends in high places and you are a foreigner with no more rights than any other guest. Obey our rules and you are welcome. That's the British way, for better or worse. Break our rules – by having your boyfriend blow your father-in-law's face off, for instance – and you'll discover what we mean by 'the full force of the law' before we deport you back to Moscow, a woman twenty years older and wiser."

The staring contest continued as Pickering gestured to the uniformed constable outside the door, who entered and then carried out the instruction to take the prisoner to the cells. Both officers then breathed out.

"You know, when I saw the Dancer's body on the floor in his farmhouse, my first thought was that we were never going to find the murderer. There was a long list of possible suspects and her name wasn't on it. Yet here we are, little more than a week later, and we've got our man."

"And woman!" Pickering laughed. "Just goes to show, follow the evidence wherever it leads."

Darling could not help but agree with that, although she spent a lot more time making her farewells to Pickering than she really wanted. When she walked out of the airport police station she was trembling and felt as though she wanted to vomit. It was strength of will rather than strength of muscle keeping her upright. The adrenalin that had fuelled her during the investigation had drained out of her, making her fear that a strong gust of wind would bowl her over. God, she felt exhausted and was not looking forward to being driven back north. She was not entirely disappointed when she found Milburn had booked them both into an airport hotel for the night and arranged for Ekaterina to be taken up to Newcastle by secure transport.

Chapter Forty-Six

Having slept undisturbed – except by the alarm on her phone – in a way she had not in a long, long time, Darling returned to Newcastle just after midday. She spent the rest of the day tidying up and chasing paperwork. Milburn had 'volunteered' to give the good tidings to the chief constable and everyone higher up the food chain with an interest in the outcome of the investigation into the Dancer's death. Darling did not object. She had no desire at all in being thrown into that pool of politics and intrigue until there was absolutely no alternative. She had hoped that Morton might have found something that might incriminate Ekaterina even more during the search of her house, but nothing had come to light there, or in her office at the security company or anywhere else they had looked. If she was a criminal mastermind, she kept her records somewhere that was, as yet, a secret. Not that there was any urgency about finding any such evidence. Wearing's detailed confession was enough to get her convicted, never mind remanded, so they could investigate further.

Trevor Sinclair, the Dance family solicitor, had turned up and tried to play the 'diplomatic incident' card, but Milburn had sent him packing with a flea in his ear, telling him essentially what she had already told his client at Heathrow – that this was England and she wasn't going to get to play any of the 'get out of jail free' cards she might have in Moscow.

Darling had just kept her head down and shifted paper, hoping nobody would see that she was so thin an edition of herself she was practically transparent. Just then, the success of her investigation felt to her like a failure – what did having Ekaterina Dance and Mark Wearing charged with murder matter in the big scheme of things? – and failure was no success at all. She racked her brain trying to remember the song those words came from, and failed, even though, on the Constabulary Duties quiz team, she was the acknowledged music expert. Eventually, though, even she had to acknowledge she was exhausted as much mentally as she was physically.

It was time to call it a day, feeling as though she did not have the strength to get up from her desk and go home. Had her office been equipped with a sofa or even an easy chair she might well have curled up in it, only it wasn't, so she cleared her desk, locked up and left the station.

She walked along Grainger Street intending to take the bus home when her phone rang. Stepping into a doorway, she answered it. Paul? Who was Paul?

"Sorry if I've caught you at an unfortunate time, but I was thinking…"

"There is a first time for everything, Reid!"

"Ha ha bloody ha. I was thinking about that drink you suggested."

Her first thought was to say 'no'. She was still in the work clothes she had worn for two days, not even a fresh bra and knickers, although she had washed them in the hotel basin and dried them overnight in front of the air conditioning. Then she almost laughed aloud at the thought Paul Reid was going to get to see her underwear any time soon, although as the thought formed itself she realised she wasn't as averse to that idea as she thought she had been for most of her life.

"I'm knackered, Paul. It's been a hectic week and a bit. I'll have to take a rain check."

"Have you ever asked yourself what that means? Exactly what is a 'rain check'?"

There was something about his tone of voice that made her giggle, and the fact that she was giggling about something a man said, at her age, only made her giggle even more. Suddenly the idea of spending some time with a man who could make her giggle was irresistible. Everyone had to giggle sometime, maybe even laugh a little. Being a detective inspector who had just solved a murder didn't mean she couldn't laugh.

"You know that comedy club by the Central?"

"I know of it. I've never been."

"How would you like to go there now?"

"Are you asking?"

"Sounds like it."

She felt herself smiling. "When can you get here?"

"In about thirty seconds."

Looking over the road she saw a figure walking towards her, one hand held to his head in the classic way of someone talking into a mobile phone, the other one raised above his head and waving.

"Are you following me?" The levity evaporated out of her.

"I'm coming towards you. How can I be following you if I'm coming towards you? Jeez, some people are just so suspicious."

"That's my job, in case you hadn't noticed, to be suspicious of strange men."

By now he stood in front of her, closing his phone. "I'm not a strange man," he said, suddenly reaching out, taking hold of her and pulling her close enough to plant a brief, soft kiss on her lips. "But I do think you needed that."

"I'll be the judge of that," she said, slipping out of his grasp.

"Judge? I thought you said you were a detective inspector!"

This time she didn't giggle, she laughed, a full-bodied laugh that made him laugh, too. A moment later, they were walking arm in arm along Grey Street, unaware of anything else in the world.

If you enjoyed this book, please let others know by leaving a quick review on Amazon. Also, if you spot anything untoward in the paperback, get in touch. We strive for the best quality and appreciate reader feedback.

editor@thebookfolks.com

www.thebookfolks.com

Also in this series

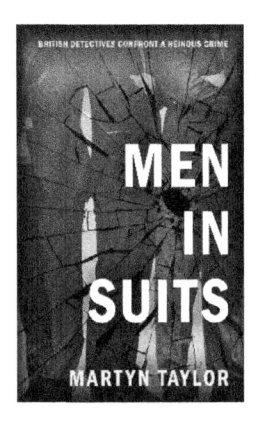

MEN IN SUITS (Book 2)

When thirteen-year-old Kimberley Ford is found murdered, DI Penelope Darling will have to keep her emotions in check to face the facts of the case. Aided by a rookie cop who is crucial to gaining the victim's schoolfriends' trust, her investigation begins to focus on a group of people in high-profile positions in society. One of them is the killer, but all have something to hide.

More fiction by the author

GALLASILL

The hanging of an innocent man seven generations ago left a curse on the two feuding local families involved. Sarah Charlton's father has hidden this family secret, but curiosity gets the better of her. When she investigates the story, she realises she is not the only one with a stake in the past.

FREE with Kindle Unlimited!

THE PRICE OF EVERYTHING

Peter Mann is a rational chap so, when his brother dies, supernatural causes are far from his mind. But when the balance of good and evil is so precarious, at what price do we not recognise the dark forces around us? That's the question that will confront Peter and his nephew Billy when a series of macabre events make them realise that true malevolence has come to town.

FREE with Kindle Unlimited!

Other titles of interest

CRIMINAL JUSTICE
by Ian Robinson

Batford walks a thin line when he infiltrates a criminal gang. He sees an opportunity to make some money and take down a pretty nasty felon, but his own boss DCI Klara Winter is on to him. Can he get out of a very sticky situation before his identity and intentions are revealed?

FREE with Kindle Unlimited and available in paperback!

OUTCAST SISTER
by James Davidson

London detective Eleanor Rose is lured back to her old city of Liverpool by Daniel, an ex-boyfriend and colleague who's in danger. It's against her better instincts, as she has no desire to confront her past. But when she gets there, he's nowhere to be found, and as she retraces his steps, Eleanor gets caught in a dark web of deceit, corruption and violence. Her half-sister, who never forgave her for leaving, seems involved too. Will their path cross? Will she find Daniel?

FREE with Kindle Unlimited and available in paperback!

THE BOOK FOLKS

Sign up to our mailing list to find out about new releases and special offers!

www.thebookfolks.com

Printed in Great Britain
by Amazon